An Amanda Knightly Mystery

Serving Up the Truth

DEBRA KLEIN

Editor: Lisa Mathews
Proofreading and manuscript development advisor: Judith Gallagher
Cover Design: Karen Phillips of PhillipsCovers.com
Inside Book Design: Sue Trowbridge, interbridge.com

Serving Up the Truth/Debra Klein — 1st ed.

Library of Congress Card Catalogue Number: 2024924930
ISBN: 979-8-9917335-0-2 (Print)
ISBN: 979-8-9917335-1-9 (eBook)

CHAPTER 1

Amanda Knightly beamed her best customer-friendly smile and repeated her question.

"After sampling our premium lunch meats, have you decided on the honey-baked ham, the prime roast beef, or the mesquite-roasted turkey? Or perhaps all three?" Amanda kept her tone congenial but firm, tapping her foot behind the deli counter at Bob's Finer Foods in the suburban village of Oak Hills, Illinois.

The young woman leaned against the glass display case, chewing on her fingernails, one by one, as if they were the special of the day. "I'll take the ham. No, wait, the roast beef. Er … let's just go with the turkey. And make it three slices, shaved thin." She let out a bored sigh, dived in for a second helping of her index finger, then wiped it across the side of her "*I'm Just Being Me*" sweatshirt.

It was one of those days. Besides her disgusting habit, the customer acted as if Amanda were her personal shopper. She seemed clueless to the line behind her getting even more restless. And she'd ordered only three thin slices. Really? Where was that part-timer? He'd supposedly made a quick dash to the cooler.

With her back to the customer, Amanda rolled her eyes as

she headed toward the slicer. She had just set the turkey breast against the blade when the young woman's voice rang out from the counter.

"Wait. Forget the turkey. I'll take the smallest container you have of potato salad. And make sure it was made today. I don't want that day-old stuff. And could you please hurry it up? I can't stand here all day." She drummed her fingers, including the one whose nail she'd just finished nibbling, on the metal countertop.

Amanda so wanted to reply, *"At your command, your royal highness"* and drop a curtsy. Instead, she steeled herself with a smile. "Coming right up."

It'd been a tough morning. Her last customer's toddler wouldn't stop sobbing "Mommy, Mommy, MOMMMYYY!" as his flustered mother tried to tell Amanda her order. Amanda was relieved when an unseen miracle worker managed to quiet him. The giggling little guy and his happy mother quickly left, deli order in hand.

Now, Amanda hoped the young woman standing in front of her would leave just as quickly, once she got her potato salad.

Amanda worked at warp speed, filling, weighing, and labeling the small container before handing it over the counter. She seared the young woman's dark eyes, curly brown hair, and turned-up nose into her memory. If she had to pick the customer most likely to get murdered by a deli clerk, it would be this one.

Amanda felt herself blush. The Deli Lady shouldn't be thinking that. She'd earned her nickname by delighting customers for the past ten years. Maybe the thrill of this job was spiraling downward more than she'd thought.

The customer started to reach for the container, then stopped. "David, David! Over here," she called, frantically waving.

The people behind her, clutching their numbers, turned to look. Amanda recognized David Stedman parked at the edge of the crowd. Her son's longtime friend was one of those guys everyone liked. He reminded her of a young Brad Pitt, minus the cocky edge. David had been the only one of Matt's friends who'd jumped in to help at their Fourth of July backyard barbeque last year. Now he stood at the back of the line, which spilled into the bakery department's display.

"David, you don't have to wait for your number. You can use mine." The young woman shouted loud enough for shoppers over at the bakery counter to glance her way.

Raised eyebrows and mumblings of "He's not butting in front of me," and "That's not fair" reverberated through the crowd.

Amanda opened her mouth, ready to remind the woman that wasn't the way things worked. But David beat her to it. "That's okay, thanks. I'll wait my turn," he called back.

"I insist," the young woman practically hollered. "Besides, we need to talk."

David, a placid smile on his face, maneuvered through the other customers, ending up next to the inconsiderate woman. "Olivia, I appreciate your offer, but I can't jump the line." His voice was even, his demeanor calm, as he pointed to the line behind them. Amanda breathed a sigh of relief.

Olivia pulled her shoulders back, eyes blazing sparks. "You've been ignoring me for the past week. I have a right to know why."

David's expression remained the same. "This isn't the place to talk."

"Fine. Then I'd better have an update by tonight." She shoved the potato salad container back at Amanda and stomped off.

Amanda pushed the young woman's rude response out of her mind and turned to David. "It's good to see you again, Mrs. K," he said with a smile. "Sorry for the misunderstanding with … my friend. I'll take her potato salad so it's not wasted and head out." He scooped it up before adding, "Say hi to Matt for me. I haven't seen him for a month."

Amanda always got a kick out of David calling her Mrs. K, like the Fonz did with Richie's mom on the old *Happy Days* TV show. "It's good to see you too, David. I'll definitely pass on your hello."

As he headed toward the checkout lines, she silently thanked him for stopping the young woman from creating a worse scene.

Amanda turned back to the impatient line of customers, cheerfully calling out the next number. Her co-worker reappeared as the cluster of waiting shoppers slowly shrank. Finally. It had been a long "quick dash." Life at the deli counter returned to normal.

At home that night, Amanda passed on David Stedman's greeting to Matt. "He said you two haven't seen each other for a while."

"My bad," Matt said, frowning. "Yeah, I was supposed to call him."

"Something else happened that I need to ask you about." She recalled David's even-keeled response toward the young woman's obnoxious behavior and her insistence they talk. "I thought I knew everyone in Oak Hills, but she didn't register with me. He called her Olivia. Do you know who she is?"

Matt leaned his tall, lanky body against the kitchen counter, grimacing as if she had described the Wicked Witch of the West. "Short, curly brown hair, kind of cute, but clueless?"

"I'd say that describes her."

"That would be Olivia Hager. She's been annoyingly crazy about David for the past year. She's always pestering him at his job at the Happy Bean over in Schaumburg. Constantly bugs him. And trust me, he has zero interest in her."

"She was pretty insistent that he give her an update on something."

"I'm sure it's about the money."

"What money?"

"David is starting up his own coffee shop and put out feelers for backers. Why he included Olivia, I don't have a clue. She gave him five thousand dollars last month. Now she wants it back."

"And he can't return it?" Amanda asked.

"He used it to grab a hot deal on equipment. It was a no-returns sale."

"This sounds like it could get ugly."

"Yep. And knowing Olivia, she'll only get more demanding. She's a real nightmare."

Based on what she'd seen at the deli counter today, Amanda didn't doubt that one bit.

———

After a restless night interrupted by police and ambulance sirens, Amanda slipped out of bed and headed down the second-floor hallway, leaving her husband, Joe, in a deep sleep. Focused on a much-needed first cup of coffee, she smiled as she passed Matt's vacant bedroom. He was already on his way to work. No surprise from her take-charge son, intent on paying off his student loans after graduating last year. Next up was moving into his own place. A familiar twinge hit her. She wasn't ready for that just yet.

She stopped at her daughter's closed bedroom door. After several knocks, followed by a low groan, she heard a mumbled, "I'm up, Mom."

Amanda leaned closer to the door. "I need to hear feet on the floor, sweetheart."

"Geez, Mom."

Amanda shook her head. Once again, Brittany was lollygagging in bed and would probably be late. Just turned twenty-one, her daughter liked to boast about experiencing life as it unfolded. Being on time to her college classes and part-time job was secondary. Whoever said girls matured earlier than boys hadn't met Brittany.

When Amanda walked into the kitchen, Matt was putting on his new black leather jacket. "I'm not sure if I'll be home for dinner tonight, Mom."

"Working late or big date?" Amanda's heart warmed at the thought of Matt's new girlfriend, Chloe Dawson. He had suddenly found a reason to be more conscious of how he dressed. At twenty-three, it was about time.

"Hopefully, I'll be seeing Chloe. But I haven't been able to reach her." He frowned and shoved his phone into his pocket. "I'll let you know this afternoon for sure."

"That works for me." Amanda pulled out the coffee can with the extra-strong dark roast blend from the cupboard. Just what she needed to revive herself. "Did you hear those sirens last night?"

"Nope. I was playing video games with my headphones on." Matt slipped in his ear buds. "Sorry, gotta go. Can't miss my train."

Amanda watched her son walk out the back door. His confident stride reminded her of a young buck ready to take on the world. She let out a sigh. Someday, her daughter would do the same. Right now, Brittany needed more time.

She tackled the thankless chore of emptying the dishwasher as the coffee brewed. Then she headed back upstairs for a shower, a steaming cup of java in hand.

Thirty minutes later, Amanda emerged feeling like a million-dollar lottery winner. The shower had stayed hot, there'd been a clean towel on the rack, and the bathroom scale was thankfully still broken. She pulled her robe tight and strutted into the hallway, barely missing her husband hurrying past.

Joe stopped to give her a quick smile. His tie hung around the collar of his dress shirt, and he had his suit jacket flung over one shoulder. He seemed tense, more so than usual this morning.

His salt-and-pepper hair looked like it'd turned mostly toward salt overnight.

"You must be off to another tough client meeting." Amanda reached out and tightened his tie. Her hand lingered on his shoulder. At the same five-foot eight-inch height, they stood eye-to-eye. "Thanks again for going over that credit card issue with me after dinner last night. I was so worried."

Joe nodded, looking deep in thought as he stuffed his right arm into his jacket sleeve. "I'll call their customer service hotline today. Tonight I'll let you know what I learn." He gave her a quick peck on the cheek and continued down the hallway. "Don't want to be late," he called over his shoulder, before he disappeared down the stairs.

She headed toward the bedroom, happy with their brief exchange. After twenty-four years of marriage, they knew each other well, especially their mutual view about money. Frugal, careful, and realistic had been their mantra. The idea that they'd be charged late fees on their Super Fuel card was bad enough. But if their interest rate went up, she'd really be upset. Even more upset than the year he'd forgotten their anniversary.

But no worries. Joe would make sure the issue was all cleared up and keep her in the loop, like he always did. After all, she'd made a few mistakes herself in the past, and Joe had never made a big deal about them.

Half an hour later, dressed in her usual go-to outfit of black pants, sweater, and slip-on sneakers, Amanda pulled her dark-blonde hair into a ponytail. With a last check in the full-length mirror, she gave herself a thumbs-up. Pinterest was right. Wearing black was the secret to hiding those ten pounds she couldn't seem to lose after turning forty-two this past fall.

Returning to the kitchen, she groaned at the scene that greeted her. Joe and Brittany had left their breakfast dishes spewed across the kitchen table. Well, she wasn't the scullery maid. Pulling out her phone, she snapped a telltale photo of the mess and captioned it *Clean me!* A quick hit of the send arrow and the ball was officially in their court.

She slipped on her coat and grabbed her backpack. Time for a brisk walk to her favorite place before heading to work, like she did every Thursday morning.

When she reached the front sidewalk, she straightened the crooked garden sign that announced "The Knightly Happy Home." Then she scooped up the *Oak Hills Gazette* and slipped off its plastic sleeve.

The headline sent a chill down her spine.

BODY FOUND IN OAK HILLS

Was this the reason for those sirens? She zeroed in on the article.

Early yesterday evening, Oak Hills Police discovered the body of Olivia Hager, 23, in a unit at Valley Lane Condominiums in Oak Hills, Illinois.

Amanda gasped. Olivia Hager! The rude young woman from the deli counter. Her fingers gripped the edges of the newspaper tighter.

Police declined to give further details. They ask anyone with information to come forward. Oak Hills Police Chief Ed Grady also told this reporter that residents should take extra precautions, be aware of their surroundings, and not open their doors to strangers.

Article continued Page 2.

Amanda lowered the newspaper. The phrase "*take extra precautions*" touched off a quiver in her gut. This sounded like a murder. And only a block from her house.

Without warning, the late March wind wrestled the newspaper out of her hands. She reclaimed the billowing pages, and bent down to stash the paper in the side pocket of her backpack.

As she stood up, Amanda sensed a sudden presence behind her. A firm hand gripped her shoulder.

CHAPTER 2

Adrenaline shot through Amanda as fingers dug into her shoulder. Instinctively, she made a fist and took a swing behind her.

"WHOA! Amanda, what's the matter with you? Take it easy, for goodness' sake."

Amanda's arm halted midway through her second swing. That gruff voice belonged to Frank Morelli, their next-door neighbor.

She lowered her arm and peered over her shoulder. Frank stepped back, his craggy face indignant. The man was a lonely widower, Joe always reminded her. He saw the elderly man as harmless but agreed with Amanda's "cranky" and "nosy" labels. She'd typecast Frank as the annoying neighbor on a TV sitcom. A true curmudgeon.

She pointed to the page. "I just learned a young woman was probably murdered a block away."

He pulled at the brim of his faded Chicago Cubs baseball cap. "Where have you been? It's all they talked about on the TV news this morning. I turned it off. Couldn't stand any more of their blabbering." Frank leaned in closer. "I wonder who'll be the next young gal to get killed."

Frank's thoughtless remark sent a second chill down Amanda's spine. Brittany flashed into her mind. And hadn't Matt mentioned that his girlfriend lived at Valley Lane condos?

"I need to be on my way." She took a step away from Frank.

He gave a loud harrumph. "I can see you're antsy, like everybody else these days. No one wants to talk. They hurry here and there, noses stuck in their phones, and—"

"Goodbye, Frank," she said, turning away with a little wave.

As Amanda hurried down the sidewalk on First Street, the dreadful news roared back into her mind. Olivia Hager, annoying customer and acquaintance of David Stedman, was dead.

After sending a heads-up text about the terrible news to her family, she couldn't dismiss the fact that it had happened in their neighborhood. And the killer was still at large and could strike again.

Amanda picked up her pace. Police had asked for anyone with information to come forward. No way would she confess to her own coldhearted musing of Olivia Hager being the customer most likely to be murdered by a deli clerk. But should she tell the police about David and Olivia's connection? Olivia had told him she expected an "update" last night.

Sailing by the row of rehabbed Victorian homes framing both sides of the street, she wrestled with the question. She decided there was no way David would have done something that heinous. The police would find whoever killed the young woman. That was their job.

Right now, she needed to refocus on her destination.

At the intersection of First and Valley Lane, Amanda glanced to her left. The five-story Valley Lane condo building stood at the end of the block. Yellow police tape curved around the front entrance, and a squad car sat at the curb. A shudder ran through her as she crossed the intersection and continued down

First Street. It'd be a long time before she set foot near *that* place.

Amanda perked up seeing the familiar *Welcome to Oak Hills Business District* sign. She continued on, past Blooming Blossoms Florist, known for its colorful bouquets and high prices, then Your Favorite Sandwich Place, the Knightly choice for quick carryout, followed by a slew of little shops and restaurants tucked along both sides of the two-block downtown.

Finally, the carved wooden sign of the Dark Roast Coffee Shop came into view, bringing a grin to her face.

Matt called it Mom's Hangout. Brittany called it Mom's Escape Room. Joe called it My Wife's Hideaway.

Amanda called it Paradise.

A chime from her phone broke her anticipation of near-Nirvana, reminding her only two hours remained before the start of her noon shift at Bob's Finer Foods.

Another nippy gust of wind barreled out of nowhere and hit her from behind. Amanda flipped up the hood of her coat.

Paradise awaited.

––––––

The rich aroma of freshly brewed coffee greeted Amanda as she pushed open the front door of the Dark Roast. The background chatter of customers followed her to the empty front counter.

"Hello? Anyone here?" she asked. Her only greeting came from a framed photo next to the register captioned: *"Nicki Lenzini, Proprietor of the Dark Roast, Oak Hills' Top Coffee Shop, Welcomes You!"*

She frowned. At least one barista always stood behind the counter. Her bestie was probably in the back office, taking care of an emergency, or else she'd be out here chit-chatting with the customers. *"A shop owner never ignores emergencies,"* Nicki always said.

"Nicki! You've got a thirsty customer waiting," Amanda called, loud enough for her friend to hear. Even with the door shut.

She did a double take when David Stedman emerged from the back, wearing the royal blue Dark Roast employee polo. Didn't he work at the Happy Bean?

"David, I didn't know you'd started working here." Amanda wasn't sure if she was more surprised that he was behind the counter or that Nicki hadn't told her about the new hire. The two of them shared all their news.

"Long story." David's abrupt tone made Amanda think this was the last place he wanted to be. The friendly smile he'd shown her yesterday at the deli counter had vanished. Something wasn't adding up. Nicki would never let an unhappy employee wait on customers.

"Is Nicki here?" she asked.

"She's running an errand. She should be back soon." He dropped his gaze to the counter.

Waiting for him to say something more, Amanda decided his last customer must have been a downer, and he needed a little boost.

"Well, I'm glad you're here." Amanda added a big grin. "The Dark Roast is a great place to work. And Matt says hi back."

David nodded in a preoccupied kind of way. Amanda hesitated. He was probably upset about Olivia Hager's death, despite what Matt said about her. That might explain his out-of-character attitude.

She couldn't hold back from giving him a concerned motherly look. "I was so sad to hear the news of Olivia Hager's murder. Looks like it hit you hard, too."

David shook his head. "I can't talk about it, Mrs. K," he said, his voice catching. His eyes glazed over as if lost in thought before he asked for her order.

Olivia's death had definitely affected him.

She turned to the menu board as a formality, already knowing she'd order a Panda Bear. The specialty latté, topped with whipped cream and drizzled chocolate, was a lot pricier in both dollars and calories than the standard black coffee. Today she justified it as a well-earned treat.

"I'll have a large Panda Bear, extra hot." Amanda slipped a fiver and two ones across the counter. "This should cover it, including something for you." David took the money and nodded. Amanda frowned. Not even a thank-you.

She watched him execute the quick, precise steps of an expert barista. He stayed focused on the filled-to-the-brim latté as he slid it across the counter. This was the dependable David she knew.

A bandage wrapped the length of David's right index finger caught her attention. "That looks serious," she said, concerned.

"It's nothing. Just a silly accident." He waved it away.

Amanda turned her attention to her Panda Bear. She gingerly touched the cup. Extra hot, but not too hot to pick up. She took her first sip. Perfect.

"Thank you. You got it just right."

She saw a spark of relief on David's face. In a flash, it was swept away. Amanda stepped back to brace herself from the sudden chill.

"Can you help me?" a white-haired woman asked, walking up behind Amanda. "This is my first time here. I'm confused by the menu." Her voice was as shaky as her hands.

David's expression immediately softened. "No problem. Happy to explain it."

Amanda felt relief that the David she knew had returned. But as he described the first coffee on the board, he tensed up, and his voice turned frosty. The older woman looked even more confused.

Oh dear, Amanda thought. David was an emotional yo-yo today. He needed help.

"The house Colombian brew is always a favorite," Amanda offered, catching the woman's eye.

"Thank you, dear. I'll try it. And young man, I'd like a small cup."

Holding back from feeling too cocky about jumping in at just the right time, Amanda glanced at the digital clock on the wall. 10:06 a.m. Her morning in Paradise was flying by.

Spotting her favorite table by the shop's front window, Amanda bolted from the counter like a racehorse charging toward the finish line, being careful not to spill her hot coffee along the way. She settled into the chair, dropped her backpack on the floor, and took another sip of her Panda Bear.

The scene in front of her consisted of a dozen or so patrons, divided between two groups of tables like ships moored at independent docks in the same harbor. Their voices converged into one steady buzz.

"Can't believe that girl was killed last night ..."

"And so close to downtown ..."

"I heard she wasn't a very nice person ..."

Amanda silently thanked Nicki for not following the trend of a blaring TV mounted on the wall. The commentary ricocheting back and forth was enough noise.

She looked to the front counter. David's expression hadn't changed. He seemed to be the only person in the coffee shop besides her not joining in on the gossip about Olivia's death.

A stab of sadness struck her as the chatter continued in the background. Everyone seemed interested in the murder, but no one showed compassion for the young woman whose life someone had cut short. It could have been anyone's daughter. It could have been her own daughter. She shuddered once again at the thought.

Trying to shut out the voices, she turned toward the large front window. Her favorite view of Oak Hills showed off its vintage buildings from the early days of the village's 150-year history. The whistle from the commuter train, on its thirty-minute run to downtown Chicago, sounded in the background.

The perfect town. Almost. Amanda frowned after counting two more "For Lease" and "Going Out of Business" signs among the storefronts that invited customers from the city and the surrounding suburbs to spend their money in the charming village. After seven recent burglaries, nine carjackings and no arrests, customers weren't coming to the shops and restaurants, which affected everyone's bottom line. It didn't help that parking was horrendous and the police were brutal about handing out parking tickets.

And now a murder.

"Oh no, not Lombardo's!" Amanda said aloud, seeing the CLOSED sign slapped across the front window. Every year, she and Joe celebrated their anniversary at the family-favorite Italian restaurant. It was their present to each other.

"Mommy, look! It's the Deli Lady!"

Amanda turned and smiled at the little girl who stood nearby, her sparkly pink kiddie headphones askew. People in Oak Hills didn't always know Amanda's name, but everyone who patron-ized Bob's deli counter knew her face. She was always flattered when people remembered her. But right now, she wanted to be incognito and read her paper.

"Why yes, Madison, you're right. But I think it's the Deli Lady's alone time. And I'd like you to finish your coloring because we're leaving soon. Can you do that for Mommy?"

With that redirect, the little girl hopped back onto her chair, plopped her headphones over her ears and picked up a red crayon.

Amanda silently thanked the woman. She'd return the cour-tesy the next time she stopped by the deli counter.

The wafting scents of her Panda Bear pulled her back on task. She leaned down to retrieve the *Gazette* out of her backpack.

As she sat up, Amanda caught David's stare from the front counter. It wasn't threatening, more of a questioning gaze. A second later his head dropped into his hands, with his elbows anchored on the counter.

Had he and Olivia had that conversation? she wondered. Had she demanded the money back again?

She unfolded the newspaper and laid it across the table. Knowing David like she did, he had tried to straighten everything out with the young woman. The important thing was for the police to catch Olivia's killer. And for these chatty customers to leave so she could read the rest of the story on page 2 in peace.

As if hearing her silent plea, all the patrons suddenly rose and left the shop. The little girl with the headphones waved goodbye to Amanda. The white-haired woman, coffee in hand, exited last.

Ah. Peace and quiet. Just she and David remained. Taking a sip of her Panda Bear, Amanda turned her attention back to the paper. Maybe she'd get a refill after finishing the story.

At the squeal of tires, her head jerked toward the front window. Within seconds, four Oak Hills police officers, guns drawn, burst into the Dark Roast.

"HANDS UP!"

Amanda's hands shot up, spilling her Panda Bear across the table and onto the floor. She watched in horror as Officer Monica Evans stepped into the mocha-brown puddle, leaving wet footprints as she hustled to the front counter. The officers behind Evans added theirs to the trail.

Amanda remained frozen. Her white-knuckled right hand gripped the handle of the empty coffee cup, which swung back and forth like a pendulum on a clock. Her left hand, palm side out, hadn't moved an inch.

David stood behind the counter, surrounded by all four police officers. They cuffed his hands behind his back.

"David Stedman, you are under arrest for the murder of Olivia Hager," an officer announced. He rattled off the suspect's Miranda rights.

As the police led him to the front door, Amanda caught David's frightened eyes and stunned face.

"I'm innocent. Please help me, Mrs. K," he pleaded as they hurried him past her.

Amanda felt a surge of adrenaline and leaped out of the chair. It crashed to the floor, the sound echoing across the shop. "Wait!" she cried, hands still in the air. "You've made a mistake. You can't arrest him."

Officer Evans turned toward Amanda, her usual friendly manner now all business. "You need to sit back down and keep quiet."

"But—"

"I strongly recommend you not interfere with a police matter, Amanda," Evans added.

"But I'm sure—"

The icy stare from Evans made her stop talking. Amanda's insides flipped as doubt, anger, and confusion surged through her.

The front window provided a ringside view as three officers led David to one of the squad cars parked curbside. She saw his head silhouetted in the back window of the vehicle as it disappeared around the corner.

Why had the police arrested David for the murder of Olivia Hager? And why was Officer Evans still standing in the coffee shop?

The front door flew open once again. Nicki Lenzini, Amanda's best friend and owner of the Dark Roast, stood in the doorway. Petite, with a dark-haired pixie cut, today she wore retro cat's-eye glasses. The leopard-patterned belt cinching her waist accented the look.

"What's going on? Why did my new barista just get hauled away by the police?" she demanded, hands on hips.

Amanda hurried toward her. "Oh, Nicki, thank goodness you're here. You won't believe what just happened."

"Try me."

"The police arrested David for Olivia Hager's murder."

"What?" Nicki's head jerked back as she turned toward Officer Evans. "Monica, what's going on?"

Amanda knew Nicki was on a first-name basis with the officer. Her bestie excelled at schmoozing people. Next, she'd offer Evans free coffee.

"Talk first, coffee later, Nicki," the officer replied. "I'd like to chat with both of you, and I don't have a lot of time."

CHAPTER 3

Amanda sat between Nicki and Officer Evans, two tables away from the remains of her spilled Panda Bear.

She watched Evans set her laptop down, noting the officer's pressed navy-blue uniform, dark hair pulled into a sleek bun, and overall professional demeanor. Absent was Evans's familiar, laid-back persona.

The officer had made it clear she was on duty.

"Consider this a friendly conversation, although I'll be taking notes," Evans began. "I'm going to ask each of you some general questions, starting with Amanda, since she was in the shop when Stedman was arrested." The officer's voice was even, yet firm. "I want both of you to let the other person speak without interrupting, so we stay on topic. Understood?"

Amanda and Nicki nodded.

Nicki raised her hand. "Before we begin, I want to say that Amanda and I have been friends for twenty years. We share everything." She cocked her head in Amanda's direction. "Right?"

Amanda nodded. "We do." Except for Nicki not mentioning

she'd hired David to work in her shop. But that was a business matter, no big deal.

Evans gave Amanda a stern look. "If you ever find yourself in a trying situation again, please remember to let the police do their job."

Amanda's cheeks burned. "I'm sorry, but I couldn't help speaking out. I still can't believe you arrested David for murder."

Evans offered a brief nod. "Let's move on. Tell me what you saw from the moment you arrived at the Dark Roast."

Officer Evans's fingers danced over the keyboard as Amanda gave her the details. Whenever Amanda stopped to collect her thoughts, the officer's fingers paused, like an actor waiting for a director's next cue.

"So what I've heard is that David Stedman is an acquaintance of your family's, and you were surprised to see him working at the Dark Roast when you arrived this morning, just before 10:00 a.m. He told you that Nicki left the shop briefly to run an errand. And you thought he wasn't his usual self when he waited on you. Is that correct?"

Amanda nodded. "Yes, that's correct." Then hesitated. *This could make David's situation worse.*

Nicki frowned. "That's not the David I saw working the front counter all morning. He knew his craft, was super nice to every customer, and had a sweet charm. That's why I felt comfortable leaving him in the shop on his own for a few minutes. In fact, I hoped to—"

Officer Evans held up her hand. "Nicki, you'll get your turn."

Nicki sighed and sat back in her chair.

Amanda saw Officer Evans knew how to stand her ground. Not someone to tangle with while in her official capacity.

Evans turned back to Amanda. "Did Stedman say anything about Olivia Hager being killed?"

"When I mentioned I was sad to hear the news of her death,

he shook his head and said he didn't know what to say. Then he asked for my order. That's all."

"Did he make any movements that alarmed you?"

"No. He acted like maybe he wanted to be left alone, other than when he had to fill a customer's order. We all have bad days at work, and under the circumstances …" Amanda paused. *That should help him.* "It's been a tough morning for everyone in Oak Hills, and I'm sure he felt the same with the nonstop talk about Olivia's murder," she added.

"Not murder, officially," the officer said. "Yet."

"Well, it was just me and David in the shop. I settled into reading the *Gazette*, sipping my Panda Bear. That's when you all burst through the front door."

The officer nodded; her face neutral. "How long have you known David Stedman?" she asked.

"Since he and my son Matt played on the high school's varsity soccer team. Matt's twenty-three, so that would make it seven years. David's been to my house many times since then. They're close friends."

Oops. Did I just point the police to a connection with Matt?

Officer Evans shrugged. "No matter. Loving grandmothers, prominent leaders, and smart college boys have all been convicted of murder. It's like the familiar saying about not judging a book by its cover."

"True. But suspects must have means, motive, and opportunity," Amanda said. "So what were David's?" *Matt did say Olivia made David's life a nightmare. And Olivia insisted she and David needed to talk last night. Plus, those five thousand dollars Matt had said she wanted back made it messy.*

Amanda squirmed in her chair.

Evans raised an eyebrow. "We understand that yesterday, around noon, Olivia Hager and David Stedman had a discussion at Bob's deli counter. Were you working at that time?"

"Yes, I was," Amanda said, not surprised the police knew about their public meeting.

"I'd like you to tell me what you heard and saw."

Amanda reiterated the scene, including David's kind, calm approach, in contrast to Olivia's curt demands.

"Did she say why she wanted an update?" Evans asked.

Amanda paused., *Matt offered the idea of Olivia wanting her five thousand dollars back last night, but at the deli counter yesterday, I didn't hear Olivia or David say anything about money.*

"No," Amanda answered truthfully. No need passing on thirdhand information if Matt was wrong. If she learned something about the money firsthand, she'd let Evans know. Hopefully, any info would help David, and not the opposite.

"Did you see either of them again?"

"I saw David when I walked into the Dark Roast this morning. I didn't see Olivia Hager again."

"Amanda, I can tell you read mysteries and watch a lot of TV crime shows. As I'm sure you know, one of my responsibilities is to collect all relevant facts for the Illinois State Attorney. One more time, do you have anything more to add before I move on to Nicki?"

Amanda forced a thin smile. "I can't forget that David shouted out he was innocent and asked for my help."

"That's a favorite trick of criminals," Evans said. "They plead their innocence to bystanders, hoping to find a soft heart."

Amanda hesitated, then smiled. "I'd also like to state that David Stedman makes a great latté." Perhaps her little joke would lighten the mood of the conversation.

Fortunately, Officer Evans chuckled. "I'll alert the Illinois State Attorney's office of that fact." She looked at Nicki. "It's your turn." The officer's fingers hovered over the keyboard again.

Amanda silently gave her friend a prize for sitting still for the last ten minutes. Well, almost still. Her bestie could have walked to downtown Chicago and back for the number of times she'd tapped her foot under the table.

Nicki adjusted her glasses and took a deep breath. "Yesterday afternoon, I was in a real pickle when my lead barista, Gina Rohmer, announced she was quitting and stomped out the front door."

Amanda's jaw dropped. "Oh no. She's your top employee."

Evans gave Amanda a stern look. "It's Nicki's turn to talk, and your turn to stay quiet."

Amanda drew a finger across her lips in a zip-the-lip gesture. The officer's stern frown remained.

She turned back to Nicki. "Is there a connection to Stedman?"

Nicki nodded. "That's the reason David was working here this morning." Her voice turned steely. "Gina quit abruptly, believing she'd been cheated out of a promotion to assistant manager and the salary that went with it. She even threatened me with a lawsuit for creating a toxic work environment."

Amanda wanted to blurt out, "That's crazy!" but held back, fearing another stern look from Evans. She'd never felt comfortable with Gina. The young woman was friendly when she wanted a hefty tip and frosty after she pocketed it. But Amanda hadn't felt it her place to tell Nicki. That separation-of-business-from-friendship thing again.

The officer shook her head. "Sounds like it's better that she quit. But I'm still unclear how this connects to Stedman, Nicki."

"He agreed to fill in as assistant manager so I could take my vacation to Florida next week. I haven't taken time off since I bought the shop five years ago. I told you about my trip plans."

Evans nodded. "Yes, I remember." She had that "*I've heard this twenty times*" expression Amanda had seen many times from Nicki's acquaintances in the past month. Nicki never quit talking about her upcoming trip.

Nicki made a face. "Obviously, the deal with David is now off. That means no vacation for me. I'm going to get dinged on the nonrefundable airfare ticket and the prepaid condo rental."

Amanda patted her bestie's arm and gave her a so-sorry look.

Evans frowned. "Stedman works at the Happy Bean in Schaumburg. But this morning he was also working for you. Is that correct?"

Nicki nodded. "Kinda. Last night I called my friend Eddie Turner, who owns the Happy Bean. I told him of my predicament with Gina quitting and no one on my staff wanting to step in as full-time manager for next week. Eddie convinced David it would be a great opportunity and it'd only be a temp position. Nothing permanent. David started this morning so he'd have a few days to get familiar with the Dark Roast before I left. I thought he was doing a great job for only being here a couple of hours."

The officer's fingers returned to the keyboard. "Had you ever met Stedman before this morning?"

"Yes. He's often on shift when I stop by to see Eddie at the Happy Bean."

"And Mr. Turner had no trouble lending out his employee to you? That seems a little unusual."

"Our shops are far enough apart that we don't compete for the same customers. As small independents, we agreed several years ago to band together to fight off the big chains. I help him and he helps me. We've made it work."

"How did Stedman seem when he arrived this morning?"

"Fine. On time. Knew his stuff. Seemed happy to be here. That's why I left him alone. I needed to run a few errands with my vacation back on." Nicki rubbed her forehead, as if trying to rid herself of a painful nightmare. "I feel dreadful about David's arrest. But now the Oak Hills rumor mill will blast me for hiring a murderer and—"

"Hold on, Nicki," Amanda broke in. "He's only been arrested." She winced when she saw Evans's frown again. "Oops, sorry."

The officer held up her hand. "Nicki, did Stedman say anything at all about Olivia Hager's death?"

"No. My focus, like all mornings, was on filling orders as fast as possible. David seemed of the same mind. Plus, I had to fill him in on managing the shop."

"Did you mention Olivia's death?"

"No. And he didn't bring it up. That's the whole truth and nothing but the truth."

Officer Evans shut the lid of her laptop and stood up. "You can save that line for the courtroom, Nicki. Thank you both for the background information. I need to head back to the station. If you remember anything else, contact me. Or you can use our new online Citizen Watch program."

"What's that?" Amanda asked.

Officer Evans pulled a stack of flyers out of her laptop carrier and tossed them on the table. "We kicked off the program last week. We're asking Oak Hills residents to report any suspicious activity to our new online site. It's an easy way for our citizens to help the police and their community."

"Great idea." Amanda skimmed a red, white, and blue one-page flyer. OAK HILLS CITIZEN WATCH headlined the sheet, followed by the web address and social media sites. The background featured a photo of the police station with a squad car parked in front.

"The site's available 24-7," Officer Evans said. "If you wish to stay anonymous, you can sign in as a guest. So far, the program's been invaluable."

Amanda's mind churned as she slipped the pamphlet into her backpack. Maybe somebody would point the police to a suspect other than David.

Officer Evans slung the laptop carrier over her shoulder. "Good luck figuring out your vacation, Nicki. I'd appreciate it if you'd check in with me before leaving town." She headed toward the front door, then turned back. "Oh, and you can reopen the shop once the floor is clean. No reason to have someone slip and fall and sue you. That would mess up a lot more than your vacation."

"Not funny, Monica," Nicki said, deadpan.

"I'm sure you'll work things out. Don't forget the Citizen Watch program, ladies. And don't be shy about contacting me personally with updates. Oh, and if I need to talk to either of you again, it will be one on one. No more togetherness."

Officer Evans hustled out the door.

When the officer was gone, Nicki sighed. "I can't believe the police arrested David inside my shop. I feel so bad for him, and even worse for that murdered young woman."

She pushed back her glasses that had slipped halfway down her nose. "This may sound cold, but I can't help being disappointed that my vacation just got tanked. I really need a break from the grind. And now I'm asking myself, what else will go wrong?"

CHAPTER 4

Amanda gave Nicki a big hug. They'd been through so many of life's major and minor disappointments together: Amanda's totaled new car, Nicki's unhappy divorce, their first gray hairs. But now …

Amanda leaned back. "It's been a horrible morning. But we'll get through it, like we always do. And I'm sure things will work out so you can take your vacation." She pointed toward the trail of wet footprints through her spilled Panda Bear. "But first it's cleanup time. I'll push the furniture out of the way if you attack the floor."

Nicki nodded and added a smile. "I can always count on my bestie to get me back on track. You're right. First things first."

By the time Nicki scurried back with the mop and pail, Amanda had pushed the first table and chairs against the wall.

"Now that it's just the two of us, what do you really think about the whole situation?" Amanda asked as she dragged a second table to the side.

Nicki attacked the biggest puddle first. "Hearing a young woman was killed blocks from my shop gave me the creeps. But I can't get my head around David being capable of murdering someone. Eddie thinks the world of him. And I've been impressed with his work ethic, from what I've seen at the Bean and here." A hint of vanilla-scented floor cleaner filled the air. "What are you thinking?"

"Notch up everything you said a million times." Amanda pushed another table out of the way. "I know David. Someone else murdered Olivia."

"What if there's solid evidence against him?"

"Like Evans said, I watch a ton of TV crime shows," Amanda said. "Everyone knows things work differently in the real world." She shrugged. "Real police only need circumstantial, or indirect, evidence to make an arrest. Solid—more direct—evidence is usually needed for a conviction in court."

She paused. What *did* the police have on David? Evans had heard about Olivia's public performance at Bob's deli counter and her insistence on an "update" from David by that night. She wouldn't be surprised if rumors about Olivia's demand for him to return the five thousand dollars had caught the ears of the police. All circumstantial evidence.

A realization suddenly hit her as if she'd been slammed with a snowball in the face.

"Nicki, I think I know what's going on. The police are acting like they have solid evidence against David, but they probably don't. We know he didn't murder Olivia. Which means the actual killer is out there right now."

"That's a scary thought." Nicki gave a little shudder.

"I agree. But maybe that new Citizen Watch program will help reveal they arrested the wrong person."

"How?"

"Anyone can submit an anonymous tip pointing to another viable suspect." Amanda pointed to the pamphlets on the table. "Evans suggested that you put them next to the checkout so people can see them."

"That I can do. But what if the tips prove David is truly guilty? Like, they lead the police to solid evidence?"

Amanda frowned. "Then he's guilty, I guess." She brightened as she pulled back another chair. "You'd be surprised what I hear over the deli counter. I could be the one to submit the tip that clears David and points the police to the true murderer."

"The Deli Lady goes from slicing to sleuthing." Nicki chuckled. "I love it."

Amanda shook her head. "I don't plan to spy through living room windows or dig through garbage cans for evidence. I'll stay in the background, keeping my ears and eyes open. When I hear or see something, I'll anonymously send in the tip to the police. They'll take it from there, and I can keep my privacy."

"Even though Evans asked us to come to her if we heard anything more?"

Amanda nodded. "I don't want the real murderer knowing I was the person who alerted the police. You know how people in Oak Hills always seem to find things out."

"David may be stuck in jail while you're snooping around, though." Nicki sighed.

"That's a possibility," Amanda admitted. "I'll need to work fast. But everything needs to be accurate. No slip-ups."

"Just like the Deli Lady." Nicki smiled.

"Exactly," Amanda said. "Thanks for the vote of confidence."

As soon as the floor was dry, Amanda and her bestie hurried to put the shop in order. Nicki turned on the OPEN sign. The Dark Roast was back in business.

Seeing the time on the shop's clock, Amanda grabbed her coat and backpack. "I've got to scoot. Sorry we didn't get a chance to talk about your vacation, but I can help you out by working a shift or two. I've done it before, remember? I just need times that fit into my schedule at Bob's."

"You know what? I'll take you up on that offer," Nicki said.

"And if you're late to work today, blame it on me," she called over her shoulder on her way to the front counter.

"I'll keep that get-out-of-jail-free card in my back pocket." Amanda grinned.

A knock on the front door interrupted their goodbye. Nicki waved the customer in with a big smile. "Welcome to the Dark Roast."

"I'm overdue for my first cup of coffee of the day, especially after the terrible news about that murder," the young man said, stepping inside the shop.

Amanda recognized the customer as Patrick Williams, the brainiac in Matt's high school class. His stylish black leather jacket gave every sign he'd grown up, except for his still-boyish face. Although once the shortest boy in the class, he must have grown a foot in the past five years. Matt had said the football jocks razzed him relentlessly because of his height, calling him "Shrimpy." She'd never believed the rumor that Patrick had taken a swing at one of them.

"Patrick, I haven't seen you since graduation day." Amanda zipped up her coat and slipped her phone into a pocket. "And yes, it was terrible news about Olivia Hager. I'd love to chat, but I have to get to work."

"Just one thing," Patrick said. "I heard the police led a hand-cuffed guy out of the front door a short while ago. David Steadman? Is that true? He and I were good friends in high school."

Amanda nodded. "You heard correctly. That's the second terrible thing that happened this morning. The police arrested David for the murder."

Patrick's jaw dropped. "That doesn't make sense."

"I totally agree with you." She handed him a Citizen Watch pamphlet. "If you have a tip that can help David, let the police know through their new online site." She slung her backpack over her shoulder. "I gotta scoot. Can't be late."

"Tell Matt I hope to see him soon."

"Will do."

———

Amanda doubled up her steps down First Street. At this pace, she'd make the green traffic light at the end of the block. Then a short walk across the intersection to Bob's. Easy peasy.

She weaved through the leisurely walkers and moms with strollers, until barely dodging a UPS delivery person who almost smacked into her. His familiar face, along with the tattoos on his hands, gave him away as a friendly regular at Bob's deli counter. Except right now, he looked the other way, as if deliberately not wanting to acknowledge her. She heard him mumble what sounded like "Sorry" before rushing off.

That was weird, Amanda thought, hurrying toward the corner. Why had he acted so strangely?

She pushed it out of her head. Probably just a bad day on the job. Hopefully not as bad as David's.

Steps before she reached the intersection, the light turned red. "Rats," Amanda said aloud. Then remembered she hadn't sent her family a text about David's arrest. Matt especially should know what had happened, if he hadn't already heard.

As she hit send on the heads-up message, she looked up from her screen. The light had turned green. That's when she noticed the two men in front of her. Both wore business suits. One had distinct reddish hair, like the village manager. The other didn't have any.

As they started across the street, Amanda followed. The redhead turned his head toward his walking companion. Seeing his face confirmed he was the village manager. Amanda's ears perked up when she heard him say, ". . . arrested a guy for that murder last night. Pretty fast if you ask me."

Amanda moved closer, pretending to be engrossed in her phone. The two men didn't seem to notice her.

"They better have an airtight case," the village manager said. "Or the police chief is going to be in big trouble."

The other suit hesitated before asking, "Even more than he is now?"

The village manager shrugged as he turned again toward the other man. "We'll have to see how things play out. Like I told the mayor . . ."

He had picked up his pace and Amanda couldn't hear what he said next. She did the same and quickly caught up to the two men. But they'd switched to jabbering about the Cubs.

She slowed down thinking through what she'd overheard. Not a surprise the village manager knew about the arrest so soon after it happened. But his comment about needing an airtight case made her pause. And what did he say to the mayor?

Last week's editorial in the *Gazette* had laid the blame squarely on the police chief for failing to stop the recent uptick in crime. The murder could be another ding against the chief if not quickly solved.

She gave a silent thanks the new Citizen Watch program accepted anonymous tips. Best to remain nameless to the police in her quest to clear David of the murder.

Amanda hightailed it into Bob's employee entrance. Time to turn into the Deli Lady, with her ears and eyes wide open.

CHAPTER 5

Amanda made a record-fast change into her employee uniform, then scanned her badge and held her breath. *Confirmed start time: 11:59 a.m.*

Saved from the dreaded late list.

She hustled toward the display cases and inventoried today's freshest meats, cheeses, salads, and desserts. Customers relied on the Deli Lady's recommendations.

Amanda seamlessly blended in with the two clerks taking customer orders.

"Who has number 18?" She flashed her trademark can't-wait-for-my-next-customer smile.

"Right here." Mr. Logan signaled with a snap of his fingers. Behind him, Mrs. Logan guarded their shopping cart with a scowl.

Amanda inwardly groaned. She truly loved waiting on customers. But not the Logans. They loved to complain if given the slightest chance. She hadn't let her guard down after their petty grievance against her five years ago. And Bob Early hated customer complaints. Even more than late employees.

"We'd like a half-pound of honey-baked ham, sliced thin,

and eight slices of Muenster cheese, sliced medium. And we don't want any ends." Mr. Logan gave a dismissive wave.

"Coming right up," she said, keeping her smile intact.

She sliced the Muenster on autopilot, thinking about the murder and the upending events at the Dark Roast. Mr. Logan met her on the other side of the counter as she weighed the stack.

"Glad they arrested that murderer at the Dark Roast this morning. He's a wretched human being who should rot in prison," he said, his voice booming. Several waiting customers stared. A few stepped to the side.

Amanda turned away, focused on wrapping the cheese. Thank goodness Bob Early insisted his staff limit chatting with customers. Otherwise, she'd be tempted to challenge Mr. Logan over David's arrest.

"All those do-gooders saying the car accident that killed his family set him off," the man went on, adding a loud harrumph.

Amanda reached for the side of ham and headed to the slicer, out of hearing distance of his opinions.

But Mr. Logan's snide comment had made her pause. That horrible accident had occurred three years ago. It was possible it was still affecting David. Something to consider.

She pondered the question as she started up the slicer.

It wasn't until the third slice that she caught the classic mistake of failing to double-check the settings. Resetting the machine to thin slices, she chastised herself. Not a good idea to rile up the Logans, and a sloppy way to start her shift. She needed to focus on the job.

Handing both wrapped packages over the counter to Mr. Logan after checking for a third time that they were correct, Amanda repeated the mandated closing line for every customer's order. "Thank you for shopping at Bob's Finer Foods." Bob Early liked his staff to be polite, no matter how trying the customer.

"Number 22?" she called out, flashing a friendly smile at her next customer.

The same tattooed UPS courier who'd almost run into her on First Street held up Number 22. He mumbled an order for a to-go sandwich. It surprised Amanda. Usually he said, "Hey, Deli Lady, what's your recommendation for today?" with a grin. When she handed over his wrapped sandwich, he barely muttered thanks.

Amanda watched him head toward the checkout. He hadn't asked for his usual half-pint serving of tapioca pudding for his toddler daughter. Something was definitely off with him.

Soon she heard several positive comments about David that revived her.

The director of the local homeless program cited his weekly volunteer work. "That young man's first question when he walks in each time is, 'What can I do that no else wants to?' Doesn't have a mean bone in his body."

Another woman called out David's support of the annual holiday run, where he led youngsters through the village streets. "They adore him. And you know kids can spot a phony a mile away."

The few comments about Olivia Hager, all negative, made Amanda rethink how victims could be victimized many times over. One woman used a coarse description of Olivia and said she'd deserved what she'd gotten. Amanda felt a bitter taste in her mouth, remembering her own reaction to the young woman's behavior at the deli counter. A good reminder never to go there again.

When the police chief and the mayor each released official statements mid-afternoon confirming David's arrest, a sigh of relief could be heard throughout the store. "Oak Hills can go back to being a safe place," many said.

Hearing the public reaction weighed Amanda down. Would trying to help David be like Don Quixote fighting windmills?

Why hadn't any talk of other suspects drifted over the counter? And what evidence did the police have on David?

As she picked up a block of cheese for the next order, a strong whiff of garlic salami drifted her way. In a knee-jerk reaction, she blurted out, "It stinks!"

Amanda slapped her hand over her mouth and surveyed the milling customers. Thankfully, no one reacted to her careless outburst. It wasn't that she hated her job. It was the whiffs of pungent cheese and garlicky meat she'd once breathed happily that now seemed to bother her.

She positioned the block of cheese on the slicer. Her stomach and mind churned with each whirl of the blade.

Was she in la-la land to think that someone might walk up to the deli counter and whisper, "I know who really murdered Olivia Hager"?

Deep in thought, she headed back to the front counter with the finished stack in hand.

As she laid the order on the pricing scale, the customer leaned over the counter and frowned. "Excuse me, but I asked for Swiss. The cheese with the little holes all over. That's not Swiss," she tsked.

"I'm so sorry," Amanda said. "My mistake." Working at warp speed, she soon handed the correct order to the irate customer. The woman played up the melodramatics, tossing the package into her cart with a sigh and a shake of her head.

Amanda's cheeks burned. Her Deli Lady reputation would be in the toilet if she didn't get back on task.

A glance at the clock showed the time was 2:55 p.m. Her feet hurt and her back ached with another three hours to go.

Break time!

Amanda walked into the windowless employee break room at the back of the store and flopped down on the well-worn plastic couch, grateful to have the room to herself. Yawning, she pulled her cell phone out of her pocket and powered it up.

A series of beeps announced that voice and text messages awaited.

She clicked on Joe's voicemail first. He was relieved she was okay and couldn't wait to hear the full story about the murder.

Matt had texted, *Unbelievable*. Brittany sent a screaming emoji and added, *I'm so creeped out.*

We'll talk at dinner, Amanda responded.

The remaining texts were from Nicki. She scrolled to her bestie's first message in the string.

Have idea- later gator. That had become Nicki's sign-off while she was planning her vacation to Florida.

As she scrolled through her friend's texts, the time stamps got shorter and the messages became more urgent. *WE NEED TO TALK!!!!!!!!!!!!* sent five minutes ago.

Amanda tapped her friend's number. "Nicki, what's the emergency?"

"Remember how you said you'd take on shifts so I could go on my vacation?"

"I remember saying a shift or two, but okay, I'll do what I can."

"Well, I've got a better offer for you."

"What's that?"

"How would you like to fill in as manager for the entire week?"

Amanda sat upright, surprised and intrigued. Then reality hit. "Thanks, but I already have a job, remember? And I don't have manager experience."

"I know that. Hear me out."

"I'm listening."

"You've got customer service down pat. There's a good reason you're known as the Deli Lady."

"True."

"And you're a regular customer, so you know our menu, the staff, and how we operate."

"Good point."

"And yes, you'd need to learn how to run the daily operations. But you're smart and I'm sure you'll catch on right away."

"I appreciate your faith in me."

"Most important, I'd trust you with the Dark Roast. Hey, you even reminded me to clean up the floor first. Plus, don't forget, I'd only be a text or phone call away. Even better, it would give you a welcome change. Bonus, there'd be no stinky smells. Just delightful aromas." Nicki took a deep breath. "What do you think?"

Amanda switched her phone to the other ear. "It all sounds enticing. But I don't see it happening. Our schedule here is already set for the next four weeks."

"Okay, let me tempt you with another plus."

"And that is . . .?"

"You always complain that Bob's very strict about employees' schedules, including lunch breaks. No exceptions," Nicki said.

"True. And don't get me going on the late list or customer complaints."

"For the next week, that won't be the case if you take on the manager's job at the Dark Roast. I'm lenient with my staff about breaks and lunch, as long as the counter is covered and it's not a peak time. But, of course, the shop comes first."

Amanda twirled her ponytail, calculating how the Dark Roast's flexible schedule would give her more opportunity to help David. Then her hand dropped. "Your offer is very tempting. And truly, I'd love to help you out. But I can't jeopardize my job at Bob's. We need my paycheck."

"I know this is a big ask, but could you take a week of vacation?"

"Nope. We have to ask for time off four weeks in advance. No exceptions."

"Clone yourself?"

"Ha-ha."

"I'll do anything to make this work," her bestie insisted.

Amanda pictured Bob Early, owner of Bob's Finer Foods. The paunchy, somewhat bald purveyor of Oak Hills' biggest grocery store prided himself on wearing the same brown polo as his employees. He cruised through the store daily, chatting with customers and workers alike, right down to the after-school baggers. He liked to pretend he was one of them, but everyone knew he did it to keep tabs on the employees and glad-hand the customers. His reputation as a ruthless penny-pincher was legendary.

She jumped up from the couch, almost dropping her phone. "I have an idea, Nicki."

Amanda laid out her plan. After she'd finished, she didn't need to see her bestie's grin to know Nicki loved it.

"I'm hanging up and calling Bob," Nicki said. "Be prepared."

CHAPTER 6

After ending her call with Nicki, Amanda did a happy dance around the break room. If her plan worked, next week she'd fill in as manager at the Dark Roast. She'd get a much-needed breather from the deli counter, and Nicki's Florida vacation would be back on. Best of all, a flexible schedule would be a big plus in searching for clues to Olivia Hager's true murderer. After she found them, David could get his life back.

Amanda grabbed a bottle of water from the employee refrigerator, Bob's only free perk for staff, and took a big gulp. She rocked on her heels until they turned numb. She stared at the notices tacked to the staff bulletin board but couldn't have repeated what they said if asked.

By the time Bob Early's admin peered into the break room, Amanda felt like a kid waiting for Santa Claus on Christmas Eve.

"Amanda, Bob wants to see you in his office."

She held back from acting too giddy as she trailed the woman down the hallway and pressed her wrinkled shirt with her hand, as if it were an iron. She picked off most of a glob of goop with her fingernail. Bob Early was still her boss, after all.

Steps later, she stood in the doorway of his office. Seated behind a massive mahogany desk, he waved her in and pointed to an empty chair. Dozens of framed photographs, all featuring Bob, lined the walls. He was either shaking people's hands, surrounded by schoolkids, or addressing a captivated audience. The man liked to remind visitors of his stature in the community.

Bob leaned into the speakerphone on his desk as Amanda sat down. "Hold on, Nicki. She just walked in."

Amanda tucked her right hand behind her back and crossed her fingers.

"I'm glad we caught you on your break. I have Nicki Lenzini from the Dark Roast on the phone. She reassured me that all is well after that brief disturbance over there this morning."

He straightened a piece of paper on his desk. "Best thing for Oak Hills is that the murderer is in jail. And don't worry, Amanda, there won't be any mention of your name in the *Gazette*. I took care of that."

Amanda mentally added Bob Early's name to her list of David-is-guilty club members. She wanted to ask how he'd managed to keep her name out of the newspaper, then scratched the thought. Not the time to sidetrack him.

"I understand you're a friend of Nicki's," he said.

"Yes, I am." Amanda kept her voice neutral, not wanting to give any hint of what she hoped was coming.

Bob got into that familiar posture of his, like a bird getting ready to preen his feathers. "I'm not sure you know that I'm the president of our esteemed Oak Hills Chamber of Commerce. We pledge to support Oak Hills businesses as we work for the benefit of all."

"That's wonderful." Amanda nodded as if hearing Bob crow about his civic accomplishments for the first time. All employees knew the routine. If Bob mentioned being president of the Chamber of Commerce, they were expected to be in awe of their boss's generous community spirit, no matter how many times they'd heard it.

"Nicki told me she learned after that little ruckus this morning she would be short-staffed next week and would have to cancel her long-awaited Florida trip. I need to add that Nicki is the Chamber's vice president. A real go-getter. I can't tell you how many times she has helped me out. When she came to me with her problem, of course my first response was to ask what I could do to help her."

He leaned forward. "And lucky for her, I came up with an idea."

Amanda kept still. *So far, so good.*

"Here's the plan," Bob said. "Amanda—that's you—steps in as the on-site manager at the Dark Roast for the next week, beginning this Saturday. Amanda will be that important physical presence in the store while Nicki gets to enjoy her well-deserved vacation. You two would keep in touch, of course, however you want to work that out."

Bob looked down at the phone. "And I think you agreed that would work for you, correct, Nicki?"

"Yes, Bob, that's correct," came through the speaker.

Bob turned back to Amanda. "You'll still be an employee of my store, of course, but helping Nicki for the week. Like the Lend-Lease agreement during World War II when the US supplied ships to help our allies. How does that sound to you?"

Amanda smiled. "Works for me. I'd be honored to help." She gripped the sides of the chair, holding herself back from jumping up and yelling, "YAHOO!" She brushed off his comparison of her to a fleet of battleships from eighty years ago. Bob loved to use World War II analogies.

Bob clapped his hands. "Sounds like we're all set. No formal announcement needed. The rest of my staff will know by tomorrow morning. I already have my grandson in mind to fill in for you, Amanda. He'll be home from college on spring break, and I guarantee he'll be a whiz on his first day." Bob gave Amanda a smug smile. "For now, keep this to yourself."

"Understood." Amanda tried not to show her disappointment at Bob's boasting that his college-age grandson could easily take on the job she'd worked hard at for ten years. Another reminder the man was clueless about employee motivation. Something to be conscious of in her upcoming week as manager at the Dark Roast.

Bob sat back with a self-satisfied grin. "I'm glad I came up with this idea. It's going to work out nicely."

"Thank you, Aman—" Nicki started to say.

"Goodbye, ladies." Bob hung up the phone and turned his chair toward his computer, his back to Amanda.

For Bob, the meeting had ended.

Amanda headed down the back hallway with a bounce in her step. Hearing Nicki's text alert, she pulled out her phone.

"YIPPEE!!!!!! Later Gator."

Amanda could hardly contain her ear-to-ear grin. "Make him think it's his idea," she'd told her bestie. "His ego will take it from there."

She couldn't help standing a little taller after beating Bob Early at his own game. Was this a sign she had the skills to be a manager? And the smarts to uncover the true killer of Olivia Hager?

Fingers crossed it did.

———

Amanda clocked out from Bob's Deli counter at 6:01 p.m. with visions of her feet up and a glass of wine in hand. What an unbelievable day.

Nicki's text alert interrupted her walk home.

Need to talk details. Tomorrow morning @8ish? Panda Bear on the house.

Amanda grinned and sent a smiley face.

Stopped by the red light, she couldn't help but see the sign pointing toward the Oak Hills Police Station, just two short blocks out of her way.

What was David doing right now? Had he gotten a lawyer? How would Illinois' new SAFE-T Act come into play, now that bail had been eliminated and judicial discretion would determine whether arrestees could be released or had to remain in jail? And what was poor David eating for dinner?

When the light turned green, Amanda turned toward the police station, then stopped. She needed to head home and get dinner on the table for her own family.

She'd check on David tomorrow for sure.

Decision made; she started toward home in the fading twilight.

Ten minutes later Amanda spotted Joe as she walked up the driveway. He was leaning over his prized 1964 Ford Mustang, affectionately named Baby. Its front end was sticking out of the garage with a spotlight attached to the raised hood.

The iconic galloping silver stallion symbol glistened on the front grille. The newly painted red body showed off the white-wall tires, completing the classic look. A whiff of motor oil greeted her. Joe had yet to get Baby's engine running.

She was surprised to see him home this early. "Did something happen at work?" she asked, stopping in front of the vintage two-door sedan.

Joe rose from the right-side panel and grinned. "Everything is fine. And since my meeting ended sooner than I expected, I got home early and--voilà!" He pointed toward their house. "The kitchen is now sparkling clean."

"Thank you," she said, glad he'd taken this morning's text seriously. Her definition of a sparkling clean kitchen was leaps beyond his, but for now, hearing he'd made the effort was a good start.

Joe reached for a rag draped over the side of the car. "Hope you're okay after David's arrest at your hideaway. I'd give you a hug, but I'd get you dirty." He held up his still-smudged palms. "I'll need lots of soap and hot water to get the grease off these babies."

"Well, I'm fine. See?" Amanda opened her arms and turned a full circle, like a ballerina performing a pirouette. She ended with an exaggerated bow, then slowly straightened up, frowning.

"But I do think it's horrible that David's sitting in the Oak Hills jail for something I'm sure he didn't do."

Joe nodded. "It doesn't make sense. He's not the kind of person who would murder someone."

"I'm sure Matt and Brittany feel the same way. We can talk about it as a family over dinner." She tilted her head, planting a coy look. "Right now, I want to tell you where I'll be working next week."

"You have a new job?" Joe took a step back.

"Not exactly." Amanda explained Nicki's offer and Bob Early's agreement that Amanda could fill in as manager at the Dark Roast next week. Nicki would match her current hourly rate.

"You've worked at that deli counter since the kids were in middle school," Joe said. "Do you really want to take on the responsibilities and hassles of being a manager, even if it's only for a week?"

Amanda took a deep breath. "Well, I am nervous, but I feel like I had a golden ticket handed to me. Plus, I'll be saving money."

"How's that?"

"Dark Roast staff get free coffee."

"Well, make sure you get the real pricey ones. That should save us a bundle." Joe gave her his teasing, lopsided smile. The one that always caught her heart.

"Ha-ha. Hilarious, but true." She held out her arms again.

"Hey, I'm ready for that hug. I don't care how dirty your hands are."

Joe hustled toward her.

Nuzzling his neck, she inhaled the spicy scent of Brut, the men's cologne he'd worn since the day they met.

Joe leaned back. "Amanda, I need to tell you—"

SCRREECH!!

Their heads jerked toward the street. A truck swerved out of the way of a cyclist, who shook his fist.

Well, that killed the mood.

Joe dropped his arms and mumbled something about Baby as he turned toward the garage. Before she could stop him, he was back under the Mustang's hood.

"Joe, what were you going to say?"

He grabbed a screwdriver, acting like he hadn't heard her.

"Don't forget, we're sitting down at seven." She hoped he heard her this time.

"Got it," he muttered, his head next to the car's engine. He looked like a skilled surgeon from the *Chicago Med* TV series, poised to perform a delicate operation on a very special patient.

Heading into the house, she reminded herself not to be jealous of the many hours Joe spent on Baby. After all, he loved her more than that car, even if he never said those exact words.

Didn't he?

CHAPTER 7

Amanda's jaw dropped when she stepped into the kitchen. The room was spotless. Joe had topped her expectations.

She was about to tap the kitchen window to get his attention when she spotted the person standing next to him. Their neighbor, Frank. The man had planted his elbows on Baby's side panel. When he stood up and wagged his finger at Joe, her husband took a polishing cloth to the smudges. For once, he appeared to be annoyed with Frank. No one messed with Baby.

Fifteen minutes later, Amanda slid the family-favorite tuna noodle casserole into the hot oven. Grabbing her wineglass, she headed to the living room where her dated but still usable laptop sat on the small corner desk. It was normally her workhorse for online shopping, but tonight she'd challenge the machine and herself with more serious searches.

The online afternoon edition of the *Gazette* didn't mention her name in the article about David's arrest, confirming Bob Early's influence. But it did have an interesting interview with David's manager.

Eddie Turner, manager of the Happy Bean Coffee Shop in Schaumburg where Stedman is on staff, stated his employee was "one of my best baristas, with a following of customers that has upped my business." He also mentioned David's willingness to take on extra shifts and mundane chores to get the job done, and said everyone liked him. "I still can't believe he could have murdered that girl," he told this reporter.

Amanda sat back. This should be a plus for David's defense.

Scrolling down through older stories, she halted at a link titled *"Local Oak Hills Family Killed in Traffic Accident."* Reading the three-year-old article rekindled the sadness she'd felt earlier.

David had lost his father, mother, and younger brother when a truck ran a red light and broadsided their car. His only remaining family member in Oak Hills was his great-aunt, Virginia Smith, shown in a family picture with her arm around David.

Amanda knew the woman, a longtime shopper at Bob's, by sight, although they'd never talked beyond a greeting or taking her order.

A creak from the front door interrupted Amanda's pondering. A sliver of light revealed it hadn't been closed all the way.

Grumbling about sending an open invitation to Olivia Hager's still on-the-loose murderer, she walked into the front foyer and firmly shut the door. Then she frowned.

Anyone could have walked through the front entrance of the Valley Lane condos. There had to be security cameras operating at the entrances, in the elevators, and maybe throughout the hallways. Surely the police had checked them out. Or maybe they needed a gentle reminder.

Tightening her ponytail, she headed back to her desk, mentally composing the right words.

She pulled up the Citizen Watch home page. The background picture mirrored that of the printed pamphlet, except for Chief Daniel Grady's stern face gazing out from the right upper corner. His tough-cop stare was the opposite of his friendly, cheerful expression as he'd waved from an old-fashioned police wagon during the last Oak Hills Fourth of July parade.

She clicked the link labeled *Submit a Crime Tip.* A pop-up form asked for the details: name and physical description of the suspect, address if known, incident or crime that occurred, and where it had been committed. The tipster info screen offered two options: Submitter's name and contact information, or Guest, the anonymous option.

Amanda hesitated. Checking the security camera footage had to be standard police protocol. Whoever read her tip would laugh at it. Or even be annoyed.

But she could casually ask Evans about the security cameras when the officer stopped in the Dark Roast.

The oven timer dinged, interrupting her deliberation. She grabbed her almost-empty wineglass and headed to the kitchen. Today had been like riding in the front car of a roller coaster at Six Flags. The shocks, the g-force, the feeling of being suspended in midair were identical.

Time to bring her family in on her unforgettable day.

With the four Knightly dinner plates soon loaded up, Amanda described the moments leading up to and after David's arrest.

Joe spoke first. "Did the police say why they arrested him for the murder?"

"No, they didn't. I still can't believe it."

Matt leaned over his plate, frowning. "This is so wrong. David wouldn't hurt a fly." He stabbed a chunk of casserole with his fork. "I can think of lots of people who might want to bump off Olivia Hager. Like I told you yesterday, that girl was a real trip."

Amanda gave her son a stony look. "That's a horrible thing to say, Matt. The poor woman was murdered. Even if she wasn't well-liked, that doesn't justify her death." She tried not to blush, remembering her own unkind reaction to Olivia at the deli counter.

Matt jabbed another piece of casserole. "Yeah," he muttered. "But everyone knew Olivia was a head case."

Amanda held up her hand like a security guard holding back an unruly crowd. "Enough on Olivia. Let's get back to David."

She told her family about David's protest of innocence and plea for her help as the police led him out the front door of the Dark Roast. Then she explained her plan to use the Citizen Watch program to help him.

"Don't worry, Mom, I'm on it," Matt said. "I'm getting all of David's friends together to figure out how to get him out of this mess. We're going to start with a GoFundMe campaign."

"That's great," Amanda said. "The more people who jump in to help, the better."

Matt frowned again. "Mom, I've got it covered."

Brittany dropped her fork. "Well, what about me? If David didn't kill Olivia, that means whoever killed her is still out there. And I could get murdered next."

Amanda touched her daughter's hand. "Trust me. I will not let that happen."

"Your mom's right, Brittany. Not to worry," Joe said. "But I have to be honest, Amanda. I'm not comfortable with you getting involved in a murder investigation. You don't have a lot of experience as a private eye. At least, not that I'm aware of."

Amanda shook her head. "Joe, don't worry. I'll be working incognito. I'm just going to keep my ears and eyes open and pass on anonymous tips through that new Citizen Watch program." She turned to her son. "And Matt, I promise I won't interfere with whatever you and your friends are doing."

Her son gave her a weak smile. Joe sighed and dished himself another helping of casserole. "All I ask is, please don't get hurt. Or get in trouble."

"That won't happen." Amanda laid down her fork. "Now I want to share my good news."

"You won the Mega Millions lottery and we're millionaires?" Matt's exaggerated grin matched Brittany's as they high-fived each other.

"Don't I wish. But sorry, no."

The two siblings sighed in mock disappointment.

"But as I started to say, beginning Saturday through next week, I'm stepping in as manager of the Dark Roast. Nicki's going to tell the staff tomorrow."

"You'll be working with Chloe," Matt said with a softness in his voice.

Amanda pictured his girlfriend, always accessorized in something pink and wearing a friendly smile. Pink had been her favorite color since she was a little girl, she'd told Amanda. Matt and Chloe had started hanging out together three months ago, and Amanda had been thrilled when Matt hinted that they might be getting serious.

"So how are things going with you two? Anything you need to tell us, son?" Joe asked.

The opening bars of Mendelssohn's "Wedding March" started up in Amanda's head.

"Nah," Matt quickly protested. "It's no big deal."

Amanda wasn't sure if she totally believed him. Maybe he just wasn't ready to say anything more right now.

She reluctantly shut down the matrimonial prelude.

"Before you leave the table, I want to remind everyone it's going to be a busy week for me. You all need to pitch in," she announced. "Starting tonight."

"Your mom is right," Joe said. "Let's move, you two."

He loaded the dishwasher while Brittany took care of leftovers and Matt wiped down the counters and stovetop.

Amanda gave them a thumbs-up. "Kudos to all of you. A great start." *Fingers crossed.*

Matt grabbed his jacket. "I'm meeting Chloe. She's still really upset about the murder, especially because it happened two floors below her condo. She can't believe they arrested David, either."

"How does Chloe know him?"

"They dated back in high school. But they're just friends now."

"Oh. Well, please tell her I'm thankful she didn't get hurt."

"Will do." He was already out the back door.

Brittany headed off to call a friend.

Joe held up his cell phone. "Darn it, Amanda. I have to answer this email from work." He hustled out of the kitchen before she could ask if he'd learned anything more about the missed credit-card payment.

When she headed into the living room, Amanda's tired eyes bounced between the corner desk with her laptop and the couch in front of the TV.

After all she'd been through today, the couch beat the laptop by a landslide.

CHAPTER 8

For Amanda, Thursday never seemed to end. And Friday started too soon.

Her phone jolted her awake. She didn't have to open her eyes to know Joe's side of the bed was empty.

Showered and dressed, she headed down to the kitchen. Seeing today's *Gazette* waiting for her on the table, she silently thanked Joe. Glancing out the window, she was surprised to see him tinkering with Baby again. *Must have a late start for work,* she thought.

She zoomed in on the *Gazette*'s front-page story of David's arrest. The article stated Stedman would be brought to a pretrial release hearing this afternoon.

Amanda nodded, remembering she'd read that the new Illinois SAFE-T Act eliminated bail. At the hearing, defendants with lesser charges would be released. Anyone charged with first-degree murder would remain in jail. The defendant would also be assigned a public defender if they hadn't hired a lawyer.

She frowned. Did David have the money to hire a private attorney?

According to the article, he could be transferred from the

Oak Hills police station to the Cook County Department of Corrections. That would mean Cook County Jail.

A shiver passed from Amanda's head to her toes. The place was so horrible, dreary and dangerous, you wouldn't want your worst enemy imprisoned there. That was how people described it. She didn't know anyone who'd been locked up in the Cook County facility. Until now, possibly.

On the next page, the headline *"Cook County Jail Strike Imminent"* caught Amanda's attention. The guards were threatening to strike over pay and working conditions, with late-night bargaining sessions ramping up.

Her shiver let up ever so slightly. If the Cook County guards were on strike, David would likely remain in the Oak Hills jail. Not good news, exactly, but better than the alternative.

Seeing the time was 7:45, she grabbed her coat and hurried out the back door, waving goodbye to Joe, who was still huddled over Baby outside the garage.

She headed down the driveway and on to the Dark Roast.

Just before 8:00 a.m., Nicki greeted Amanda with open arms. Today her friend wore her black, boxy, I-mean-business glasses.

Amanda glanced around the busy shop, reveling in the chatter and laughter while breathing in the spicy, nutty, and chocolatey coffee aromas. Another day in Paradise, with one slight difference.

Nicki handed over a name tag that said "Amanda"—and just below it, "Manager." She grinned. "This makes it official. I had it shipped priority mail."

Amanda gave her friend a big hug. Nicki stepped back first. "We only have an hour, so let's get started. But first, how about that Panda Bear?"

"Sounds great!" Amanda replied.

They toasted each other in Nicki's cramped office and went to work. First up, the upcoming week's shifts. Checking the sheet in front of her, Amanda frowned. "Why am I only working until noon on Sunday when the shop is open until 3:00?"

"I don't want you to miss your weekly visit with your mother. We both know she's challenging, but she relies on you."

Amanda didn't answer right away. Her mother wasn't chatty. She had few interests and even fewer friends. Whenever Amanda brought up questions about the past, especially about her father, her mother really clammed up. But she did rely on her only child.

"You're right," she reluctantly agreed. "Let's keep going."

An hour later Amanda sat back, her yellow pad bulging with pages of notes on manager responsibilities and overall operations. "Whew! There's a lot to learn."

"You'll do great," Nicki said. "Get here by 6:00 tomorrow morning and we'll cover the rest before the 7:00 a.m. open."

Amanda raised a teasing eyebrow. "Okay if I come in my pajamas and slippers?"

Nicki smirked. "Nice try, but no. It's Saturday, so you get an extra hour to sleep in. Same with Sunday. But starting Monday, you'll need to be here by 5:00 for the 6:00 a.m. open. And no pj's." She wagged her finger at Amanda.

Amanda made a pretend annoyed face.

Nicki chuckled and handed her several Dark Roast polo shirts. "Two things I need to caution you about. First, I know you plan to keep your ears and eyes open so you can help David. That's okay, as long as you do it discreetly. Keep your focus on the Dark Roast."

"No problem."

"Second, never ask Evans about the investigation when she stops by," Nicki said. "I don't want to call any more attention to the Dark Roast than needed. It's not true that all publicity is good."

Amanda nodded. "Understood."

Nicki's smile returned. "How about a refill on that Panda Bear? On the house, of course."

"Absolutely, thanks. I'll be super energized for the rest of the day."

Amanda hurried home, holding tight to her Panda Bear, along with the yellow pad crammed with notes. The closed garage door and the van parked in their driveway meant Joe had taken the train to work. The van was hers.

She hustled inside the house. Time to do a little online sleuthing.

Within a minute, she found the address and phone number for Virginia Smith, David's great-aunt.

"Hello," a woman's crisp voice answered after four rings.

"Is this Virginia Smith?" Amanda asked.

"Yes. To whom am I speaking?"

"My name is Amanda Knightly. My son, Matt, is a close friend of your nephew."

"What do you want?" The woman's tone sounded accusatory now.

"I was in the Dark Roast yesterday when the police arrested David. I thought you might want to know what I saw and what he said to me. I live in Oak Hills and can be at your front door in less than ten minutes."

Silence.

"If that works for you, of course," Amanda added. "I'll only take a few minutes of your time."

"I'll expect you at ten o'clock sharp." The call was disconnected before Amanda could say goodbye.

At 9:59 a.m. Amanda pulled in front of a tiny, well-kept house on the west side of Oak Hills. Second thoughts made her queasy. Virginia Smith had always acted a bit distant at the deli counter. Would she think it rude that Amanda had invited herself to her house? Should she drive off and call back with a lame excuse?

Seeing the woman staring out at her through the sheer front curtains, Amanda unbuckled her seatbelt. Too late to back out now.

Virginia stood in the partially open front door as Amanda reached the top step of the porch. Along with her coiffed silver hair and regal posture, the woman's sad, deep blue eyes broadcast caution. She was clad in dress slacks and a coordinated blouse. Amanda guessed her age to be early 80s.

The woman continued her haughty stare, then gave a nod, like a queen granting an audience. "You're the Deli Lady at Bob's," she said, with a condescending clip in her voice.

"Yes, I am."

Virginia's eyes narrowed. "I've been warned about talking to you."

"By whom?" Amanda asked.

"Let's just say I know people in high places. But they haven't lifted a finger to help David."

Virginia hesitated, then pulled the door wide open. "Since you took the trouble to call before stopping by, it's only polite I invite you inside. I'll make a fresh pot of coffee." The snippy tone remained.

Seated at the kitchen table, Amanda laid out yesterday's events, including David's protest of innocence and plea for her help. She kept her voice calm, not wanting to alarm the woman.

At first, Virginia showed no sign of emotion. Until a tear rolled down her cheek. Then she opened up like a burst dam.

Amanda soon understood Virginia's initial reluctance to meet. Yesterday morning, the police had arrived at her front door minutes after David left for the Dark Roast. "I thought I was helping the police. I didn't know I was helping them arrest my nephew!"

The police had asked for her consent to search the house, and she'd innocently agreed. They'd checked out David's bedroom, the garbage, and around the outside of the house. They hadn't seemed to find what they wanted and soon left.

Amanda nodded. Maybe the gossip she'd overheard yesterday about a missing piece of evidence was true.

She learned David's one phone call after his arrest had been to his great-aunt. His quivering voice had scared her.

"He had grown into a fine young man. Then that horrible car accident happened three years ago." Virginia traced the rim of her coffee cup with her finger.

"We formed our own little family," she went on, breaking the silence. "He moved into my home, taking over all the chores I couldn't handle anymore. He worked several jobs, re-enrolled in college, and pulled his life back together. I felt better, too."

Amanda kept still. She sensed Virginia hadn't let out everything bottled up inside her.

"Then, out of nowhere, came this arrest." Virginia shook her head. "But I know he didn't murder that girl. That's not my David."

"Not the David I know, either," Amanda said.

Virginia's hands tightened into fists, and she banged the table. "I knew Olivia was nothing but trouble. Months ago, he told me she wouldn't leave him alone. She just wouldn't take no for an answer." She shoved aside her coffee cup.

Amanda kept quiet, waiting for Virginia to calm down.

"I apologize for getting angry," the woman said at last. "I truly appreciate that you came to my house. The police wouldn't tell me anything." She gave Amanda a weak smile. "Thanks for letting me blow off steam."

"I understand your frustration. I'm frustrated, too," Amanda said. "But I'm curious about something. Did David mention seeing or doing anything unusual on the day of the murder?"

"I'll tell you what I told the police. He worked his regular 9 to 5 Wednesday shift at the Happy Bean over in Schaumburg."

"What time did he get home?"

"Just after 10 p.m. I was watching the local nightly news on TV. David seemed excited about filling in as manager at the Dark Roast, starting the next day." Virginia sighed. "He promised he'd give me special service if I stopped by the shop."

Amanda tucked away Virginia's comment about special service. Next week she'd keep David's promise of special service for his aunt if the opportunity came up.

"Did he tell you where he was Wednesday night after his shift ended?" Amanda asked.

"No. And I didn't ask him." Virginia gave Amanda a motherly glance. "I try to give him his privacy."

Amanda nodded. "Understood. By chance, did you notice anything different about him?"

"I saw a deep cut on his right index finger that seemed to be bleeding. I asked how it happened. He said it was no big deal. I suggested he bandage it, and we left it at that."

Amanda made a mental note. The same injury she'd seen this morning. "Did you ever meet Olivia Hager?"

"No, and I never wanted to after what David told me about her."

"How did David know her?"

"Through high school, although he barely knew her then. He told me she started coming to the Happy Bean a couple of months ago and pestered him a lot. One night she confided she had no friends and was lonely. When she started to cry David felt sorry for her. He took her out to dinner after his shift ended. He said he only thought of her as someone who'd needed a friend that night, and nothing more."

"So, they never dated?"

"Not that I'm aware of." Virginia hesitated before drawing in a deep breath and letting it out slowly. "I shouldn't be telling you this, but David needed backers to start up his own coffee shop, and Olivia was his first investor. She gave him five thousand dollars in cash. I asked him where she got all that money, but he told me he didn't know. That made me feel uneasy."

"What happened to the five thousand dollars?" Amanda had Matt's answer, but she wanted Virginia's.

"David used it to snap up a great deal on equipment, which he stored in my basement. But on Tuesday night, the day before the murder, he mentioned to me that Olivia was acting as if she owned him because of her investment."

"Did he say anything about returning Olivia's money to her?"

"No, he didn't. And I didn't ask. That was David's business, not mine." Virginia's regal arched eyebrow reappeared. "Now before I answer any more of your questions, I have a few for you."

"Go ahead."

"You're known as the Deli Lady at Bob's Finer Foods because you do a great job helping shoppers," Virginia said. "I'm unclear how that translates into you helping David. Advising him that Black Forest ham is the special of the day isn't going to get him out of jail."

Amanda couldn't hide a chuckle. "You're right. Here's my plan." She explained the Citizen Watch program. "You'd be amazed what I hear shoppers say while they're in line, because they forget I'm there."

"But the police have already arrested David."

"Yes, but a lot can still be uncovered that will point to someone else."

Virginia nodded. "All right, I understand the how part. Now I need to know the why. Let's be honest. Why are you interested in helping a twenty-three-year-old man? I'm sure there will be talk about that."

Amanda paused for a moment. "That's a valid question. Like I told you earlier, I know your great-nephew through my son, Matt. They're close friends. Plus, I can't ignore that he asked for my help as they led him out of the Dark Roast in handcuffs."

Amanda shrugged. "If people want to think the worst, you can't stop them. I believe David is innocent and his plea was sincere. If it were my son, I'd want someone to do the same for him."

Virginia nodded, then gave Amanda a sheepish glance. "My apologies. I completely forgot that you said they were friends. Please excuse me for sounding skeptical. You're right. David can use all the help he can get."

"You should know it's not just me jumping in," Amanda added. "Matt is right now rallying their friends to set up a GoFundMe campaign. The money they collect can help pay his lawyer. Which reminds me. Who is David's lawyer?"

Virginia folded her hands. "I'm embarrassed to tell you he doesn't have one. I've made several inquiries, and the retainer fees are far beyond what either David or I can afford." She sat still for a moment. "Is it true David will be assigned a public defender by the court, and there'll be no fee?"

Amanda nodded. "Yes, it's true."

Virginia let out a long sigh. "Thank you for clarifying that point. It makes me feel a little better." She sat up straighter. "Now I need to ask for your help myself."

"Of course."

"Could you drive me to the police station so I can talk to David in person? I want to see him, if only to give him encouragement. I'm afraid to drive with my emotions on edge like this. I'll only stay a short time."

Amanda hesitated. She couldn't be late for her noon shift at Bob's.

She checked her watch. If they kept the visit brief, she'd make it to work on time and keep last night's promise to check up on David today. She'd figure out later how and when to tell Nicki about being at the police station.

"I'd be happy to, but we need to leave now," Amanda said. "I can't stay longer than thirty minutes."

Virginia reached for a cane leaning against the wall. Amanda frowned. She never used a cane at Bob's.

"This is my insurance policy that I don't get any malarkey from the chief about needing an appointment. He's going to rue the day he tangled with my family," Virginia said.

Amanda smothered a laugh. This lady had a crafty side.

"Oh, and I mustn't forget my handicapped parking pass. Might as well give them the full show." Virginia reached for the blue plastic tag on the kitchen counter and stuffed it in her purse.

Amanda's innards tingled. It would be an interesting visit to the police station.

CHAPTER 9

Amanda hung Virginia's disabled parking placard from the rearview mirror after parking the van in front of the Oak Hills police station.

"Time to start the show!" Virginia grabbed her cane and stepped onto the pavement. She took a few wobbly steps and halted.

Amanda held out her arm for support. "Don't worry about me. I'm just fine," Virginia said under her breath, with an added wink.

By the time they stood at the front desk inside the lobby, Amanda knew Virginia would put on an Oscar-worthy performance.

The nameplate identified Officer Lee as the person on duty.

"My name is Virginia Smith. I'm here to visit my nephew, David Stedman," she said in a weak voice, wiggling her cane as if to steady herself.

"What time is your appointment?"

"Appointment?" Virginia's eyes watered, her voice shaky. "Oh, my goodness. I'm sure Chief Grady told me I could come by anytime. It's very important that I talk to my nephew right away." She dabbed her eyes with a handkerchief.

Amanda bit her lip and held back a snicker. Virginia was quite the actor.

"No appointment, no visit," the officer said flatly, as if this wasn't the first time he'd heard Grady's name used to try to bend the rules.

"Officer, could you possibly make an exception in my case?" Virginia gave him an optimistic look, like a dog hoping for a bone.

The officer let out a loud sigh. "Okay, I'll check. But don't get your hopes up." He pointed to a row of benches lining the wall. "Take a seat over there."

He turned aside and picked up the phone. Ten feet from where Amanda and Virginia stood, a heavy door swung open, stenciled with the warning *Entry Only with Police Authorization* in large red letters. Two police officers emerged through the open doorway.

"Follow me," Amanda heard Virginia whisper.

Miraculously, Virginia sprinted like a teenager toward the open door, the cane dangling off her arm like an artsy bracelet.

Amanda hesitated for a second, remembering Joe's request for her to stay out of trouble. But no way could she miss whatever might happen next.

She hustled to the door behind David's great-aunt.

Virginia smiled as they hurried by the two perplexed-looking officers who had stopped in the doorway. "Thank you so much for your kindness," she said. "We're late to our meeting with Chief Grady." Her voice dripped with sweetness.

"Second office on your right," one officer offered with a smile. The other nodded.

"Wait! Ladies, you can't go—" The click of the closing door cut off Officer Lee's urgent directive from the lobby desk.

Amanda's heart pounded, but she followed Virginia into the chief's office.

The placard on the large desk in the middle of the room read: *Chief Dan Grady*. The heavyset leader of the Oak Hills Police Department sat behind it, frowning as he pressed a phone receiver against his ear. His spanking-white police dress shirt blended in with the stacks of papers and folders on the over-flowing desktop. To the side, a desktop monitor coated with a layer of dust appeared more ornamental than functional.

"They're in my office right now, Officer Lee," Grady said, his frown lines deepening. "I expect a report on my desk before the hour is up on why visitor protocol wasn't followed. Make sure the two officers that allowed them through the door are included." The chief slammed the receiver into the phone's cradle and turned toward Amanda and Virginia.

Feeling the tension in the room, Amanda didn't move. If there was ever a time to act invisible while keeping her ears and eyes wide open, it was now.

"Hello, Virginia."

"Hello, Dan."

"Congratulations. You just christened our newest officer on how not to handle unexpected visitors." The chief leaned back and crossed his arms, broadcasting his irritation.

"As your mother's best friend," Virginia cast her eyes skyward, "… bless her soul." Then she met his gaze. "I shouldn't have to make an appointment to see my great-nephew."

"And I explained when you called me last night that we follow police protocol here."

"Is it police protocol to lock up an innocent young man because I gave them consent to search my home?" She wagged her finger. "And they weren't tidy about it, I'll have you know."

Grady took a deep breath. "They followed strict police proce-dure, Virginia. I can't discuss the details. But perhaps there's something else I can help you with before an officer escorts you and whoever this is to the lobby?"

Amanda gave a weak smile at the chief's acknowledgment of her presence. His focus, fortunately, remained on Virginia.

"As his only living relative, I demand to see David right now." Virginia jammed her cane into the floor.

"As I told you last night, appointments must be made at least twenty-four hours in advance to validate your credentials. Visiting hours are 10:00 a.m. to 2:00 p.m. I'm sure Officer Lee would love to help you understand how it works." The chief's voice carried a hint of sarcasm.

"You know me personally, Dan. That should be validation enough."

The chief didn't answer.

"Well, I think your mother would be ashamed to hear you kept me from seeing my family over some silly rules." Virginia jammed her cane once again into the floor, harder this time. "I must see my David. Immediately."

The chief leaned back in his chair again, and his attention shifted to Amanda. "I didn't catch your name."

"Amanda Knightly," she said with another weak smile. *So much for being invisible.*

The chief sat straight up. "Ah, the Deli Lady. I've heard about you."

Virginia leaned over the desk. "Leave her out of this, Dan."

The chief scowled.

Virginia flashed a self-righteous grin. "Your resistance to my simple request has gone far enough. Your mother would agree."

Grady tidied several sheets of paper on his desk before looking up. "I'll make a one-time exception. Ten minutes. That's it. And my permission doesn't include the Deli Lady joining you. Understand?"

"I guess I'll just have to make the best of it."

After watching her performance, Amanda could guarantee Virginia would.

"Oh, and one more thing you should know," the chief said. "Your nephew's pretrial release hearing has been pushed back to Monday because of courthouse building issues. He'll remain here at the jail through the weekend. Visitors are allowed on Saturday, not Sunday. And don't forget, you'll need to make an appointment twenty-four hours in advance. No exceptions next time."

The hearing delay was disappointing. But it gave Amanda an idea.

After watching Virginia get escorted through security doors for her visit with David, Amanda stopped at the front desk and asked for clarification on visitor rules. Mission accomplished; she plopped down on a bench to wait for Virginia.

After checking her watch for the fourth time, Amanda started to worry she'd be late to work. Plus, it was long past Chief Grady's ten-minute deadline for Virginia's visit with David. Oh, to be the proverbial fly on *that* wall.

A side door burst open and Chief Grady strode into the lobby. He stopped in front of Amanda and leaned in, towering over her like a skyscraper. "I understand that during Stedman's arrest you told Officer Evans they had the wrong person," he said, his voice steely.

Amanda drew back, then caught herself. He might be the chief, but she knew how to handle tough customers. She looked him directly in the face. "Yes, I did. Because I know David didn't kill Olivia Hager." She kept her tone friendly but firm.

Grady didn't move, but the sudden twitch in his left cheek gave him away. "Deli Lady, this is an official police case. Let my officers do their jobs."

He vanished as quickly as he'd appeared through the same side door.

Amanda took a deep breath. Well, that was unexpected. Did

the police not want villagers to get involved and use Citizen Watch? She noticed Officer Lee didn't react. He probably felt the same way as Grady, she thought.

As she checked her watch once again, Virginia returned to the lobby leaning heavily on her cane. Her face was tear-stained and her expression pensive. The feisty-royal-lady facade was gone.

Amanda hurried to her side. "Is everything okay?"

Virginia nodded but didn't speak until they'd sat down on a nearby bench. The visibly shaken woman pulled a handkerchief out of her purse.

"We sat on opposite sides of a table in a very cold room. They handcuffed David with his hands on the table. He refused to look me in the face. I was told there couldn't be any physical contact between us, but I couldn't help myself. I reached out and barely touched one of David's fingers. Of course, the officer in the room was cross with me, but we both needed that physical reconnection. It broke the ice, and the floodgates opened."

Virginia dabbed her eyes.

"David sobbed for a good minute. I cried with him," she said. "Then he started talking nonstop. He said the police had told him things would be easier on him if he confessed. But he kept telling them he had nothing to confess to."

Virginia gripped the handkerchief tighter. "I told him he shouldn't give up. That he needs to keep telling them the truth."

Amanda waited until Virginia wiped away her tears before asking what David said next.

"He said he was sure his friends had given up on him by now."

Amanda shook her head. "Like I told you, my son is pulling their friends together to set up a GoFundMe campaign for his defense."

"I told him that. But he didn't react. Like he didn't believe it," Virginia said. "Even so, David knows asking you to help was impulsive. But he was glad you and I connected."

She folded her hands again. "I'm very worried about my nephew, but I'm starting to have a hard time handling all this stress. I feel I need to choose between visiting him tomorrow or being at his pretrial release hearing on Monday. It's too much to do both."

Amanda nodded. "I have good news. While you were with David, I made a 1:00 p.m. visitor appointment for tomorrow. I promise to let you know what he says."

Virginia's face lit up. "Oh, thank you. That's a relief to hear."

"I'm glad," Amanda said. "But now I need to get you home. I can't be late to work."

After Virginia gave a safe-in-the-house little wave from inside her front window, Amanda pointed the van toward Bob's.

Virginia's performance had invigorated her, and the chief's surprise confrontation had upped her motivation to find Olivia's murderer. No more just keeping her ears and eyes open and sending in anonymous tips. She was leaping in and hanging on for the ride.

CHAPTER 10

Amanda focused on keeping her customers happy as she worked Friday's shift at Bob's. Tomorrow she'd start her week at the Dark Roast, but she'd need her deli job back once that ended. Living on Joe's salary alone wasn't an option for the Knightlys. Inflation and out-of-the-blue house repairs had battered their family savings over the past couple years.

Clocking out at 6:00, Amanda was ready to celebrate a mistake-free shift. But before she could head home, she needed to stock up on weekly staples. She traversed Bob's aisles like an Olympic skier in a race for the gold, then headed to the checkout with a loaded shopping cart.

"Your total is $234.15," the teenage cashier said.

Flinching at the amount, Amanda slid the well-worn household credit card she and Joe used for most of their purchases through the card reader.

"Your card got declined," the cashier said in a flat voice.

Amanda frowned. "That can't be. Let me try again." She slid it once again through the card reader.

"Nope. Didn't go through that time either." He gave her a told-you-so look, with an added snip of impatience in his voice.

"Perhaps there's something wrong with the card reader or your register?"

He shrugged. "No one else has had a problem today." The bagger at the end of the checkout, along with the three shoppers in line behind Amanda, leaned in as if not wanting to miss the unfolding drama.

Her cheeks burning, Amanda dug out her backup credit card, to be used only in an emergency. Which this had become.

"That one worked." The cashier handed her the receipt. "Thanks for shopping at Bob's Finer Foods," he mumbled, reaching for the next shopper's first item.

Minutes later, with five bags of groceries loaded in the back of the van, Amanda climbed into the driver's seat and glanced in the rearview mirror. Her cheeks were still an embarrassed hot pink. What just happened?

To be fair, she should give Joe a chance to explain. After all, he hadn't gotten upset when she'd forgotten to shut off the sprinkler last summer. He'd joked the backyard had turned into Lake Knightly, the sixth Great Lake.

As she drove home on First Street, the setting sun colored the western sky in pinks and purples. Catching sight of the Valley Lane condo building encased in the glow, Amanda tossed aside yesterday's vow to never set foot where the murder had happened. A lot had changed in the last twenty-four hours.

Making an abrupt right turn down Valley Lane, Amanda parked along the curb outside the five-story building. The same building where Matt's girlfriend Chloe lived, and where he'd probably been many times.

The yellow caution tape was gone. Trimmed bushes and a polished bronze plaque announced *Valley Lane Condominiums, 103 West Valley Lane.* No one would guess a murder had occurred here barely two days ago.

Anxious and curious at the same time, she opened the front door and stepped into a tiny, unadorned, rectangular entryway.

Two cameras, mounted above on opposite corners, stared down at her. Aha! There *were* security cameras. So, it would make perfect sense to casually pose her question to Evans about possible recordings.

A checkerboard of locked mailboxes was embedded in the wall to her right. The opposite wall displayed the building directory. The simple tiled floor and red brick walls added to the no-frills appearance.

In front of her a glass-paneled door guarded the entrance to a cozy inner lobby, where a plush couch and two side tables sat against the wall. A rose-colored carpet runner led to an elevator at the other end of the room. To the right of the elevator door, a steel sign with the word STAIRS pointed to a dark hallway.

Amanda pulled, then pushed the glass door's handle, but it wouldn't budge. Then she noticed a small black pad mounted next to the door. Entry required a security card or getting buzzed in by a resident. Although the security measures hadn't kept Olivia Hager safe, she thought grimly.

She zeroed in on the resident directory, needing only three steps across the tiny entryway to reach it. The *Gazette* article had reported the police found Olivia's body in a unit, but hadn't given the number. But her name might still be listed.

Amanda discovered Olivia Hager had lived in 305. On either side of her were Phil Wharton in 303 and Max Paxton in 307. Maria Sebastian lived across the hall in 306. One of them had to have seen or heard something the night of the murder.

Then again, it wouldn't be a stretch that one of Olivia's neighbors could be the killer. She filed that possibility on her mental list.

A quick glance at the rest of the third-floor listings gave her a jolt. Eloise Rohmer lived in 309, just two condo units from Olivia. Could she be related to Gina Rohmer, Nicki's former star employee who'd suddenly quit and almost ruined her Florida vacation plans?

Amanda pulled her phone out of her coat pocket and snapped a picture of the list.

"Amanda Knightly? What are you doing here?"

Amanda spun around. Gina, Nicki's ex-employee, stood behind her, wearing a Cheshire cat smile. She was dressed head to toe in black running gear, with a towel wrapped around her neck. Trickles of sweat ran down her face.

Amanda silently chastised herself. She'd been so engrossed in taking a photo of the directory she'd missed hearing the outside door open.

"Why, hello, Gina. I didn't know you lived here." Amanda slipped her phone back into her coat pocket, hoping the young woman wouldn't figure out she was snooping.

"My sister lets me stay at her place when I'm between apartments."

"Is that Eloise Rohmer in unit 309?" Amanda could feel Gina's stare. *Oops. TMI.*

"Yes. But that's none of your business." Gina's stare turned into a glare. "And why were you taking a picture of the residents' directory?"

Busted. Amanda forced a smile. "I wanted to visit a friend on the third floor, but I don't have her unit number in my phone. I took a picture so I'd have an easy reminder. I have a terrible memory." *Does that sound plausible?*

"What's your friend's name?"

Amanda's brain whirled. *Who lives across the hall from Olivia? Think, think.*

Gina raised a doubting eyebrow.

The name popped into Amanda's head. "Maria Sebastian." *Whew! That was close.*

"That's very interesting. Maria lives across the hall from Olivia in unit 306." Gina smirked. "Well, she *used* to. Before Olivia was murdered."

She leaned in and lowered her voice. "Trust me, no one in

this building is crying about that. She caused a lot of pain to a lot of people. I won't miss her."

Amanda froze. Gina had zero sympathy. And Amanda hadn't forgotten the young woman's fake smile when she waited on customers at the Dark Roast. Like the one she flashed right now.

"Were you staying at your sister's place the night of the murder?" Amanda tried to make it sound like a casual question that anyone would ask.

Gina snickered. "I told the police everything I know." She pulled a security card out of her jacket pocket before flashing her fake smile again. "I'd love to chat, but I need to get ready for the late shift at Le Grand Café. If you haven't heard, I'm no longer at the Dark Roast. I'm so glad to be out of that rat trap."

Security card in hand, Gina had just turned toward the glass door when it burst open, almost hitting her head. "Watch it, buddy," Gina growled.

Amanda recognized the silver-haired man with a face like a gnarled tree trunk. He was Raymond Cartel, Nicki's go-to maintenance man at the coffee shop. Nicki went on and on about how he'd show up any time she called him. She also bragged that his handyman skills had saved the Dark Roast from several catastrophes in the past year.

Nicki's maintenance man looked to be in his eighties. Carrying a toolbox and dressed in bib overalls and a long-sleeved gray T-shirt, Raymond took slow, short steps across the tiny entryway, now claustrophobic with three of them crammed into it. He gave Amanda a blank glance and Gina a sneer. Then he exited through the building's front door.

"That's our maintenance guy. He's a real creep," Gina said.

Amanda tucked away that comment as Gina tapped her security card against the black pad and the glass door clicked open. The young woman walked through the doorway into the cozy inner lobby, pulled the glass door shut behind her, and strolled down the rose-colored carpet runner to the elevator.

That stopped any chance of sneaking into the building once Gina was out of sight, Amanda realized.

But Gina probably knew more than she'd told the police. Amanda definitely needed to figure out how to run into her again.

She watched Raymond Cartel plod along the sidewalk outside the condo building and disappear from view. Nicki always sang his praises and Gina called him a creep. Two polar opposite views on the same man. What was the real story?

She hurried to the van, mulling her next move.

Number one was to get to the bottom of the five thousand dollars. Virginia had disclosed only that Olivia had lent David the money. She hadn't said anything about Olivia wanting it back.

What really happened Wednesday night? David didn't seem in a position to return Olivia's five thousand dollars. Had she truly needed it or had she only wanted to get David's goat by demanding it?

More importantly, what did the police know about the investment, and were they using it as a motive?

Amanda shook her head. She'd stay with the Olivia goat theory and keep digging.

———

Ten minutes later, Amanda stood in her kitchen, frowning as she told Joe of her humiliation at Bob's checkout.

He shrugged. "Must have been the card reader."

"Nope. I tried twice. Declined both times. Thankfully, my other card worked." She crossed her arms and gave him the Look.

"It could be a bad chip. Did you have the card near a magnet?" he countered with a raised eyebrow.

"It's been in my purse where I always keep it."

Joe waved it off. "I'm sure it's a minor issue. I'll straighten it out with the credit-card company right away. No problem, honey."

Amanda leaned against the kitchen counter. "Come on, Joe. You know I don't like being called 'honey.' You only say it when you want to avoid something. My question to you, my loving husband, is … What's really going on?"

Joe smiled. "With all you have on your plate, I didn't want to bother you with anything else."

"What didn't you want to bother me about?"

"Well," he started, then dropped the smile. "Our household credit-card issuer has a new online site. They haven't credited our automatic payments for the last three months, and—"

Amanda's eyes almost popped out of their sockets. "*Three months?* Why didn't you notice this until now? Or tell me about it?"

"They told me we could still use the card. Obviously, that wasn't the case today. I'm sorry you were put in a bad spot."

Amanda frowned. "This is the second issue with payments I've learned about in the last week. Should I be worried there's something bigger going on?"

Joe shook his head. "I have everything under control. I'll hound them until it gets cleared up. In the meantime, make sure you use the emergency backup card for the next few days."

Amanda bit her lip. She'd readily agreed to let Joe handle all their finances when they were first married. It made sense with Matt a honeymoon baby, Brittany a surprise fifteen months later, and Joe a newly minted CPA. Through the years he'd always shared their financial numbers with her and never missed a payment.

But now something was out of whack.

She gripped the edge of the kitchen counter as the terrifying scene from her childhood roared back into her mind.

Her mother sobbing. Their furniture tossed on the apartment

building's sidewalk. Neighbors gawking. The landlord shouting that they were deadbeats for not paying the rent. Her small hands trembling as she clutched her mother's skirt.

"Hey, are you okay?" Joe put his arm around her. Just before their wedding day, she'd told him why money was a touchy subject for her. He'd promised she'd never have to worry. And she hadn't. Until now.

"I've been better." Amanda let go of her vice-like grip on the counter as the painful memory faded.

Joe raised his hand. "You have my word. No more money issues."

"Okay. Thanks." Amanda gave him a faint smile. Best to keep her worries at bay for the moment. She'd take a more active part in their finances. But not just now.

The atmosphere in the kitchen remained chilly throughout dinner. Amanda had planned to tell Joe about her visit to the police station with David's great-aunt, but her still-uneasy insides squashed that idea.

Amanda pushed her empty plate aside just as Matt burst in through the back door. His girlfriend, a pink scarf framing her rosy cheeks, followed.

"I hope I left my credit card in my pants pocket," Matt said as he headed upstairs.

Joe trailed after Matt. "I'll help you search." Joe looked relieved. He'd just been handed a great excuse to escape the frosty room.

"Chloe, take a seat." Amanda gestured to the chair next to her. She was glad Matt and Joe had exited. Chloe might open up more about Olivia if it was just the two of them.

"I heard the good news that you'll be the manager at the Dark Roast while Nicki is on vacation," Chloe said with a happy giggle as she sat down. "The roster has us both on tomorrow's early shift."

Amanda grinned. "I can't wait." She paused. "I hope you

don't mind me asking how you feel about Olivia Hager's murder? Living in the same building, I'm sure it was terrifying."

Chloe's giggling stopped abruptly. "It was. The police questioned everyone. I'm on the fifth floor, so I couldn't tell them much."

Amanda nodded.

Chloe also believed David was innocent. Her voice tightened when she talked about Olivia. They had both been speedsters on the high school cross-country team, and Olivia never liked to lose. After graduation Chloe had encountered her in action at local coffee shops and bars.

"In action? What does that mean?" Amanda asked.

"How she operated with guys." Chloe explained how Olivia targeted her man of the month and bragged she would make him fall for her, even if he didn't show interest at first. "For her, it was all about the conquest. She was relentless. Texted them hundreds of times a day, followed their social media accounts. Stalked them, basically."

"That sounds like a lot of work on her part."

"It was. But the crazy thing was, Olivia *only* loved the pursuit. When a guy finally showed any interest, she'd shut them down in a cruel, public way. She seemed to enjoy it." Chloe paused. "Not that she deserved to be murdered, of course."

Amanda nodded. "It does sound like Olivia knew how to rile people up."

"She really got to Gina Rohmer, too." Chloe filled Amanda in on how five years ago Olivia had stolen Gina's high school prom date. She threw herself at the guy and a week before prom, he dumped Gina and hooked up with Olivia.

Gina already had her dress, shoes, and jewelry, including a pricey tiara. She'd also spent a ton of money at a tanning salon. Plus, Gina had really liked the guy.

"Sounds like real mean girl stuff," Amanda said. "Although Gina could have gone with a group of friends."

"Sure. But Gina wasn't going to give Olivia the satisfaction of showing up dateless. She vowed revenge from that day forward. Right up until Olivia's murder, Gina still talked about wanting to kill her."

"Did Olivia and that guy stay together?" Amanda asked.

Chloe shook her head. "She dumped him the day after prom."

"This is disturbing to hear," Amanda said. "Do you think the police know about Gina's grudge?"

"I mentioned it to them. Not sure if anyone else has."

Before Amanda could ask any more questions, Matt bounded into the kitchen, followed by Joe.

"Success!" Matt shouted. "Found my credit card."

"Where are you two off to?" Amanda asked as he and Chloe headed toward the back door.

"Manny's Pizzeria, to kick off the GoFundMe campaign for David's defense."

Chloe tugged at Matt's sleeve. "We need to get moving. We don't want to be late." Amanda hid her smile. Chloe and Matt made a good team.

Matt paused. "Like I told you last night, Mom. We're helping David. You don't need to do anything."

Amanda shrugged off her son's comment. She was in too deep to stop now. Especially after hearing Chloe's story about Gina.

———

A few hours later Amanda was sitting in front of her laptop, checking out the *Gazette's* evening online edition. The front-page story reported that David's pretrial release hearing had been pushed back to Monday due to courthouse building issues, confirming Chief Grady's statement.

Hearing the front door open, she looked up.

Brittany stood in the living room doorway. Before Amanda could ask about her evening, her daughter gave a bubbly recap of how she'd run into Matt, Chloe, and all their friends at Manny's Pizzeria.

She'd talked the whole time to one guy, who had driven her home. He even walked her to the front door."

Brittany clasped her hands together. "Tomorrow night he's taking me out to dinner and then to the newest clubs in downtown Chicago."

"What's his name?"

"Patrick Williams. He's, like, the politest guy I've ever met, Mom."

"Manners are a nice thing for a guy to have." Amanda was secretly pleased. Maybe Patrick was a perfect match for Brittany? Then she caught herself and chuckled. She could be the mother in a Jane Austen novel, eager to find an eligible suitor for her daughter.

Brittany stopped on her way upstairs, still grinning from ear to ear. "He's at least five inches taller than me, too. I can wear my highest heels!"

She suddenly looked panicked. "Oh, no! I have nothing to wear!" As she rushed up to her bedroom, the words "I need to shop tomorrow" drifted back downstairs.

Amanda shook her head and turned to her laptop again, happy her daughter was happy. She still needed to pull together a list of questions to ask David tomorrow, but her tired brain told her to quit for the day.

She pushed aside her guilt. She'd wing it. Sometimes that was the best way to go.

CHAPTER 11

At the break of dawn on Saturday, Amanda quickly walked down the quiet streets of Oak Hills, her nerves on overload. Reaching the Dark Roast's entrance, she stopped.

Could she succeed as manager for the next week? And help David at the same time?

She squared her shoulders. Yep, she could do both. Plus, she'd be in Paradise. Who wouldn't want a one-week gig in their favorite coffee shop?

Nicki swept open the front door and waved Amanda inside. "Welcome to your first official day at the Dark Roast, Ms. Manager."

Nicki's oversized glasses frames were a colorful blend of flamingo pink, ocean blue, and sunshine yellow. Her sleeveless sundress was patterned with a spray of colorful seashells. Jingling bracelets decorated her arms.

"I can see you're ready for that long-awaited Florida vacation. Well, almost," Amanda teased, pointing to her bestie's black legwarmers under her sun dress. Nicki assured Amanda that she'd strip them off, along with her winter parka, as soon as the plane took off.

Nicki pointed to the line of coffee urns standing at attention like soldiers ready for battle. "We have one hour before the shop opens. Then I'm out of here. It's time to get the coffee started."

After a quick refresher for Amanda, the percolating pots perfumed the shop with tempting aromas. Amanda and her bestie sat at a table, steaming coffee cups in hand.

Nicki pushed a black binder labeled *Dark Roast Procedures* toward Amanda. "This is your go-to handbook. Don't forget, I'll be available through text, instant messaging, or a phone call."

Amanda sized up the thick manual. "That's a lot of procedures."

"That's because there's a lot to running a business. But I can see you're determined." Nicki gave her a thumbs-up. "It looks good on you."

Amanda returned the gesture with a simple "Thanks."

Then Nicki's smile dimmed. "Remember, as manager, you're on call 24-7, no matter what the schedule says. Today your shift technically ends at 4:00 because I didn't want you overwhelmed on your first day. Luckily, Chloe was a sweetheart and agreed to stay on the last two hours by herself. It's usually a slow time then anyway. You two work out your lunch breaks."

Nicki peered at Amanda over the top of her glasses. "With Chloe working the full day, I strongly recommend you give her an extra-long lunch."

"I was already thinking that," Amanda said.

"If there's a problem, no matter the time, I expect you to handle it. Make sense?" Nicki added.

"Got it."

"And remember, the customer is always right." Nicki raised an eyebrow and smiled. "Or at least you let them think that."

"Like we do at Bob's. Or at any business, if they're smart."

Nicki nodded. "You'll do just fine. But don't forget, your number one job next week is to manage the Dark Roast. Keeping your ears and eyes open and picking up tips for David's case is second. But let the detectives investigate. As manager, you have to be neutral."

"Understood." Amanda straightened the napkin under her coffee cup to avoid looking at Nicki. No need to tell her friend about her one o'clock appointment at the Oak Hills police station to talk to David. Technically, it'd be her lunch break.

"I love my staff," Nicki continued. "They're all level-headed. No big egos." She paused, then added, "Except for the person who conned me."

"You mean Gina, right?"

"Yes. I truly believe that young woman is capable of anything. And I do mean anything."

"Even murder?" Amanda asked.

"Yes, even murder, horrible though it sounds. It's only a gut feeling. But like I said, that's for the police to determine. You need to focus on the Dark Roast."

"Understood." Amanda already had a mental list she'd tallied up on Gina. Her heartless comments about Olivia in the Valley Lane Condos entryway. Staying with her sister two doors from the murder scene. Boasting of still wanting to kill Olivia after a prom fiasco five years ago. And now Nicki, a sharp people person, had just said Gina was capable of anything.

Amanda had her potential first suspect: Gina Rohmer.

———

Chloe hustled into the Dark Roast just before opening, wearing a pink floral coat and carrying a small bundle of *Gazettes*. Amanda had recently swayed Nicki to support the local paper, despite the dwindling interest in print news. She'd cited the newspaper as an important voice for their small village, and Nicki had agreed.

"Amanda, the Dark Roast is all yours." Nicki slipped her winter parka over her shoulders and grabbed her to-go coffee.

"Sun, here I come!" With hugs for both of her employees and a cheerful wave, she was out the door.

After turning on the OPEN sign, Amanda glanced at the *Gazette's* front page.

Olivia Hager Case Update! the headline shouted, outlined in red ink.

The Gazette has learned several Oak Hills merchants have reported finding anonymous notes on their premises. Each contained stick-on letters pasted on a single, standard letter-sized page with the same message: "Stedman is guilty." The Oak Hills police are investigating.

Updates to come as details are released.

Amanda cringed. Someone really wanted David to take the rap.

Stepping outside, she checked the perimeter of the building. No letter. Just a small, empty potato chip bag. *Why did other merchants get a message but not us?* she wondered as she headed back into the shop.

The rest of the morning flew by in a blur. Between the missing supply of to-go cup lids, a temporarily stopped-up sink, and an irate customer who loudly complained about getting the wrong order, Amanda was relieved to survive her first morning at the Dark Roast. She was even getting comfortable with this manager thing.

Her confidence didn't waiver standing at the Oak Hills police station front desk just before 1:00 p.m.

"My name is Amanda Knightly and I have an appointment to see David Stedman."

After showing her photo ID and signing in, Amanda walked through the metal detector and surrendered her purse before an officer escorted her through a set of locked doors and into the interview room. He gestured to a metal chair at a rectangular steel table.

As she sat down, Amanda pulled her coat lapels over the

Dark Roast logo on her shirt. Nicki had made it clear. Keep the coffee shop out of whatever she did to help David.

"Wait here. We're bringing the prisoner. You'll get ten minutes." The door slammed shut.

She surveyed the room; its walls were bare except for the large mirror behind her. No doubt one-way glass, just like on TV. Several officers were invisible behind it, ready to watch and listen. Most definitely, Chief Grady was one of them. A steel-gray speaker was embedded in the wall next to the mirror. Cameras peered down at her from each of the corners.

Amanda fidgeted as the cold chair sent goosebumps up her backside. A pang of uneasiness shot through her.

Should she walk straight out of this room and just worry about her own life? Was she making things worse for David?

She'd almost convinced herself to bail when the door swung open. Another Oak Hills officer steered David, dressed in jail scrubs, into the room.

To Amanda's surprise, her son's friend had a sneer on his face she'd never seen before. His eyes were colder than her metal chair.

Amanda braced herself. *He's probably more scared than you. Not the time to run out on him.*

David dropped into the chair opposite Amanda. His hands fell into his lap.

"Hands on the table, Stedman. You know the rules." The officer planted himself in front of the closed door.

The clatter of handcuffs against the metal table rang through the room. Amanda immediately noticed that David's right index finger was minus its bandage, revealing a nasty, raw cut running its length.

Amanda focused on David's bowed head.

"Eight minutes left, ma'am," an unknown voice called out.

Amanda almost jumped out of the chair before realizing the time check had come through the speaker embedded in the wall.

The officer standing at the door didn't react. David glanced up, then dropped his attention back to the tabletop.

Amanda was ready to protest that David had just arrived, but she quickly changed her mind. The police were in charge. Best to move on.

"Hello, David. It's good to see you." Amanda heard the fakeness in her chipper tone.

Silence.

"You asked for my help when you were being arrested."

Silence again.

"I'm here to find out how I can help you." This time her tone was firmer and not as fake.

David's head stayed bowed for what seemed like forever. "Thanks for coming. But no one can help me," he finally mumbled.

"Why do you say that?" Amanda said, relieved he'd at least spoken.

He fidgeted in his chair. "Because I'm the fall guy they're pinning that murder on."

Amanda frowned. This wasn't going well.

"Seven minutes," came through the speaker.

She turned toward whoever was on the other side of it. "Thank you for reminding me," she said in her best customer-friendly voice.

She turned back to David, forcing a smile. "So we use our time wisely, how about if I ask the questions and you give me a yes or no?"

He shrugged, still staring at the table.

"Six and a half minutes," the speaker's voice added.

This was not going as well as she'd hoped. She refocused on David's downcast head. "Did you know Olivia well?"

He raised his head ever so slightly, revealing a wry smile and sad eyes.

"What do you think, Mrs. K?"

"I'll take that as a yes." She was making progress. He'd acknowledged her and said her name.

"Did she try to contact you on the day she died?"

"You heard her. You were right there at Bob's deli counter."

"I meant after that."

"She would never leave me alone."

"Another yes." Time to redirect the questions.

"Do you know Gina Rohmer?"

"Of course I do. That crazy girl is almost as bad as Olivia."

"Four minutes. No extra time," the speaker said.

"If I told you there might be other viable suspects, what would you say?"

David looked up. "Yippee," he mumbled, and looked down.

"Good. You're excited about that." Amanda took a deep breath. "You should know, David, that Matt and all your friends set up a GoFundMe campaign to finance your defense and—"

His head jerked up. "My great-aunt said that, but I didn't believe her. Thought she was just trying to make me feel better."

"Your friends don't believe you killed Olivia."

His face brightened. "Well, that's great to hear." He leaned forward. "So when am I getting out of here?"

"I don't have an answer to that question," she said in a quiet voice.

David sat back as his face fell. Then he leaned forward and banged his handcuffed hands against the table. "It's super that my friends are backing me. But I know those things take time. And right now, I'm stuck in that creepy cell."

He pushed his chair back and stood up. "Officer, I'm finished here. This is a waste of time."

Amanda held up her hand. "Please, David, don't go. Your great-aunt Virginia wants to know all about our visit. She'll be disappointed to hear you broke off our talk early." Amanda wasn't ready to give up. Using Virginia's name might guilt him into staying.

David dropped back into the chair. "I don't want to disappoint my aunt." He took a deep breath. "I also need to apologize for being rude to you." He gave Amanda an embarrassed look. "I really do appreciate you coming to see me."

"Less than three minutes left," the speaker said.

David sat up straight. "What's your next question, Mrs. K?" His tone had changed from snotty to inquisitive.

"Do you know Raymond Cartel?" Amanda asked, talking faster.

David frowned. "Who?"

"I'm taking that as a no."

"Two-minute warning."

Amanda bit her lip. She had so many questions. Time to ask the most important one before it was too late.

"Who do you think killed Olivia Hager?"

Silence.

"Did you hear my question?"

"Thirty seconds . . ." warned the speaker.

David shook his head. "I've tried to figure that out for the last two days. I've got nothing." His voice held a hint of hope. "If you can find out who murdered Olivia, I'd be forever grateful."

"Who should I talk to?" she said.

David nodded. "Try Eddie Turner, the owner of the Happy Bean. He knew Olivia and how obnoxious—"

"Time's up!" the speaker announced. Amanda groaned inwardly.

The officer pulled David out of the chair and toward the door. "Stedman, let's go."

David's head swiveled back toward Amanda. "There's the maintenance man at Valley Lane Condos. Olivia called him handsy. She wanted him fired. Same for the UPS delivery guy. She accused both of them of—"

David's voice cut off as the officer led him out of the room.

Amanda wobbled as she stood up, stiff from the uncomfortable chair and the emotional ups and downs she'd just been through.

On the way back to the Dark Roast, her too-brief visit with David kept looping through her brain in overdrive.

No surprise Gina Rohmer was also on David's bad list. If only there had been time to ask more questions about her.

The maintenance man had to be Raymond. Nicki sang his praises, but why had Olivia referred to him as "handsy"?

And who was the UPS delivery guy?

She hadn't asked about the money Olivia had invested in David's start-up and supposedly wanted back. And he wisely hadn't mentioned it. Did the police know about it?

Most troubling was the deep cut on his finger, which had started to heal. When, where, and how had that happened?

Another question she didn't want to ask in front of the police. Although they'd probably already asked him.

And what had the police found at the crime scene?

Her questions kept multiplying like rabbits.

Her first call would be to Eddie Turner at the Happy Bean.

CHAPTER 12

Amanda returned from her interview with David with more questions than answers. She made sure to thank Chloe for keeping the shop running smoothly. The pleased young woman hustled out the door for her extra-long lunch break.

Soon after Chloe's return an hour later, Saturday's usual mid-afternoon lull struck. Three customers nursed their drinks, focused on their laptops and phones. A relaxed stillness hung in the air. Amanda didn't complain. She needed the mental break.

Throughout the day, Chloe had refreshed her on steps for the trickier coffee orders. For the past hour, Amanda had taste-tested the double espressos and robust ground-bean blends, plus the extra espresso shots added to the cappuccinos. It led to a whopper of a caffeine buzz.

She decided to take advantage of the coffee high and dive into the coffee shop's procedure manual. But the dry text only made her eyes blurry, and she closed the cover.

Chloe stood next to her, stifling a yawn as she pushed back her cuticles for the nth time. Amanda itched to get a hint of her feelings for Matt. Not to be nosy, like Joe would say, more being friendly. But she quickly dropped the idea. The Dark Roast wasn't the place to ask.

"Since it's so slow, why don't you take a quick inventory of the supplies in the storeroom?" Amanda asked Chloe instead.

"Sounds good to me." Chloe headed toward the back hallway.

Amanda set aside the manual and mentally rehashed her visit with David for the twentieth time. She was glad he'd started talking in those last minutes. When she'd called Virginia on her walk back to the Dark Roast, the woman had sounded relieved but still concerned. Amanda's heart had warmed when Virginia confessed how happy she was that Amanda had jumped in to help.

She fussed with the to-go cup sleeves while contemplating how to hint to Matt he should visit David, in case he hadn't thought of it himself.

Then there was Joe. Last week, he'd chided her about over-mothering their adult children. She needed to back off, he'd reminded her. He'd probably be upset to learn she'd visited David in jail. Not a good idea to tell Chloe either, because she might let it slip to Matt. And Nicki wouldn't be happy to learn she'd visited David at the police station wearing her Dark Roast polo, even though she'd covered it up.

Best not to let any of them know for now, she decided.

Amanda glanced at her phone for the third time in an hour. Eddie Turner still hadn't returned her call.

A pang of doubt stabbed her like a bee sting. Digging for clues and suspects never seemed this difficult on TV. It was even harder than trying to please a grumpy customer.

Her musings were interrupted when the front door opened. Raymond Cartel, Nicki's maintenance guy, hobbled into the shop as if in pain.

Amanda automatically stepped around the counter with her hand outstretched to offer help. "Good afternoon. Can I—"

Raymond's stony expression made her step back.

"Where's Nicki?" he spat out.

Amanda didn't flinch. "She's not here, but I'd be happy to—"

"Who are you?" he demanded.

Amanda kept her smile as she dropped her hand. Nicki had introduced her to Raymond multiple times, but yesterday he hadn't seemed to remember her when he walked through the Valley Lane Condos entryway. Now today he did the same. It irked her once again, but she pushed it aside. He was Nicki's fix-it guy, after all. Not a smart idea to get snippy when she might need him for an emergency.

"I'm Amanda, Nicki's friend and acting manager this week while she's on vacation."

"Humph. Yeah, now I remember her telling me something about Florida."

Amanda stepped back behind the counter. "Can I interest you in our specialty coffee of the day? It's called—"

"Nah! I want my usual. Black, small, house brand. And make it hot. Don't give me any of that warmed-over stuff." Raymond's voice was gruff, with added impatience.

"Would you like that to go?"

"Of course. I have work to do. What's the matter with you?" The deep wedge between his eyebrows deepened.

"Coming right up." Raymond was almost worse than the Logans at Bob's deli counter. Or their curmudgeon neighbor, Frank. Even the UPS guy had been grumpy recently. And Oak Hills was supposed to be a friendly town.

Less than a minute later, Amanda pushed his hot, black, small house brand to-go over the counter. "Three dollars even, please."

Raymond stared at Amanda. "Nicki doesn't charge me," he said.

"Oh. Then I won't either," she quickly replied. Best not to

have a scene. She made a note to check with Chloe on who got free coffee.

Raymond leaned forward, almost nose to nose with her. A musty basement smell filled the air between them. She tried not to cringe.

"Heard there was some commotion here on Thursday and someone got arrested." The old man's face tightened, as if he were gritting his teeth.

Amanda leaned back. "Yes."

He glanced over both shoulders, then turned back to Amanda. "Bet the Oak Hills police got it all wrong." His voice had lowered to a gruff whisper.

"Why do you say that?" Amanda tensed ever so slightly.

"I've heard all the gossip." He took a deep breath. "The cops are missing a big piece of evidence. It's 1944 all over again."

"What happened in 1944?"

He waved the question off. "Never mind. I've said too much already."

Amanda frowned. What was the missing evidence, and how did it connect to something that happened years ago?

His hand brushed the pile of Citizen Watch pamphlets as he reached for his coffee. "What're these?" he muttered.

"Brochures about the new Oak Hills Citizen Watch program." She handed one to him. "The police are asking everyone—"

"Phooey! I want nothing to do with the police." He shooed the brochure away as if it were a fly. With his hot, black, small house brand in hand, he shuffled to the front door, grumbling the entire way.

"How did things go with Raymond?" Chloe, back from the storeroom, hoisted two large containers of coffee beans onto the side counter.

"What do you know about that guy?" Amanda asked, returning the rejected Citizen Watch brochure to the pile.

"Nicki loves him. Swears he's the best handyman she's ever had, even though he must be in his eighties. He's good with minor jobs, like fixing jammed doors, cleaning drains, or repairing loose chair legs and wobbly tables." Chloe stooped down to push one of the containers onto the open lower shelf.

"By chance, does he have a nickname?" Amanda casually straightened the pile of brochures.

Chloe reached up and grabbed the second container. "Yeah. Handsy Ray. Someone said he tried to get a little too friendly with them." She shook her head. "But I never saw anything, and he's never gotten anywhere near me." She pushed the second container next to the first. "How did you hear about that?"

"Someone mentioned it today." Amanda cleared her throat. "What else do you know about him?"

Chloe stood up, brushing off her hands. "He does maintenance work for several apartment and condo buildings in Oak Hills. I see him around Valley Lane Condos all the time."

"Does he live there?" Amanda asked.

"No. He has an old house on Birch Court, a couple of blocks from here. Nicki said he's been fixing it up for the past year."

"Does she give him free coffee?"

Chloe nodded.

"Does Nicki know about the 'handsy' rumor?"

"I don't know." Chloe paused. "I've never said anything about it, though. I don't even know if it's true, because the person who said it isn't that reliable. And Nicki runs this place on a tight budget. What Ray fixes stays fixed." She leaned back, crossing her arms. "What do you think of him?"

"He wasn't exactly friendly when I got his coffee. And he never seems to remember who I am. But nothing beyond that."

"Did he go on and on about the good old days?" Chloe smirked.

"He hinted about something happening in 1944 and then wouldn't say anything more."

"You're lucky. Once he gets going about the good old days, as he calls them, he never stops." Chloe cocked her head. "After we left your house last night, Matt mentioned you're trying to help David, too. Is that why you asked me those questions?"

Amanda nodded. "I'm just trying to understand what really happened to Olivia."

"Well, I think that's great. Matt isn't happy about it, though."

Amanda paused. "Matt is confident in his own abilities. Plus, I think he's concerned for my safety. But I truly believe David is innocent and I want to help him if I can."

"Well, Olivia filed a complaint with the Valley Lane condo board, accusing Raymond of shoddy work. She posted a copy of the complaint in the lobby a week ago, along with a petition demanding they fire him. Yesterday the condo board canceled the complaint. Of course, everyone knew why. Olivia was the only one who complained. And now she's … gone."

Amanda tucked away that interesting update. A large group had just walked into the Dark Roast and it was time to refocus on work.

On her walk home after her shift ended, Amanda texted Nicki.

Miss ya bestie! So far, all okay. No more murders yet! LOL. Enjoy your first night on vacay!

After hitting the send arrow, her thoughts continued to churn.

Maybe Raymond's ramblings about 1944 were a cagey diversion to throw people off. Maybe he'd tried to reason with Olivia about her petition to have him fired. And Olivia had put him down, humiliating him as she seemed to like to do. With his total access to the building, he could have easily slipped away, unseen, after—

Amanda halted in the middle of the sidewalk.

She had suspected it. Now she was certain. Raymond Cartel could have murdered Olivia Hager!

CHAPTER 13

Pumped that she now had two potential suspects, Amanda once again took a detour to Valley Lane Condos on her way home. Her feet hurt and her brain needed a break, but finding witnesses who could support David's claim of innocence had priority.

Pulling open the front door, she stepped once again into the tiny, unadorned entryway. The glass-paneled door continued to guard the entrance to the cozy inner lobby. She turned to her left and took three short steps to the resident directory. She buzzed Maria Sebastian in 306, the neighbor across the hall from Olivia's condo.

No answer.

She tried a second time. Nothing.

It was the same for Olivia's neighbors on either side: Phil Wharton in 303 and Max Paxton in 307.

Buzzing Maria Sebastian one last time, she didn't hear the inner lobby door open and flinched at the familiar voice behind her. "Amanda Knightly. I didn't expect to see you here again."

Amanda spun around with a smile. "How nice to see you again, Gina."

"I'd love to chat, but I can't be late for my four o'clock shift at Le Grand Café." Gina struck a pose in her dressy jet-black trousers, with a crisp white blouse tucked into the waistband. Her long wavy hair, pulled back, showed off dangling gold earrings. It looked as if she'd spent hours piling on her make-up, with false eyelashes that could be mistaken for fuzzy caterpillars nestled across each eyelid. The word "overdone" popped into Amanda's head.

Gina let out a long, contented sigh. "The customers leave me great tips, and the boss says I'm doing super. And it's only my third day."

She gave Amanda a smug look. "If you're still trying to buzz Maria, I'm sorry to break the news, but she's in Wisconsin visiting her grandchildren. My sister gave me the update."

"Oh, silly me for not remembering." Amanda hoped she sounded embarrassed. At least she'd picked up a clue about the woman's age.

She was about to say goodbye when she spotted a delicate, gold-etched heart locket on a double rope gold chain, suggestively dangling in the V-neck of Gina's blouse. "That's a beautiful necklace you're wearing," Amanda said.

The young woman broke into a 1,000-watt grin. "It's my good-luck charm. I fell in love with it at first sight."

"Was it a gift?"

Gina's smile disappeared. "Well, yes … it was. I just got it a few days ago." A guilty expression popped out on her face before she averted her gaze from Amanda.

"Does the locket have a picture of the special person who gave it to you?" Amanda couldn't help yanking the young woman's chain, so to speak. Nicki would want her to.

Gina glared. "It's really none of your business who I got it from. And frankly, I think you need to quit loitering around here with your nose in the resident directory, or I might have to report you to the management."

She crossed her arms. "If Maria is your friend, you should have her phone number."

Amanda painted on a pretend smile. "I wanted to surprise her in person. But I'll be on my way."

As she hurried home, Amanda vowed to search online for the phone numbers of the three neighbors. Maybe Chloe would have a resident directory.

The last thing she wanted was to run into Gina a third time in the condo building. The young woman would probably be delighted to report Amanda for loitering, as she'd threatened. Or worse.

Amanda couldn't pinpoint why, but something felt fishy about that necklace.

———

In her bedroom, Amanda swapped her work clothes for comfy jeans and a sweater as she checked off today's wins. Survived first shift as manager. Broke through to David. Homed in on Gina Rohmer and Raymond Cartel as potential suspects.

It had been a good day overall, despite her disappointment at not yet getting in touch with Olivia's neighbors. Had the police had better luck?

Heading down the hallway, she glanced into her daughter's bedroom and shook her head. No surprise, it looked like a tornado had passed through. In the middle of the clutter, a dressy black jumpsuit, tags still attached, hung on the outside of her closet door. Brittany's sparkly stiletto heels were lined up directly below.

Amanda heard her voice cheerfully warbling behind the adjacent bathroom door and smiled. Happy daughter, happy mother.

Joe glanced up from the newspaper as she walked into the living room. "How was your first shift, Madame Manager?"

Amanda flopped onto the couch. "Challenging, but I got

through it. My head is bursting with everything I need to know about managing the shop."

"Sounds like you need a cup of coffee."

Amanda gave Joe the stink eye. "You're kidding, right?"

Joe chuckled. "Yeah, I couldn't resist. Can I offer you a glass of wine instead?"

"That sounds wonderful. A cabernet, served in one of our Waterford goblets. From our wedding gift stash, remember? This is a special occasion. I want to be pampered."

Joe's hand brushed her shoulder as he left the living room. For a brief minute, she questioned if he was trying a little too hard to be nice after the credit-card snafus. But right now she just wanted to chill out.

When her eyes drifted shut, a replay of her regular deli customers' reactions to seeing her behind the counter at the Dark Roast today started in her head.

Hey, aren't you supposed to be at Bob's Finer Foods?

Amanda would explain she was helping a friend, then ask for their order.

They'd wink and say, *I'd like a half-pound of Virginia cured ham ... No, wait a minute.*

And they'd all chuckled.

She'd played along all day. Customer service could happen in many ways, she'd reminded herself after hearing the same questions at least fifty times.

Joe interrupted her daydream. "Amanda? Here's your wine."

She opened her eyes and reached for the glass. "Thanks, I so need this right now." She took a long sip. "But we can't get too comfortable. Patrick Williams will be here in thirty minutes. He's taking Brittany to dinner and then clubbing in Chicago."

"That sounds like fun. Which reminds me, what are you making for dinner?" Joe plopped back in his chair.

Amanda raised a teasing eyebrow. "I'm not making anything. You're making reservations."

"I didn't know reservations were needed for the drive-thru at Burger Heaven." Joe broke out his lopsided smile.

"Ha-ha. Nice try. We're eating inside if we dine at Burger Heaven."

"I'll make sure we get a table with a view."

"Well, Mr. Romantic, will we gaze on the exciting pop dispenser, the always delightful condiment corner, or the dark hallway to the restrooms?"

"The hallway is my favorite," Joe with a wink.

Amanda held up her hand. "I'm calling a truce. But don't grab the van keys yet. I want to wait until Patrick picks up Brittany. She might need me for something at the last minute."

Joe turned quiet before saying, "She's twenty-one, Amanda. It's time you started to let your baby go."

Amanda gave him an unconcerned wave. "Brittany hasn't been on a date in over a year, and I can tell she's very nervous. I'd like to be here when he picks her up, just in case."

"Matt told me Patrick bought a slick new two-seater Porsche about a month ago. Seems he's doing very well at one of the big accounting firms in the city." He grinned. "Expensive sports car equals a good catch for my daughter."

Amanda rolled her eyes. "That's old-fashioned thinking, Joe. Brittany will have her own career and buy her own sports car someday soon."

"You're right," Joe said. "My bad. But I'd love to take a ride in that car."

"Well, it's only their first date. And don't let Brittany hear you say he's a good catch. It's an automatic turnoff if parents like the guy, remember?"

"Understood."

Joe leaned over and kissed Amanda. She felt herself blush. It was the first time he'd done so since she'd first questioned him about that credit-card issue four days ago. The longest time a wedge had ever been between them. She kissed him back. Being mad didn't help anyone. It wasn't as much fun, either.

At exactly six o'clock the doorbell rang. Joe headed to the front door.

"Hello, Mr. Knightly. I'm not sure if you remember me. I'm Patrick Williams."

Joe waved him inside. "Of course I remember you. You're a little early."

"I didn't want to be late, Mr. Knightly."

"Please, call me Joe." The two men stiffly shook hands as Amanda joined them.

Patrick turned toward her. "How was your first day at the Dark Roast, Mrs. Knightly?"

"Good. And please, call me Amanda." She decided Patrick had a knack for dressing sharp, yet casual. He wore a fitted brown leather jacket, pressed white dress shirt unbuttoned at the collar, sharply creased pants, and polished loafers. A light, woodsy aftershave complemented his smart appearance.

When he fidgeted with the jacket sleeve, Amanda couldn't decide if he was nervous or overly fastidious. Either way, he had dressed as if he wanted to make a good impression. He'd succeeded with her.

"I'm a big fan of the Dark Roast," Patrick said. "By the way, Brittany told me you're helping David. I'm on Matt's GoFundMe campaign."

Before Amanda could respond, Brittany started down the staircase, then teetered as a heel caught the edge of the top step.

Patrick flew up the stairs like Superman, catching Brittany before she tumbled down. He gently escorted her the rest of the way.

Brittany thanked him as she caught her breath. Amanda and Joe added their appreciation.

Patrick helped Brittany with her coat and the two headed out the front door. As they walked down the porch steps, she slipped her hand over Patrick's arm.

Closing the door, Joe shook his head. "He seems like a nice enough guy, but he's sure particular about his appearance. My grandfather used to straighten his shirt cuffs like that."

"Being conscious of your appearance isn't a bad thing. You're lucky we had a second date after you showed up in those threadbare jeans. Plus, the faded sweatshirt and ratty gym shoes you always wore."

"Hey, I loved those shoes. I never took them off."

"That I can believe." Amanda gave Joe a wry smile. "But back to Patrick. I was impressed with his quick reaction when our daughter almost tumbled down the stairs. At least we know she's in safe hands."

"True. So are we ready to hit Burger Heaven?"

Amanda tried not glance at her laptop on her desk. Right now David probably sat in a jail cell eating who knew what, and she'd soon be chowing down on her favorite greasy cheeseburger and fries. More frightening was David's potential transfer to Cook County Jail if the guards didn't go on strike.

The idea gave her a jolt. When they got home, she'd tackle the top to-dos on her list: finding the phone numbers of Olivia's neighbors and snooping through social media sites.

"Yes, I'm ready for dinner," she answered.

As Amanda and Joe drove to Burger Heaven, back-to-back text messages arrived on her phone.

Chloe's text arrived first. *Shop closed for tonight. All in order.*

Amanda smiled. Today Chloe's stock had gone up even further in her eyes.

The second text was from Nicki. *LOVE the heat. LOVE my condo. LOVE it here! Later gator.*

Amanda's smile grew. Nicki had put endless hours and

energy into the Dark Roast over the past five years. She'd more than earned a great vacation.

As they munched on their burgers and shared a large order of fries, Amanda and Joe's conversation stayed on safe subjects: the changing weather, the Cubs' upcoming season, and a new mystery series they wanted to stream. Neither of them brought up the credit-card fiasco. Amanda didn't want another dinner ending in frozen silence, and she suspected Joe felt the same.

Back home, she hustled to her laptop while Joe headed to the garage and Baby.

After several frustrating attempts, she found phone numbers for Maria Sebastian, Phil Wharton, and Max Paxton. It was too late to call tonight, so she'd contact them tomorrow.

Next, she snooped through Gina's social media. It amazed her what she could see without having to friend her. Amanda learned Gina wasn't in a relationship but hoped to be soon, hated her old job, loved the new one, and liked to post pictures of herself. Nothing Amanda didn't already know.

The same necklace Amanda had seen dangling from Gina's neck only a few hours ago also appeared in the young woman's profile picture. She held up the gold-etched heart locket with an "I bet you're jealous" smirk.

She certainly had acted very coy about who had given it to her. Perhaps it wasn't a gift? Maybe she'd stolen it. Or maybe it was somehow even involved in Olivia's murder?

Amanda sat back and shook her head. Connecting the necklace to Olivia was a huge leap. She'd need solid proof before trying to introduce that wild theory.

A quick check of Olivia's social media sites was a bust. The young woman had zilch connections. Surprised, Amanda reconfirmed twice she hadn't misspelled Olivia's name. Still nothing. Well, that was interesting, she thought.

She pulled up the Oak Hills Citizen Watch website. According to Gina, the police already knew that she'd stayed with her sister on the same floor as the murdered woman. Chloe had said she'd told the police about Gina's continual comments about wanting to kill Olivia—five years after a spoiled prom date. Wouldn't the police see this as a motive and question her further? Or perhaps they needed another confirmation.

Amanda clicked on the online submittal link and a blank form popped up. After keying in Gina Rohmer's name, she gave a brief description of Gina's rumored threat to Olivia and hit the submit button. The police now had two confirmations on the same motive.

One down, one to go.

Amanda pulled up a second blank form and keyed in Raymond Cartel's name.

Chloe had said Olivia filed a formal complaint to the Valley Lane condo board about Raymond's supposedly shoddy work. Olivia had also posted a copy of the complaint in the lobby, along with a petition demanding Raymond be fired. But no one signed it. Yesterday, the condo board had canceled the formal complaint. The coincidence was something the police should know about.

She checked "Guest" for submitter's name to keep her identity secret. Then she hit the submit button, satisfied.

She'd only just begun.

CHAPTER 14

Amanda punched the alarm and rolled over to Joe's side of the bed. Empty. She threw off the bedcovers and peered out the bedroom window. No surprise, he stood over Baby with a wrench in his hand and a spotlight clipped to the raised hood.

Amanda hurried across the back deck in Sunday's awakening daylight, giving her ponytail a tight tug.

Joe glanced up from under the Mustang's hood and hustled toward her. He wore a grin like a rookie who'd hit a home run. "You might not believe this, Amanda, but Baby is ready to show her stuff. I want to take you for a drive and then stop for breakfast." His left arm gestured toward the car, like an usher showing a patron to their seat.

"Joe, I'd love to. But I'm opening the shop today, remember?" She pointed to the Dark Roast logo peeking out from under her coat.

Seeing his eyes lose their twinkle, she touched his arm. "Can I get a rain check? Nicki insisted on arranging today's schedule so I could leave at noon and not miss my weekly visit with my mother. I'll be home by mid-afternoon, promise."

"Sure. That works." Joe's grin reappeared. "Catch you later." He strode back to the garage.

That's one of the many reasons I love the guy, Amanda reminded herself as she hiked to the Dark Roast. He rolled with the punches.

Seeing the coffee shop's sign pushed her thoughts into work mode. Yesterday had been like a dress rehearsal, with Nicki not yet gone. Today she'd have a solo performance.

Her steps quickened as her stomach turned uneasy. This morning she'd work alongside Zak Walker, one of her favorite baristas. She loved joking with him as a customer. How would he respond to her being his temporary manager?

Minutes later, Amanda and Zak stood side by side in front of the line of empty coffee urns. His man bun held back his auburn-verging-on-orange-tinted hair and a rainbow of jeweled studs curved around his earlobes. Colorful tattoos traveled down both arms to the top of his hands. He could have been headed to a rock concert, except for the Dark Roast polo.

Amanda always found Zak comfortable being his own person. Right now, though, he lacked his usual casual ease. He rocked back and forth like a tennis ace tensed to receive a serve at Wimbledon.

"Now that you're my manager, I don't know what I should call you," Zak said.

"Call me Amanda. Like you always do."

His wary demeanor loosened up a little. "Uh, sure. If you'd like, I can explain how Sunday morning works."

"That would be great. If I'm doing something wrong, let me know. Deal?"

Zak broke into a genuine smile. "Deal."

A surge of adrenaline hit Amanda. She could do this manager thing.

The two prepped side by side, accompanied by the clang of

coffee urns. Their laughter and the aroma of freshly brewed coffee filled the little shop.

Zak held up his hand. "As part of your training, I need to fill you in on the fun facts I've collected about coffee. I've won over tough customers sharing them."

"You never shared fun facts with me," she said, pretending to pout.

"Because you're always a good customer."

"Whew! That's a relief to hear. Okay, start at the top of your list."

Zak nodded. "Legend has it a goat herder in Ethiopia noticed his goats appeared to dance after eating the berries of the coffea plant. Notice it's pronounced *coffea*, with an 'a' at the end. A local monastery heard about the goats. One monk made a drink from the seeds in the berries and it kept him up at night. The devoted monk appreciated the extra hours. Thus, the original cup of coffee was born."

"That's a great story. What's next on the list?"

Zak wagged his finger at her. "Only one tip at a time. I'll share the second one at our next shift together."

Amanda smiled. "I can't wait."

With everything in order ten minutes before the shop opened, Amanda wanted to put their bonus time to good use. Her son kept putting her off whenever she asked about the GoFundMe campaign.

But just like Nicki, she knew Zak loved to talk. A first-year law student, he'd been tagged the legal expert for the campaign.

When she casually asked about the fundraiser for David, he took the bait.

Zak reeled off that they'd received almost $1,000 in only two days. They planned to use the money to hire a lawyer, who'd promised to charge the minimum fee. "David deserves more than a public defender who's already overloaded with cases."

"I totally agree," Amanda said. "But I'm curious. You don't live in Oak Hills. How do you know David?"

"We met at the Happy Bean over in Schaumburg. He's a great guy. Like all of us, maybe not a saint. But there's no way David murdered Olivia Hager."

"Did you know her?"

He nodded. "She hung out at the Happy Bean. I almost asked her out once, but she made it very clear she had no interest in me. She only wanted David and went after him mercilessly. Honestly, a few times I wanted to tell her to lay off of him. She was relentless. I could tell David didn't like her bugging him, either."

Zak frowned, rubbing the back of his neck as if agitated. Amanda tried not to stare. His reaction to Olivia Hager's pursuit of David troubled her. Plus, Olivia had put him down. The guy probably had a bruised ego.

Zak dropped his hand and gave her a funny glance. "You're sure asking a lot of questions."

"You're right, I am. I was at the Dark Roast when David was arrested. He cried out for my help and I'm keeping my ears and eyes open for him."

"Okay. Then it makes sense."

"Can I ask a couple more questions?"

"Sure. Fire away."

"I'm curious if you were at the Happy Bean this past Wednesday, the day of Olivia's murder."

He nodded. "Yeah. I subbed for another barista. Olivia was her usual self. She hung out by the counter, annoying David and holding up the line. I even heard her tell another woman to back off because she was talking to him."

"That sounds pretty aggressive. Did anyone tell her to tone it down?"

"In my opinion, the manager should have called her on it. Instead, he pressured David to drop off Olivia's debit card at her condo. I'm sure she'd purposely left it behind. My shift ended at three. That's when I got asked to fill-in at my other part-time job delivering packages for UPS. A driver had a family emergency close to the end of her shift."

"Did you make a delivery to Valley Lane Condos?" Amanda kept her expression neutral. She didn't want to consider Zak a suspect. But she had to ask.

"Yep, just after four o'clock. It was a quick in and out. Sam Robertson usually handles that route. He's been a driver for several years. Quiet, keeps to himself, a great guy." Zak frowned. "About a month ago, Olivia tried to pull a fast one on him."

"How?"

"She tried to claim a package he'd delivered was tampered with. Said an expensive necklace was missing from a three-piece jewelry set. Insisted the package had been opened and re-taped. Olivia filed a police report and personally took it to top UPS management and even complained to one of those TV stations that promise to solve your consumer problem."

"What happened?"

"Sam told me he was afraid he'd lose his job. He believed Olivia had the necklace and cooked up that scheme so she wouldn't have to pay for it. Then someone solved *his* problem, when Olivia was murdered."

Zak took a deep breath. "I know that sounds kinda cold. But I felt sorry for the guy. I'm sure the police pulled him in for questioning. I need to call him."

"Do you know what the necklace looked like?"

"Never saw it. But he said it was gold with some kind of fancy locket."

Amanda's internal antennae shot up. That sounded just like Gina's new necklace.

Zak nodded. "Sure, I'll ask Sam and let you know what he says."

"Thanks. In the meantime, I have one last question for you.

Are you aware of any security cameras at Olivia's condo building?"

"That's a whole different story—"

The shop's front door pushed opened. Time to welcome their first customer of the day.

The entire morning had a steady flow of patrons, as Amanda and Zak worked the front counter in tandem. At one point, she heard Zak argue with a customer about a Cubs' pitcher. The irritated patron grabbed a to-go lid and hurried out the front door as if he couldn't get away fast enough.

Where were those fun coffee facts for tough customers? Amanda wondered.

She frowned when Zak calmly turned to the next customer in line and asked for their order as if nothing had happened. Nicki had warned her to watch for Zak's occasional heated opinions. She'd said he sometimes lacked an internal alarm when to back off, but he didn't stay angry for long.

An alarming scenario hit Amanda.

Zak had made a delivery to Valley Lane Condos late Wednesday afternoon. Maybe after being buzzed inside, he stopped by Olivia's to say a friendly hello. Maybe she brushed him off. Maybe humiliation and his hot temper had driven him to murder her in a fit of rage. Maybe being part of the GoFundMe campaign and getting a private lawyer for David were just a big cover-up.

Maybe Zak hoped to get away with the murder of Olivia Hager.

A pang of dread crossed her mind. *Please, please, not Zak.*

She tried to push the idea out of her head but couldn't. It seemed far-fetched and yet plausible.

Soon a party of three on their way to a singing gig burst into a familiar, old-time folk song while waiting for their orders. Amanda hummed along, glad for the diversion. She made herself stay in that zone for the rest of the morning.

Just before noon, Chloe arrived to take over Amanda's shift. Wearing a cream-colored cape trimmed in pink faux fur, accented with a pink knit cap, she could have been featured in a fashion layout. For a moment, Amanda envisioned herself in Chloe's outfit. An image of a wayward pink flamingo popped into her mind. Nope. Not happening.

As she donned her practical black coat, a text arrived from Nicki.

80s and sun. Pool perfect. Later gator.

The attached selfie showed Nicki perched on the edge of a beach chair, wearing an ear-to-ear grin and reflective aviator sunglasses. She toasted the camera with a tall, frothy, tropical drink, accented with a miniature purple umbrella. A skewer of orange, pineapple, and melon slices cascaded down the side of the frosted glass. Amanda sent a smile emoji, happy for her friend.

At noon Amanda left the Dark Roast, relishing her three-block walk down First Street to home. It was sunny, with a hint of spring in the air. The start of the change in seasons invigorated her.

Reaching Valley Lane and First Street, she caught sight of Olivia's building down the block and winced.

Security cameras. Zak hadn't answered her question. Tomorrow morning on their shift together, she'd ask again.

Arriving home, it didn't surprise Amanda to find the garage door down and the house quiet. Joe was probably showing off Baby somewhere, Matt would be at his indoor soccer league, and Brittany should be headed to work.

Changed into her Sunday-going-to-see-Mother outfit, she stepped into the upstairs hallway at the same time Brittany sauntered out of her bedroom wearing a T-shirt and pajama bottoms. Amanda leaped sideways to avoid a collision.

"Aren't you scheduled to work today?" Amanda asked, frowning.

"No worries. I've got it under control." Brittany tousled her hair as she yawned.

Amanda couldn't hold back. "How did it go last night with Patrick?"

In a nanosecond, sleepy Brittany turned into beaming Brittany. "I had a great time. We ate at this fancy restaurant off Michigan Avenue and then hit four clubs. He's so different from anyone I've ever dated. Really mature, but he also likes to have a good time."

"I'm glad it went well." Amanda waited a beat, not wanting to seem nosy. Which Joe would have said she was. "Do you plan to see him again?"

"Definitely. We're meeting for coffee after I get off my shift. No big deal. I like him, but I don't want to get serious."

"By serious, you mean where he wants to see you all the time?"

"Yep. He already texted me three times this morning."

"Well, be honest with him, Brittany. Let him know how you feel. You said he's mature, so I'm sure he'll understand."

Brittany made a face as if Amanda had just said the dumbest thing possible. "Mom, I'm not ready for any big talk with Patrick. I just want to have fun. He even hinted about showing me his new place. I'm not interested in getting that close right now." She stretched her arms over her head. "What time is it, anyway?"

"It's 12:15."

"Oh, no! I can't be late again." Brittany charged down the hallway and slammed the bathroom door.

Heading downstairs, Amanda was glad she'd held back from reacting to the casual mention of Patrick's invitation to his new place. That was Brittany's decision to make, after all. If she wanted her mom's advice, she'd ask for it. Hopefully.

Once in the kitchen, Amanda skimmed the Sunday *Gazette* Joe had left on the table. The headline *"Olivia Hager Case*

Update" was outlined in red ink, boxed in the top right corner of the front page once again.

The Gazette has learned several additional Oak Hills merchants have discovered anonymous letters on their premises. All were identical to the ones found Saturday morning, with the message "Stedman is guilty." The Oak Hills Police continue to investigate.

More to come as details are released.

Amanda groaned. Someone really wanted David put away for good. Could that someone be Gina or Raymond, or possibly the UPS driver? Or please not Zak? Or was it someone she hadn't yet considered?

As far as she knew, the Dark Roast still hadn't gotten an anonymous letter. At least yet.

CHAPTER 15

Amanda drove her usual half-hour route to her mother's home on the northwest side of Chicago. Today she mulled over the questions she wanted to ask her mother about what had happened in 1944 in Oak Hills that Raymond Cartel had hinted might relate to David's predicament. She knew her mother's family was originally from Oak Hills.

But getting information wouldn't be easy. Her very private mother never wanted to talk about the past. Amanda knew she'd have to be patient.

While she was stopped at a red light, a scene at a nearby park caught her attention. A little girl squealed in delight as a young man, probably her father, pushed her swing higher and higher.

Amanda felt a familiar jab in her heart.

Higher, Daddy.

You mean all the way to the sky, Amanda?

Yes, Daddy!

Anything for my little girl.

The next morning, her father had walked out the front door, never to return.

Amanda's hands tightened on the steering wheel. Her mother never talked about her father's disappearance. Maybe someday she would.

Today Amanda wanted to focus on Oak Hills in 1944. One step at a time.

At 1:00 p.m. sharp, Amanda parallel parked in front of her mother's Chicago-style bungalow. It was identical to all the others on the block, except each had been built with a different color of brick.

Her mother opened the front door. "Hello, dear."

Amanda recognized her mother's Pendleton wool two-piece suit from her days as a teacher in the Chicago Public Schools. A resale shop would label it a classic.

"Hello, Mother," Amanda said as she stepped inside.

Her proud Baby Boomer mother had never been a hugger. And she had steadily lost her "boom" in recent years due to never-ending health issues. Only recently had she accepted Amanda's offer of help with her weekly shopping. Like many city dwellers, she relied on public transportation, calling taxis an unnecessary expense. Getting on and off a CTA bus was challenging enough for her now and almost impossible with shopping bags.

Amanda drove her mother to the local supermarket, followed by a stop at the neighborhood drugstore. Shopping done and groceries put away, mother and daughter headed to the mom-and-pop restaurant around the corner, as they did every Sunday. Amanda's mother liked the routine, she always said.

"Are you ladies ready to order?" Their usual waitress had her pen and order pad in hand.

Her mother's order never changed: breaded pork chop dinner and salad with French dressing. "Don't forget the scoop of vanilla ice cream for dessert. That's my favorite part," she always added.

Amanda liked to vary her order. "This week I'll take the grilled chicken sandwich." Her belt buckle pressed against her waist. "And can I substitute fruit for the fries?"

"It's an extra two dollars."

"That's fine." She silently groaned. Paying extra for fruit when she craved the greasy, hot fries with gazillions of calories that came with the meal wasn't fair.

Her mother smoothed her napkin over her lap. "How's the family?" she asked.

Amanda gave updates on Joe, Matt, and Brittany. Her mother showed little reaction other than to nod.

Every Sunday Amanda experienced the same disappointment. She loved her mother for her strength during their hard times, her work ethic, and her straight-to-the-point answers. Yet Amanda yearned for the loving heart she remembered. It hadn't shown itself since the day her father vanished.

When the waitress delivered their orders, their stiff small talk continued: the weather, the popular mystery her mother was reading, and Amanda working as the manager at the Dark Roast for the week.

"That's nice, Amanda." She didn't ask why her daughter had switched jobs for the week. That would have been prying and none of her business.

It wasn't until the end of their meal that Amanda decided it was time to bring up Raymond's story.

"When Joe and I bought our house in Oak Hills, I remember you told me my grandparents once lived there but moved to Chicago right after you were born. Do I have that right?"

The spoon in Amanda's mother's hand hovered over the scoop of vanilla ice cream. "Why, yes, that's true."

"Did they live in Oak Hills in 1944?"

"Yes. They both grew up in the village. In 1944 my dad was twelve years old and my mom was eleven. They were already sweet on each other, as they said in those days."

Amanda took a deep breath. "A man by the name of Raymond Cartel told me something happened in Oak Hills in 1944 that involved the police and missing evidence in a crime."

Her mother frowned. "I don't know anybody by that name," she said. "But then, I wasn't born yet."

"I was hoping you'd heard your parents mention it."

Her mother laid down her spoon. "Why are you asking these questions, Amanda?"

"Because the police have locked up a young man in the Oak Hills Jail for a murder that I believe he didn't commit. Raymond said it reminded him of what happened in 1944, but he wouldn't say anything more. If I can learn what injustice happened back then, I could make sure it doesn't happen again now." She reached out and gently touched her mother's hand.

After a long silence, her mother spoke. "I'm not sure if it's wise to get involved, Amanda. There's a reason everyone in our family keeps to themselves."

Amanda frowned. "But I don't know what that reason is."

Her mother stared down at her coffee cup. "I guess it's time I tell you. All I know is, my father helped a stranger back in 1944 and it backfired on him. The Oak Hills police charged him with a crime he didn't commit. He served time and afterwards moved out of Oak Hills."

She looked up again. "It sounds as if this Raymond Cartel was talking about your grandfather."

Amanda felt as if the air had been sucked out of her lungs. "Although it was painful to hear, thank you for telling me."

Her mother stood up with her ice cream untouched. "It's time to go home, Amanda."

"I agree." Amanda took her mother's arm and guided her to the van.

When Amanda walked in her back door several hours later, Joe greeted her with a hug. "Normally you're home from your mother's long before now," he said, stepping back. "Is everything okay?"

"My bad. I should have called. Today we needed some extra time."

"Your mother isn't one to vary her weekly schedule. Or be too chatty."

"You're right. You won't believe what she told me." Amanda dropped into a chair. "My grandfather was falsely convicted of a crime in 1944 and served time."

Joe looked shocked. He pulled a chair next to hers. "And you knew nothing about this?"

She nodded. "All these years she's kept it a secret from me. Now I finally understand why my family always insisted we keep to themselves. They were ashamed. And yet I was always the exception. I liked to be with people."

"That also explains those do-not-get-too-close-to-me vibes that I always pick up from your mother."

"It makes me even more determined to find out how David could be connected," Amanda said.

"Did you get any hints about how your grandfather's and David's situations are alike? And where Raymond Cartel fits in?"

Amanda shook her head. "I need to do more digging. I plan to comb through the library archives."

Joe's long sigh filled the air. "What if the person who murdered Olivia Hager finds out you're on an all-out quest to clear David's name? They may come after you. Have you thought about that?"

"Yes, I have. But I don't plan to accuse anyone to their face. That's where the Citizen Watch site comes in."

"Like I said the other night, be careful. I'd hate to have to find a new wife if something happened to you." He gave her his lopsided smile again.

"Real funny! But I'm glad to hear you're being practical."

"Now who's trying to be funny?" Joe teased, then dropped his smile. "But seriously, a quick kick to someone's shin can slow them down. Although I hope you never find yourself in that position."

"I'll remember that."

"And being 'anonymous' doesn't mean the Oak Hills Police can't find out who sent in a tip. Plus, I hear Chief Grady is relieved they have a suspect behind bars. If you rile them up enough, you might end up in the jail cell next to David."

Amanda shook her head. "That won't happen. I promise. David will soon be a free man and you can tell me I did the right thing." She tugged at her ponytail and gave Joe a smile. "And now I'm ready to cash in my rain check for a ride in Baby."

"Yeah, well, hold on to your rain check. When I took Baby out for a trial spin, she wasn't running right. It'll probably be a couple of days before I can honor the offer." He bowed his head and extended his arm like a courtier in the Middle Ages. "I hope that meets with your satisfaction, m'lady."

"I'll excuse you this time, Sir Joe. But any more delays and it will be off with your head!" She flourished her arm upward as if brandishing a sword.

"With your permission, I would like to return to the garage to fix the royal coach."

She gave him a regal nod. "Your request is granted."

They both chuckled.

A half hour later Amanda sat back in her desk chair, feeling triumphant. Finally all the scattered phone notes, mental reminders, and spur-of-the-moment questions from the last four days were on one to-do list. Potential suspect names filled a second list.

Then she sighed as stark reality hit. She'd be on overload this week between managing the Dark Roast and digging for more evidence against her list of suspects.

Shutting down her laptop, she chuckled despite her worries.

Maybe she should slink around Oak Hills camouflaged in a black overcoat with the collar turned up, a fedora to hide her face, and sunglasses to hide her eyes. The Knightly van would be her James Bond car.

Forget being the Deli Lady. She'd be the Sleuth Lady!

CHAPTER 16

Amanda unlocked the front door to the Dark Roast early Monday morning, focused on getting the shop ready for the 6:00 open.

Zak trailed behind her, disheveled and groggy. His usual neat man bun had turned into a squashed mini pumpkin hanging off the back of his head. Strands of hair fell into his face. His wrinkled polo needed an iron. Half-shut eyes signaled that he hadn't gotten enough sleep.

"Is everything okay?" Amanda asked, her concerned-mom alarm on high alert.

"I overslept. I'll be right back." He headed to the bathroom and came out two minutes later with his bun intact and his polo straightened. He looked and acted like he'd finally woken up. He quickly tackled the opening checklist tasks, offering no further explanation.

Amanda bit her lip. She so wanted to ask him more questions, maybe give him some advice. Nicki's voice rang in her head: *Keep a professional distance. You aren't here to mother the employees.*

Working side by side, Amanda limited their conversation to getting the Dark Roast ready for the morning rush. When she asked about his next coffee tip, he perked up.

"The world's most expensive coffee is Kopi Luwak, also known as cat-poop coffee," he said.

Amanda made a face. "Yuck. How do cat poop and coffee fit together?"

"Great question. Asian palm civets digest the coffee-plant berries, which ferment in their bodies before they poop them out. The fermented pooped beans are collected, washed, and roasted. It's priced at $600 a pound if collected from cats in the wild. For caged civets, the cost is only $100 a pound, but it brings up the question of animal cruelty. Both versions are considered extremely tasty and full-bodied. I haven't tasted either of them, though, and I doubt Nicki will ever offer it here."

"Ugh. It sounds terrible—and a little too pricey for Dark Roast customers. Plus, how would Nicki list it on the menu board? Pooping Delicious? Pooped for You? Pooped Your Way?" She giggled and slapped her hand over her mouth.

Zak grinned. "Best Poop on the Menu? Roasted Not Flushed? Here's the Real Poop?"

They both bent over in laughter. Amanda stopped chuckling only when she unlocked the front door.

The line of customers headed to work never seemed to end. Some took the commuter train to downtown Chicago, others drove to work, and many headed back home to their remote work desks. All anxiously checked their phones for the time. They needed their coffee *now*.

By 8:30 the rush trickled off, and the shop hummed as regulars settled into their daily routine.

"Whew! I survived my first workday shift." Amanda leaned against the front counter. "It's worse than the crazy noontime crowd at Bob's deli counter. Dare I say I'm pooped?" she said in a wry voice.

Zak chuckled. "Good one. I feel the same." He grabbed a napkin and swiped his perspiring forehead. "No need to hit the gym after the Monday morning surge."

Amanda's hand flew to her mouth. "Oh, no! We were so busy, I forgot to mention our special visitors. They're due any minute."

As they rushed to get everything in order, Amanda explained that Nicki had given her a heads-up late last night to expect Sarah Morrison and her pint-sized students at mid-morning. The owner of nearby Fun Times Preschool liked to take her young charges on short walks around Oak Hills once the tease of early spring arrived. It was a reward to both herself and her pupils for enduring cabin fever over the cold Midwestern winter months.

Amanda and Zak had only enough time to pull together the tables before the front door burst open. A salt-and-pepper-haired woman strutted in wearing a mustard-gold sweatshirt with *Learning Is Fun* stamped across the front and a flowing, multi-colored skirt. A big smile broadcast her delight to be at the Dark Roast.

Trailing behind her, a parade of giggling, fidgety youngsters held hands two by two, wearing miniature versions of the sweatshirt with an array of leggings and sweats. A laid-back young woman with purple strands in her dark hair anchored the back end. She'd paired the preschool's sweatshirt with frayed jeans. She seemed more interested in casing the shop's menu than watching her charges.

The teacher greeted Amanda as her students' excited voices notched up the noise level multiple decibels. Turning toward her boisterous charges, she wagged her finger. "Children, remember you need to be on your best behavior. Use your inside voices, please."

The youngsters took that reminder as permission to run, skip, and twirl in all directions. The assistant remained focused on the menu board as if it were a priceless Monet at Chicago's Art Institute. Amanda wasn't sure if the young woman was enraptured by the Dark Roast offerings or just needed a break from the preschoolers.

She was grateful their other customers chose to ignore the commotion. A few smiled. One even remarked, "Aren't they adorable. Chock-full of energy."

"Thank goodness I got the heads-up from Nicki," Amanda said under her breath to Zak. "We need to corral them."

But the children had already taken over the Dark Roast. Every inch became a new place to explore as they moved on to the next corner or table.

Several ended up behind the front counter. One boy ran off with the computer mouse; another started to play with the keyboard. Amanda feared the daily sales totals would be a catastrophe.

She stopped two students headed for the storeroom and made sure the few remaining patrons didn't become open game.

It didn't take long for Amanda to realize that the head teacher had a hands-off approach toward overseeing her students. Nicki had hinted as much. "Sarah likes the kids to experience life" was Nicki's view. Amanda tagged it as chaos on steroids.

After Amanda and Zak set down ten small warm cocoas and two coffees on the pulled-together tables, Sarah and her purple-streaked assistant got their students to sit. Amanda breathed a sigh of relief as the chaos subsided.

The students started out angelic, quietly sipping their hot cocoa. Until one little boy decided to slurp his drink loudly, which made the other students giggle. Before long they all turned into noisy slurpers, and pandemonium reigned once again.

Soon puddles of spilled cocoa covered the tables and floor. By now all the patrons had decamped, except for the guy with ear buds holed up at a back corner table. Amanda saw Sarah's assistant escape toward the restrooms.

Sarah Morrison stood serenely at the front counter, the kids' laughter and shouts echoing behind her. "We all loved our visit. Thank you so much. I'll make sure Nicki knows what a great job you did." Sarah beamed.

"Thank you. I appreciate that." Amanda tucked several wayward strands of hair behind her ear and yanked her ponytail tight. She caught sight of Zak trying to stop two students from climbing on the tables. Sarah's helper was still missing.

It worried Amanda that no new customers had come into the shop since it had been overtaken by the preschoolers. Word must have gotten around Oak Hills to avoid the ruckus. Their sales numbers for the last hour would be dismal.

Sarah leaned in toward Amanda. "Nicki told me you hope to prove David Stedman didn't murder Olivia Hager. Is that correct?"

Amanda nodded. "Yes. I can't believe David is capable of murdering anyone."

Sarah hesitated. "I also want the right person to be charged. But I don't want Olivia's reputation dragged through the mud any more than it's been. She worked for me at Fun Times."

Amanda's eyebrows rose. "I didn't know that."

"There's a lot of things people didn't know about Olivia. She was a very private person. Yes, she could be rough around the edges, but I think it had to do with her upbringing. Unstable home, parents needing help themselves, living one step above poverty. Her life was worse than a horror movie."

"I can understand how that would damage someone," Amanda said, thinking how her own life had turned upside down the morning her father had walked out the front door, never to return.

"People don't seem to know Olivia had a special gift with children. She understood when they were having bad days, had a sixth sense when they acted out because something bad happened at home, or maybe they were scared for no reason. In the two years she worked for me, she blossomed and chipped away at that rough exterior."

Sarah shook her head. "When I heard she was murdered, I was heartbroken. Such a waste of a promising young life."

Sarah's words rekindled Amanda's memory of the day she'd met Olivia. A harried young mother, with a wailing preschooler hanging onto her leg screaming "Mommy, Mommy, MOMM-MYYY," had tried valiantly to give Amanda her order. When the little guy's crying turned into giggles, Amanda had heard the mother profusely thanking the next customer behind her for stopping his tantrum.

Olivia.

She hadn't put the pieces together until now. Olivia had been the unseen miracle worker.

"I totally agree. Olivia's murder was very tragic. Hearing her life had started to come together makes it even more so." Amanda was regretting that she hadn't known about the other side of Olivia the day she first met the young woman. "I'm wonder—"

Just then, two giggling little girls plowed into their teacher, almost knocking her off her feet.

"Do I see two busy students behind me?" Sarah teased, smiling at them.

After a gentle reminder to be more careful, the girls ran off and the purple-haired assistant reappeared. "I've got this," she said.

Sarah turned her attention back to Amanda. The teacher quietly said, "It's times like this that I miss Olivia." She paused for a moment, then asked, "But you were starting to say something?"

"I'm wondering if there's anything else you can tell me about Olivia."

"Well, she quit her job by sending me a text. No warning at all. I tried to reach out numerous times, but she had shut the door."

"You never heard from her again?"

"She hadn't responded to any of my calls for the past year. It didn't surprise me too much because Olivia was a very private person. And she'd been hinting about an idea for an ebusiness. I recently heard her startup online venture was already profitable. I'm happy it worked out for her."

"I didn't know she'd started her own business."

"It had something to do with brokering supplies of some kind. I don't know the name of the company."

Amanda immediately thought of the five thousand dollars Olivia had invested in David's start-up coffee shop. If her business was profitable, she probably hadn't needed the money back. Had she pressed David to meet Wednesday night only because she truly wanted to see him? And somehow it hadn't gone well for either of them?

A chorus of children's laughter jolted Amanda back to the present.

Sarah turned to the pandemonium and clapped her hands. "Children, it's time to find your partner and walk to the front door. Christopher, that means walk, not run." A wiggling two-by-two line formed and headed to the front of the shop, led by the assistant.

Sarah turned back to Amanda. "It's back to school and quiet time before lunch. Then they'll start getting charged up for our Wednesday morning visit."

"Where to?"

"The police station. We have a ten o'clock appointment with Chief Grady. He gives the children a special talk every year. Each student gets a toy police badge as we leave. They look forward to it."

Amanda held back from rolling her eyes. If only she could see the chief's face when the children let loose at the police station.

As the entourage from Fun Times Preschool filed out the front door of the Dark Roast, Amanda glanced over at Zak.

He threw up his hands. "They're more work than the Monday morning crowd!"

"I agree. But Sarah told me how much they enjoyed their visit. She'll also tell their parents, and the kids will mention it to their parents as well, which means lots of good publicity for the Dark Roast. And I'll make sure Nicki knows how hard you worked to pull this off on short notice."

Zak's scowl disappeared. "Thanks. I appreciate it." He reached for the cleaning supplies. "I'll tackle the mess they left."

Amanda hid her smile. A reminder for a fledgling manager that positive words could be a valuable incentive.

As she wiped down the front counter, Sarah's recollections of Olivia Hager ran through her mind. The teacher had presented a picture of a sensitive, talented young woman who wasn't afraid to go in a totally new career direction. Amanda was sorry their only meeting had given her such a negative impression.

A steady stream of customers returned, keeping Amanda and Zak hustling for the rest of the morning. The all-clear that the preschoolers had exited the Dark Roast must have sounded through the village.

Amanda figured the toughest part of her day was over. But then the Logans, her nemeses at Bob's deli counter, burst into the coffee shop. They didn't ask if it was okay before taping a poster advertising this Friday's Senior Center Spring Fling across the front door.

Knowing Nicki saw the support of civic events as good for business, Amanda nicely asked the Logans to move the large poster to a bulletin board so it didn't block the view into the shop.

Before they agreed, they made a couple of snide remarks that upset several customers. The two were still grumbling when they left. They didn't make a purchase either. And here she'd thought she had the week off from the Logans.

During the brief lull that followed their departure, Amanda asked Zak about the security cameras at Valley Lane Condos.

"Useless," he said.

Amanda frowned. "How is that?"

"They don't work. Never have. They're only decorations. Everyone knows that. Even the police."

Amanda felt like she'd run into a brick wall. Thank goodness she hadn't sent in that tip. The police would have howled with laughter when they read it.

"Did you have time to ask your friend about the necklace?" she asked.

Zak shook his head. "Sorry. Last night I was heads-down, studying for a big test on constitutional law. I'll try to get in touch with him tonight."

Was the test the reason Zak had shown up so raggy this morning? Why hadn't he said so? Something seemed out of whack with him.

The part-timer arrived, relieving Zak. He scooted out the front door, passing by Officer Evans walking in.

"Good to see you." Amanda held back from calling the officer Monica, like Nicki did. She normally would have taken the initiative, but her Sleuth Lady campaign to help David made it feel like a suck-up move. For now, she'd wait it out.

"Good to see you too, Amanda. I'm on break and thought I'd stop in for a quick cup of coffee." Evans scanned the shop. "I see you're keeping the Dark Roast humming while Nicki's on vacation. Nice job."

Amanda beamed. "Colombian blend, correct? And room for cream?"

The officer nodded. "You're also on top of customer

service." She touched the stack of Oak Hills Citizen Watch brochures on the front counter. "Perfect place to put them where customers can see them. Let me know when you need more."

Amanda slid the steaming cup over the counter. "I will. By the way, this is on the house."

"Thanks." The officer stuffed several bills into the thank-you jar that looked equal to the posted price. "I always return the favor by making sure employees know I appreciate their efforts." She smiled. "By chance, can you join me?"

"I'd love to," Amanda said, curious. She signaled the part-timer to take over the front counter and led Evans to a patch of empty tables.

As they sat down, Evans launched into small talk: Nicki's vacation, spring arriving early, the Chicago Cubs and White Sox back from spring training. Amanda sensed it was only a warm-up to what Evans really wanted to ask.

A brief pause filled the air as Evans took a sip, then said, "With the number of people who come into the Dark Roast, I'm thinking you may have heard some comments on the Citizen Watch program."

Aha!

"Customers have picked up the flyers," Amanda said. "I've only heard positive comments, if that's what you want to know."

"I'm interested in knowing if people find the online site easy to navigate. It's a brand-new system, and now's the time to get it fixed if needed."

Amanda nodded. Where was this conversation going?

"I know someone who sent in a tip," she said. Which was true. And also, the perfect opening to a question she wanted confirmed. "They wondered what happens after that?"

"We read every tip and determine next actions," Evans said. "Except for those from obvious pranksters about sighting Elvis, or some such nonsense." They both chuckled. "But overall, the tips have been helpful." Evans fiddled with her coffee cup before adding, "By chance, have you heard any talk about Olivia Hager's murder here in the Dark Roast?"

Amanda sat back. Why were the police interested in chatter at the coffee shop about Olivia's murder? Time to answer a question with a question.

"No," Amanda answered, truthfully. "But I'm curious. Is the evidence strong against David?"

In a flash, Evans shook her head. "You know I can't discuss details of the case with you, Amanda." She took a sip of her coffee and slowly set the cup down.

Another aha! Her swift denial could signal the police didn't have an airtight case.

Evans cleared her throat. "What I can tell you is that we need tips based on facts and not hearsay. That's especially true for guest submitters, because we can't contact them with follow-up questions."

"Guest submitters stay anonymous, right?"

"Yes, they do. But as you know, no one is truly anonymous on the web." The officer took another sip.

"Understood." That confirmed Joe's warning that the police could uncover her identity if they needed to.

Evans pushed her chair back. "I've stayed longer than I intended. But I'm glad we talked. And thanks again for the coffee."

"I have another quick question, if you have one more minute," Amanda said.

"Of course."

"I understand Chief Grady is a hands-on guy. Keeps printed copies of everything. He doesn't like to read on a screen."

Evans nodded. "The chief isn't a techie. Being in the job over twenty-five years gives him the clout to work the way he's used to."

"I can relate. I like to hold the newspaper in my hands," Amanda said.

Politely declining Amanda's offer of a refill, Evans headed out the door. Amanda returned to the front counter.

She'd been put on notice that Chief Grady wouldn't be happy about frivolous tips taking up his staff's time.

But she'd also learned of a new place where the Sleuth Lady could snoop.

CHAPTER 17

Finally able to take a break mid-afternoon, Amanda hightailed the van to the Happy Bean, the Schaumburg coffee shop where David had worked as a barista until his arrest four days ago.

She envied the number of couches, chairs, and tables scattered throughout the popular shop's cavernous main room. It could hold three times as many customers as the Dark Roast. A chalkboard on the back wall advertised an extensive menu of baked goods, salads, and sandwiches, immediately making her hungry.

Four employees, in sky-blue polos embellished with the shop's logo of a coffee bean, raced back and forth behind the long front counter. A line of customers five deep waited to place their orders. The pickup line had just as many, all heads-down on their phones. Amanda caught an energy like the Dark Roast's, but on a much larger scale.

A couple walked in behind her, then a threesome, followed by four parents with strollers. Nicki would kill for this much business mid-afternoon, she thought, then winced. Correction: *would love to have.*

A dark-haired, buff guy with *"Eddie"* and *"Owner"* stitched on his blue polo, approached her.

"Amanda Knightly?" he asked. She tried hard not to stare. Nicki was right. He could be a twin of that hunky *Chicago Fire* actor, right down to his light-green eyes. Amanda braced herself. No fawning like a starstruck groupie. Well ... maybe just a little.

"You must be Eddie Turner." She couldn't stop grinning like a giddy teenager.

Eddie nodded. "Sorry for not getting back to you. It's been very hectic." He gestured toward the hallway. "We can talk in private in my office."

Seated in a chair facing his desk, Amanda assumed a confident and friendly demeanor. The Sleuth Lady wanted to put her interviewee at ease. "Thanks again for taking time to meet with me. I can see you're a busy guy, so I'll keep it short. I'm open to hearing anything that might help me clear David Stedman of the murder charge."

Eddie folded his hands and gave her a wry smile. "Nicki talks a lot about you. I'm glad we finally got to meet."

Amanda wanted to ask why he hadn't returned her calls until after Nicki had intervened last night. But she held off. "I'll make sure I thank Nicki for connecting us," she said instead.

"I'm still thanking her. She saved my life after that *Gazette* reporter quoted me in last Thursday's online edition. I'd said I couldn't believe David would murder Olivia. It got me in real hot water."

"How's that?"

"The next day, the Cook County Department of Public Health called. Seems someone reported seeing a rodent in the Happy Bean. That meant the shop would be closed until a thorough inspection occurred." Eddie leaned forward. "Conveniently, their crews were booked solid. So we would have been shut down for three weeks before they'd even begin."

"And I'm thinking there wasn't a rodent?" Amanda asked, eyebrow raised.

"You got it." He pointed his thumb at his chest. "*I'm* the rat for telling the reporter that David was innocent, in so many words. Somebody got this crazy idea that I purposely wanted to make the police look bad. When Nicki pulled some strings, suddenly an inspection wasn't needed. It was all a big mistake. Or so I was told."

"Nicki's a good person to have on your side, that's for sure." Amanda mentally notched up Nicki's connections once again, not surprised her bestie hadn't mentioned the incident. When it came to business, there were some things Nicki rightly kept to herself.

"I have to warn you. I'm going to tell you exactly what I told the police. Don't expect any new information from me."

Amanda nodded. "Understood. Tell me about David."

Eddie took a deep breath. "David is one of my best baristas. He has a following of customers, especially women. Plus, he knows how to make a great latté. And he has those clean-cut, Captain America looks. On top of that, he's genuinely nice to everyone."

"What kind of worker is he?" She was confident she knew the answer but wanted it confirmed by his boss.

"David never hesitates to work extra shifts or help with mundane chores to get the job done. I told the police he got that nasty cut cleaning up someone else's broken glass that morning. He took it in stride, bandaged it up, and took on Nicki's temporary manager gig the next day. But somebody didn't like what I told the reporter."

Amanda breathed a quiet sigh of relief. Good. Of course, David hadn't injured his finger harming Olivia. But he could have left a trace of blood at her place. Not good.

"Who do you think was behind that rat story?" she asked.

"It could have been anyone. All part of doing business these days. But don't get me started."

"Another question, then. Can you tell me what happened here on the day of Olivia Hager's murder?"

Eddie straightened a couple of sheets of paper on his desk before looking at her. "I still can't get any of it off my mind. That afternoon Olivia stopped in briefly. She could be a difficult customer sometimes, but given how much she spent here on a regular basis, I didn't discourage her from coming into my shop."

"She bought the pricier coffees and food?"

"Yeah. And always wanted David to wait on her. He was usually very good about it. But that day, I'm not sure what got into him, but he told her to quit it."

"Did he say those exact words?"

"Well, something like that. Maybe a little blunter."

"Then what happened?"

"She complained to me that David hadn't returned her debit card. She threatened to post a restaurant review stating my barista stole it and warning people not to trust the Bean. Finally, she left in a huff."

Eddie shook his head. "Bad online reviews can kill a business. I panicked. Then David found her debit card, wedged next to a display on the front counter, as if it had been stashed there on purpose. I was suspicious about what really happened but brushed it aside. With his shift ending, I asked if he could drop it off with Olivia on his way home. He protested but then agreed. Reluctantly, I need to add. What happened next, no one knows."

Amanda remembered the noontime encounter at the deli counter that same day when Olivia had demanded they meet that same night.

"Do you remember what time he left to deliver the card to Olivia?" she asked.

"It was 5:00 p.m. when his shift ended."

"Got it. Have you ever seen David do anything out of character for him?"

"Like I said, David is genuinely nice to everyone. But a couple of weeks before the murder, he seemed preoccupied."

"What happened?"

"Olivia, as usual, was bugging him. It was late at night, almost closing. She claimed her car was dead. He offered to check it out, and they headed for our back parking lot. I was in my office, focused on getting payroll locked and loaded, when I heard a car start."

Eddie squirmed. "I looked out the window and saw the two of them in the front of Olivia's car, kind of jostling back and forth. I thought they were joking around like kids can do. The next thing I knew, there was a lot of shouting in the back hallway. I heard Olivia say, 'Don't put your hands on me ever again!' I honestly heard fear in her voice. When I hustled out of my office, the two of them were in a shoving match, right there in the hallway."

"That's scary."

"Yeah. Both were red-faced. They quickly stepped apart when they saw me. David shouted Olivia had attacked him. She yelled back that he was a liar. Finally, he admitted he pushed her first. She turned all lovey-dovey and said no, she was sorry she'd pushed him. Even tried to give him a hug. I figured it was a misunderstanding that had gotten a little too physical. You could tell she really liked the guy, and I think that's why she never filed a complaint."

Eddie shook his head. "I told David I never wanted to see that behavior again from him. I thought about not telling the police about the incident when they interviewed me, but I had to."

"Did anyone else witness this?"

"A couple of regulars could have heard the shouting, I guess, but they couldn't have seen it. They didn't react, as far as I know. When I went back out front, everyone had left.

Eddie's phone pinged. "Sorry, can we wrap this up? That's my alert that the high school let out. We've become the local hangout, and it's all hands are on deck when they arrive."

"Do you have time for one more question?"

"Sure, but make it quick."

"Did you ever see anyone else show anger or frustration with Olivia?"

Eddie pushed back his chair and stood up. "That's a question the police never asked me. But if I tell you, it's between us. I don't want it to end up in the *Gazette*."

"Promise," Amanda said, raising her hand.

"I can think of two somewhat regulars who always seemed to have their eyes on Olivia. One is a quiet guy. Brown hair, thin, obviously interested in her, but I don't know his name. The other is a really pretty girl. Dressed in pink a lot and focused on her laptop. I'm guessing she was in school. Not sure what her interest was in Olivia, though."

"Did David seem to know either of them?"

"The quiet guy, a little. But he showed no interest in the girl. Now that you ask, I haven't seen either of them here for the last couple of weeks."

Eddie stepped toward the doorway. "Sorry, I gotta go."

Remembering Zak's agitated response to Olivia's name on Sunday morning, she had to squeeze in just one more question.

Amanda rose from her seat as well. "This is my absolute last question. I swear."

"Ask it, then," Eddie said, sounding impatient as he edged closer to the door.

"Did you ever see anything happen between Zak Walker and Olivia?"

"Nah." Eddie shrugged. "Zak practically drooled over Olivia. Made it real obvious. But she treated him like dirt. And with his personality … well, I was always a little nervous he'd do something stupid. But he never did, that I saw. I've learned some kids need more time to grow up."

Eddie's phone pinged again. "I really have to go. Thanks for stopping by."

Driving back to the Dark Roast, Amanda sorted through the highs and lows of her conversation with Eddie.

Somebody clearly didn't like statements about David's innocence. She shuddered, knowing Nicki would never forgive her if the Dark Roast were closed down for imaginary rodents because her sleuthing had upset some unknown person.

As for the two customers who'd been watching Olivia, the quiet, brown-haired guy could be anyone. The girl who dressed in pink sounded like Chloe. But lots of girls wore pink. And why would she hang around the Happy Bean? She'd ask Chloe about it tomorrow.

Stopped at a traffic light on First Street, Amanda remembered Eddie's comment on Zak's quick temper. The young man's reaction on Sunday morning hadn't been a one-off. A valid reason to keep him on her suspect list, despite her reluctance.

She also couldn't erase Eddie's revelation that David had reacted physically against Olivia, no matter which of them had started the altercation.

A new scene started playing in her head. The night of the murder, perhaps Olivia had once again pressed David for the five thousand dollars. David didn't have the money to repay her, and he wasn't interested in her romantically. Plus, she was driving him crazy. Things had gotten emotional again and —

As she parked the van by the Dark Roast, Amanda tried to push the frightening scenario aside. But she couldn't.

The halo on David's head now had a crack.

CHAPTER 18

After closing the Dark Roast, Amanda headed home. Joe, Matt, and Brittany all had other plans for dinner, and she welcomed the time alone. The online *Gazette* reported the outcome of David's pretrial release hearing this afternoon hadn't gone the way she'd hoped.

Settled into the living room couch, she couldn't shake her disappointment. Matt would be upset, too. Same for Virginia, who'd planned to attend. So far, David's great-aunt hadn't called her with an update.

Joe's arrival home interrupted her musings. He soon asked about David's release hearing.

Amanda frowned. "The judge ruled his felony charge meant he'd stay in jail."

Joe gave a low whistle. "Any good news?"

"David finally got assigned a public defender. His arraignment will be scheduled next."

"Overall, that's more bad news than good."

She nodded. "You're right. But there was one huge piece of good news. That threatened strike by the Cook County jail guards is on. Which means David will stay in the Oak Hills jail until a deal is reached."

"Was the rest of your day any better?" Joe plopped down next to her on the sofa.

"It was nonstop!" She threw up her hands. "Thank goodness for the multiple Panda Bears I sipped throughout the day. They kept me going."

"But you said you love working there."

Amanda nodded. "I do. Although I can't help feeling the learning curve is like trying to walk up the 103 floors to the top of the Sears Tower. And I'm not even halfway there."

Joe raised an eyebrow. "You mean the Willis Tower, right?"

Amanda winced. "Oops. My bad. Old habits die hard."

Police sirens suddenly wailed in the distance. Amanda jumped off the couch and scurried to the living room window. She watched as two Oak Hills squad cars sped down the street, trailed by an EMT van with its lights flashing. The caravan appeared to turn onto Birch Court, two short streets south.

The street where Raymond lived.

Amanda headed to the front door and grabbed her jean jacket from the hall closet. "I'm going to check it out."

"Are you becoming an ambulance chaser now?" Joe gave her a wry glance.

"Call me whatever you want. But it could have a connection to David."

"Sounds like you're grasping at straws."

"I'm only going to see what's happening."

"Uh-huh. Sure."

Amanda gave him a dismissive wave and headed out the door.

Three minutes later, with twilight beginning to darken the sky, Amanda rounded the corner onto Birch Court.

Police cars and the EMT van blocked the street. She hustled toward the commotion of officers and paramedics standing in the home's driveway, which bordered an overgrown yard in desperate need of a lawnmower.

"What happened?" Amanda asked one officer.

"Ma'am, please stand back. We're still investigating." He waved Amanda away. A second officer approached the first. Amanda overheard them say *Raymond Cartel* before both officers got called away.

She felt a tap on her arm. "You're the Deli Lady, aren't you? I'm Raymond's neighbor."

The woman wore a winter parka, hood up, scarf wrapped around her neck. Her gloved hands held a leash attached to a yellow lab.

Amanda couldn't believe her luck. Dog walkers were often the first to know what was going on in the neighborhood. "That's right, I'm the Deli Lady. Did I overhear the police mention Raymond's name?"

"Yes, you did." The dog pulled at its leash, tail wagging. "Thor, sit," the woman commanded. Thor plopped down on the sidewalk with his tail stilled. His head rested on his paws and he had a doggy pout.

"How do you know Raymond?" the neighbor asked.

"Through a friend. I hope he's okay."

"Me, too. That's why I'm still here. Although Thor isn't happy."

Thor confirmed his displeasure with a loud woof. The woman gave his leash a gentle tug. "This is what I know so far," she said, and pointed to a two-story Victorian with a wraparound front porch. "I live in that corner house. Thor and I got as far as the house next door to Raymond's when I heard him yell at someone to get out of his backyard. He sounded mad. I couldn't see the person."

"Then what happened?"

"After a couple of seconds of silence, I heard Raymond call for help, this time sounding scared. Thor started barking, and I immediately called 911. The police and EMT van got here right away."

Amanda and the neighbor watched as two paramedics transported Raymond on a stretcher to the open doors of their EMT van. His eyes were shut, and his head was wrapped in white gauze. He didn't stir, but his chest rose and fell in a steady rhythm. A good sign, however small, Amanda thought.

"Will he be okay?" a man called out.

"He's being transported to Northwest Hospital," the EMT answered before turning his attention back to his patient.

"Hopefully it's not anything too serious," Amanda said to the neighbor.

The woman nodded. "Raymond's been an asset to our little block since he moved into this run-down house a little over a year ago. Fixed it up on the inside. This year he planned to tackle the outside, which right now makes the place appear to be abandoned property."

Amanda took a quick survey of the jungle-like lot and dilapidated garage. "There's a lot to be fixed."

"I agree. But he knows what he's doing. I've hired him for repairs at my house. Charges me a fair price. Likes his privacy, but I don't see that as a bad thing."

Two Oak Hills police officers pulled Raymond's neighbor aside and out of hearing distance from Amanda. She watched the woman give animated responses to their questions as other officers scoured the ground with flashlights and secured the yard and garage with yellow caution tape.

A short time later, the police left and the crowd dispersed. Raymond's neighbor told Amanda she'd learned nothing new from the police, then continued her walk with Thor wagging his tail once again.

Amanda was the last to leave as twilight turned to darkness.

Walking back down Birch Court, she felt a chill as she called Nicki's cell. Was it because the nighttime temperature had taxed her jean jacket? Or because her original suspicions about Raymond had been turned upside down? Now he also appeared to be a victim.

"Amanda, I'm surprised to hear from you." Nicki sounded concerned. "I got the text we closed on time. Don't tell me something happened at the Dark Roast afterwards?"

"No worries. The Dark Roast is fine. But something happened to Raymond Cartel."

Amanda told her friend what she knew. Nicki reacted as she'd expected.

"Who would do that to such a sweet man? I wish I could talk to him. But he has a hard time hearing me on my cell. I'll call the hospital tomorrow morning, after he's had a night of rest, and let you know what they say. I almost wish I were there."

"You shouldn't feel guilty enjoying your vacation, Nicki," Amanda said. "Speaking of your vacation, how's it going?"

"It's … ah … good."

Amanda frowned. "Really? Only good?"

A long sigh came through her phone. "Truth is, I fell asleep while catching rays by the pool. I woke up looking like a red tomato from head to foot. My skin feels like it's been seared on a barbeque grill."

"Oh, Nicki, that's terrible. But you know the drill. Slather on lots of aloe lotion, and by tomorrow you'll look and feel much better."

"You're right. So far, my treatment consists of downing ice-cold tropical drinks."

"That works, too. But no alcohol. It'll only make things worse."

"Really? Now that's bad news," Nicki moaned.

"I know. I hope you feel better soon. But before we hang up, I need to circle back to Raymond," Amanda said. "When he came into the shop on Saturday, I kinda felt … or maybe thought …"

"Spit it out, Amanda. Felt or thought what?"

"I heard some things said about him that made me uneasy."

"Well, he can be grumpy. And I know my staff isn't keen on him because his personal hygiene isn't always the best." Nicki was silent for a moment before adding, "But he's a wizard at fixing things at reasonable rates. And he's an all-around nice person."

"A woman I met on the scene told me he's a great neighbor. Perhaps I'm being silly."

"Amanda, is it his nickname that's bothering you?"

"You know about that?"

"Oh sure. Handsy Ray. Because what he fixes stays fixed. I've heard it twisted to a different meaning, and I think it's just nasty gossip. Personally, I haven't seen him do anything out of line or had any employees tell me otherwise. As an extra precaution before I hired him, I checked if he had any criminal history. And he doesn't. Now, if you hear or see something otherwise, let me know right away. Otherwise, once you get to know the man, I think you'll like him."

Amanda made a mental note to encourage Chloe to tell her if she heard anything concrete about the rumors. She decided to put off telling Nicki about Raymond's connection to her grandfather until she knew more.

"I have good news about Zak, though." Amanda gave her friend the highlights of the Fun Times preschoolers' visit. "He did a great job." She didn't mention he'd made her suspect list. Why rile up Nicki about another employee possibly getting arrested? Her bestie's vacation was already not going as well as she'd hoped.

"I heard the same about you from Sarah Morrison."

"Thanks," Amanda said, pleased the woman had followed through on contacting Nicki. "And I'm sending thanks back at you for getting Eddie Turner to return my call."

She gave Nicki a summary of her visit to the Happy Bean.

"Glad you two connected, Amanda. He's a person of his word," Nicki said.

By this time, Amanda had reached the corner of Birch and First. "Nicki, I'm almost home."

"Before we hang up, I want you to know I'll keep you in the loop on how Raymond is doing in the hospital. That way you can focus your full attention on the Dark Roast," Nicki said.

"That sounds like a good plan."

Amanda's thoughts were jumbled as she slid her phone into her jacket pocket. Chloe's troubling remarks about Raymond had been way off from what she'd heard tonight from his neighbor and—

WHAM!

Amanda's right shoulder met with a fierce push. She stumbled forward, tried to catch her balance, then fell to the sidewalk, striking her knee. She glanced up in time to glimpse a figure clothed head to foot in black running gear, baseball cap covering their head, sprint down First Street in the opposite direction from her house. She caught the glint of a shiny silver label on the back heel of her assailant's running shoes.

"Hey, watch where you're going!" Amanda yelled at the fleeing runner, now almost out of sight.

She braced her hand on the sidewalk and gingerly stood up. *What is with people these days? Zooming here and there, no consideration for others.* Amanda winced. She sounded like their cranky neighbor, Frank.

Steadying herself from the shock of getting hit from behind and pushed to the ground, she almost missed the piece of paper lying on the ground next to her foot.

Stedman is guilty. Give it up.

Shivers ran up and down her spine as she hobbled home with the paper clutched in her hand.

Maybe Joe was right.

Whoever killed Olivia Hager might come after her next.

CHAPTER 19

Amanda stood in front of the full-length mirror on the back of the bedroom closet door. She turned her head right, then left, then faced straight ahead. Whew! No visible trace from last night's attack.

She pressed down on her right knee and felt only a slight ache, even with the bruise she'd spotted in the shower. Thank goodness for her favorite sweatpants, the ones Brittany always groaned were hideous. They'd cushioned the blow.

As she slipped her Dark Roast polo off the hanger, a nagging feeling hit her. She'd lied to Joe when she limped through the front door. She'd said a wayward jogger had run into her, but she'd held back from showing him the note. After all, why upset him after a long day at work?

Pulling the polo over her head, she couldn't ignore the real reason. She hadn't wanted to hear "I told you so." Or worry him unnecessarily.

Amanda couldn't resist opening her bottom dresser drawer and grabbing the clear slider bag once again from under the folded pile of T-shirts. For the umpteenth time, she stared at the letter-sized sheet of paper inside, with stick-on letters spread across the middle. It could have been made by a first grader, except for the message.

Stedman is guilty.

The same sentence the *Gazette* had reported written on the letters left outside those Oak Hills businesses. Had to be from the same person.

But the *Gazette* hadn't mentioned the second sentence that stared up at Amanda, written just for her.

Give it up.

She gritted her teeth. Nice try, but not happening. This letter and the cowardly attack last night wouldn't stop her from trying to find Olivia's killer. She shoved the slider bag back under the T-shirts and slammed the drawer shut.

Phooey on that weasel's threat! She'd figure out who pushed her down and left the personal warning. After all, she was the Sleuth Lady.

On second thought ...

It wouldn't help David if the letter was stashed in her dresser drawer. It was evidence that belonged with the police. Otherwise, she could be accused of obstructing a criminal investigation.

Amanda reluctantly dragged the slider bag back out, then carefully stowed it in the side pocket of her backpack. She'd drop it off with Evans before heading to the Dark Roast. But knowing the officer would question the *Give it up* addition made her nervous.

A brief text from Nicki eased her worry about Raymond. He'd spent a quiet night in the hospital, with no visitors allowed. Nicki reiterated she'd keep checking on Raymond so Amanda could focus on the Dark Roast.

As she walked down the hallway deep in thought, Brittney popped out of her room dressed in jeans, a fashionable top, and ankle boots, as if headed to work. Amanda's eyebrows rose in surprise. Brittany's shift started at noon on Tuesdays. Normally, she'd still be in bed.

"What's got you up so early?" she asked her daughter.

Brittany yawned with her eyes half-open. "Patrick wants to meet for coffee at the Dark Roast before he starts work. I think he said 8:30. I can't remember."

"Brittany, it's 8:30 now."

"Really?" Brittany yawned once again. "I'm still sleepy. Maybe I'll text him and tell him I can't make it."

"At a minimum, let him know you're running late." Amanda tried to keep the edge out of her voice. Her daughter shrugged and disappeared back into her bedroom.

Headed to the first floor, Amanda couldn't ignore her disappointment at Brittany's nonchalant reaction. What had cooled her interest in Patrick after a great first date? Joe would tell her it was none of her business. Let their daughter figure out her own life, he'd say. She always argued back that everyone wanted the best for their children, no matter how old they were. It was one of the few topics they disagreed about.

Remembering Joe had mumbled something about taking the train, Amanda grabbed the key fob to the van and hurried outside. Backing down the driveway, she sent a silent thank you to Nicki for her 9:00 a.m. start after yesterday's thirteen-hour day. The extra hours of sleep had revived her.

Having the van today was another plus. She could quickly drop off her letter at the police station and not be late to work. During her lunch break, she'd drive to the hospital and check on Raymond. At the end of the work day, she'd squeeze in a trip to the Oak Hills Library to uncover what happened in 1944.

Today having wheels wasn't a luxury. It was a necessity.

The first yellow forsythias bloomed along First Street as she drove toward the police station. Spring had sprung. Her favorite season. For a few brief minutes, all thoughts of Brittany, the jogger who'd shoved her to the sidewalk, and Raymond still in the hospital evaporated. Her shoulders relaxed.

By good luck, Evans was available and escorted Amanda to

an interview room. The officer's "*I'm on duty*" demeanor slipped briefly when she learned about the jogger and their personal warning to Amanda. Evans cautioned her to be more careful. "Don't hesitate to call 911 if you feel you're in danger."

Evans's pointed questions forced Amanda to face the fact she was keeping her ears and eyes open to find a murderer. A murderer who could also kill her.

When Amanda pressed to learn if the police knew any more about the letters, Evans's lips tightened. "We have no new information." She promised she'd let Amanda know of any official updates.

Driving to the Dark Roast, Amanda felt a mixture of relief and disappointment. The evidence was rightly in police hands, but she'd have to wait to hear the outcome.

The atmosphere at the Dark Roast, along with an extra-large Panda Bear, soothed her ruffled feelings and charged her up for the start of her workday. Nicki had scheduled Zak and a seasoned part-timer to work this morning's opening. The shop was humming.

"What's today's tip?" she asked Zak as he donned his jacket. His short morning shift had ended with Amanda's arrival.

"Okay, here's one everybody likes," he said. "Starbucks was founded by two teachers and a writer. What better professions for people needing coffee?"

"So true," she said.

Zak told her he'd made contact with a potential lawyer for David, and it looked promising. Then he said he had a crazy day ahead, including a class project on torts, and rushed out of the shop.

She spotted Patrick at her favorite table by the window. He peered outside as if searching for something or someone, then checked his phone. He looked like a sad puppy crossed with a very disappointed suitor.

Had Brittany forgotten to text him she would be late? Or

couldn't make it? Amanda felt sorry for Patrick and unhappy with her daughter.

She headed to the empty table next to Patrick, where the chairs had been left askew. Forget Joe and his nagging to stay out of their children's lives. She'd straighten things out, along with the chairs.

Grabbing the closest one, she purposely scraped the legs against the floor.

Patrick looked up at the screeching. "Oh, hi, Mrs. Knightly. Can I help you with that?"

"Hello, Patrick. Thank you for the offer, but I've got it." What was Brittany thinking? The guy was so thoughtful.

He stood up. "I guess I'll get going."

Amanda nodded. "If you don't mind my asking, did Brittany get in touch with you this morning? She said something about meeting for coffee."

His hurt expression told her Brittany hadn't. "No. But I can't wait any longer. I have to get to work."

Amanda leaned a tad closer, like an undercover agent about to pass on a secret. "As her mother, I need to tell you she's not an early riser. She's definitely a night owl."

Patrick immediately lost his disappointed expression. "Thanks for letting me know. I'll remember that."

"Can I get you a to-go refill before you head out?"

"Thanks, that would be great." He smiled. He picked up his satchel and brushed off the bottom and sides, although it appeared spotless to Amanda. The guy was definitely fastidious. Could be a turnoff for Brittany.

A few minutes later, Amanda hummed the tune to "Happy" as she straightened the stack of cups and lids behind the counter. Patrick had left the Dark Roast a happy guy.

How could Joe say anything was wrong with that?

Then she frowned.

Was her daughter just stringing Patrick along? Being

thoughtless wasn't right, no matter the circumstances. She'd talk to Brittany about it tonight. She'd keep it to a friendly, spur-of-the-moment mother-daughter chat. No reason Joe needed to know, and that way she'd avoid his usual lecture.

When she checked the neighborhood section of the *Gazette,* a brief three-line entry about an injured older Oak Hills resident didn't include Raymond's name. The police chief said his officers were investigating what happened and understood residents' concern.

A second text from Nicki reported Raymond had continued to improve. But he still couldn't have visitors. That changed Amanda's lunch plans.

After working through the noon surge, Amanda grabbed the van's key fob, ready to head to the Oak Hills Library instead.

A phone call from Virginia Smith for an impromptu lunch of homemade vegetable soup changed her lunch plans one more time. She'd get a delicious meal, along with Virginia's in-person update on David. The library could wait until she closed up the Dark Roast.

"Smells wonderful," Amanda said, sitting down at Virginia's kitchen table. "This is a real treat."

"I couldn't think of a better person to share it with than you. Especially with everything you're doing for David."

Amanda felt warmed by both the hearty soup and Virginia's kind words.

"There's something you need to know," Virginia said. "It's about Bob's Finer Foods."

"Oh?" Amanda said, very curious.

In between spoonsful of soup, Virginia reported the chaotic scene during her usual Monday trip to Bob's deli counter. "I couldn't believe it. All the clerks were running around like chickens with their heads cut off."

Virginia sat back with a knowing smile. "You're sorely missed."

Amanda grinned. "Thanks for the heads-up." *Let's hope Bob Early misses me too,* she thought.

Virginia's smile vanished as she laid down her spoon. "I wanted to tell you about David's pretrial release hearing."

She reiterated what Amanda had read in yesterday's *Gazette:* David had been appointed a public defender, and the judge had ruled David would remain in jail.

"What else happened?" Amanda asked.

Virginia frowned. "His public defender was a disaster. I heard later the guy is overloaded with cases."

Amanda held up her hand. "You don't have to worry about him. David's friends already have enough donations for their GoFundMe to bring in a private defense lawyer. He should be in contact with David soon. What happened next?"

"I hightailed it back to the police station, hoping to see even a glimpse of David in the lobby. I knew he'd be upset."

"Did you get to see him?"

Virginia nodded. "As they brought him back into the station, a reporter asked Grady how the murder was committed. David yelled, 'I'm innocent!' at the same time Grady said 'No comment.' Then the public defender rushed in and shouted, 'Don't say a word!'"

Virginia let out a long sigh. "Everyone was so tense. It's getting hard to stay positive."

Amanda placed one hand gently over Virginia's. "I've been thinking maybe we need to do a little digging."

"Ohhh." Virginia's hands stilled.

"Can you be at the police station tomorrow morning, just before ten o'clock? And don't forget your cane."

"What are we going to do?"

"If our timing is right and all the pieces come together, we'll find out what the police really know," Amanda said.

Virginia smiled as the Sleuth Lady mapped out her plan.

CHAPTER 20

Returning to the Dark Roast after her impromptu lunch with Virginia, Amanda was relieved to get Nicki's call. Raymond could now have visitors. She was also thankful to hear Nicki's sunburn had turned from painful to tan.

"I know you already took a lunch break, so consider this a work assignment," Nicki said. Amanda heard splashing water and laughter echoing in the background. "Just make sure Raymond's on the mend and well cared for."

Amanda didn't protest. She truly wanted to see him in person and make sure he was on the mend. It'd be a bonus if she could ask questions about what happened in 1944.

On the drive to the hospital, Amanda couldn't push aside a twinge of guilt. She'd sent Raymond's name to the police as someone with motive and opportunity to murder Olivia. Evans had said the police checked out all tips. Had the police talked to him before he was assaulted or after?

Minutes later, Amanda stood in the doorway of Room 419. Raymond was in bed, propped up by two pillows. His face looked pale and his eyes were slits. A mounted TV screen on the opposite wall played a hospital drama.

"Hello, Raymond," Amanda said quietly from the door. She couldn't help feeling concerned by his appearance.

His head jerked toward the doorway. "What do you want?"

"I'm Nicki's friend, Amanda, remember? She asked me to come by to see how you're doing."

Raymond wiggled his shoulders and edged up on the pillows. "Well, if Nicki can't be here, I guess you'll have to do. No reason for you to stand in the hallway and shout at me." He waved her inside.

Walking into the room, she heard the TV doctor declare that an operation was necessary to save the patient's life. "It'll be a tough operation. But I'm sure I can do it," he boasted to a fellow physician.

"Wait a minute," Raymond said. "Now I remember you. We talked about that arrest in Nicki's coffee shop, didn't we?"

Amanda nodded. "You're right. It was last Saturday. I'm here now to find out how you're feeling and if you need anything."

"The food's okay, and everyone's been nice enough. I need nothing except to get back to work, that's for sure." Raymond touched the bandage on the left side of his head. It extended from his hairline to his ear. "My doctor wants me to stay one more day because I'm a little shaky walking. I'm getting discharged tomorrow morning."

"That's good. Is someone driving you home?"

"One of my neighbors offered. You know, it's important to have good neighbors. At one time that's what Oak Hills was all about. But then ... well, never mind. I'll get off my soapbox." Raymond pulled the blanket higher up on his chest.

Amanda pointed to the bandage. "I can see you took a nasty hit."

"Doc thinks they hit me with something hard. Probably a rock. Once I yelled for help, the coward skedaddled."

"Did you see their face?"

"Nope. That gutless creep wore a baseball cap, pulled down

so I couldn't see anything. Dressed all in black. I couldn't tell who they were."

Amanda felt a gut punch. The description sounded like whoever had pushed her down and left the threatening letter. She'd seen only their back, but they were dressed in black, head to foot. In the dark she couldn't even tell if they were male or female.

"Do you have any idea why this person was in your backyard?" She tried to keep her voice calm.

Raymond wagged his finger at her. "You sure ask a lot of questions, and you're not even a police officer."

"Guilty!" Amanda held up both hands and smiled. "You got me."

Raymond chuckled. "Well, at least you have a sense of humor. If you and Nicki are friends, that means you're a good person, too."

"As Nicki's friend, would it be okay if I asked a few more questions?" Amanda asked.

He gave her a wary glance. "Sure, but not too many more. The police grilled me three times today. I already told them I didn't know who it was or why they attacked me. That creep could have just asked me what they wanted. That would have been a lot easier."

Raymond frowned. "And then the police had the audacity to ask me what I knew about Olivia Hager's murder. Like I'm a suspect now." He let out a snort. "Where'd they get that idea?"

Amanda hoped her cheeks weren't too red. "Well, thank goodness you're going to be okay." She took a deep breath. So, the police had acted on her anonymous tip.

Time to steer the conversation in a different direction. "Raymond, did your attacker leave anything behind?"

He gave her a sharp look before asking, "How do you know about that?"

"Just a hunch."

"Well, you must be a mind reader. They left a piece of paper that said Stedman is guilty with those goofy stick-on letters. I found it jammed into the handle of the back screen door last night and stuck it in my pants pocket right before I got hit on the head."

Amanda frowned. "Where is it now?"

"The police have it. A nurse had found it at the bottom of that closet over there just before they showed up. Must have fallen out of my pocket when someone hung up my pants last night, I'm thinking. The police took it with them. And I hope that's the last I see of them today."

Raymond yanked the covers under his chin, which Amanda took as a signal he was done talking about it. At least the police had more evidence, probably from her same attacker.

Amanda was hoping to ask about 1944 and the connection to her family's history when his eyelids got heavy. It was time to leave. "You need to rest so you'll be well enough to come home soon. I know Nicki wishes the same. And I'll check in on you again."

She was heading toward the door when Raymond called out, "Wait. There's one other thing you might want to know."

She hurried back to his bedside. "What's that?" she asked, trying not to sound anxious.

He shook his head and waved his hand at her. "Oh, never mind. Just an old man's imagination. Not worth saying." He pointed to the TV remote at the bottom of his bed. "But you could help me by shutting off that darn television. It's driving me crazy."

Disheartened he'd changed his mind about saying more, she hit the Off button just as the TV patient opened his eyes and smiled at the doctor. The operation was a success!

Laying the remote on his tray, she saw Raymond was already asleep, his breathing even.

She tugged at the zipper on her coat. Darn it! What else had he wanted to tell her? What else should she have asked?

As Amanda drove out of the parking lot, she wanted to believe Raymond hadn't murdered Olivia. If he was telling the truth about the piece of paper and hadn't written it himself, he was not a likely suspect. Unless he was targeting David to throw suspicion off himself. Arrgh! She needed to be sure, like the TV doctor who had been sure he could save the patient's life. At least that story had turned out well.

After driving home, Amanda left the van in their driveway and took a welcome walk to the Dark Roast. She needed the exercise to clear her head after all that had happened so far today.

———

Several hours later, Amanda locked up the Dark Roast and started her three-block walk back home. The pounding of shoes hitting the pavement behind her came out of nowhere. She couldn't step aside fast enough before the person collided with her shoulder. Hard.

Twice in twenty-four hours.

"Hey. Watch where you're going!" Gina Rohmer glared at Amanda as she took a step back. Dressed in all black, with her hair tucked into a black baseball cap overlaid with a hoodie, she panted like a black leopard on the hunt for prey. Except she wore neon green running shoes.

"Really? I think you ran into me." Amanda didn't hold back the sarcasm in her voice.

"You don't have to be so snippy," Gina said. "When I have my ear buds in, I zone out everything around me." She jammed her hands on her hips. "You need to share the sidewalk with other people, you know."

"Luckily, I think I'm all right." Amanda rubbed her shoulder.

No surprise Gina hadn't offered an apology or asked if she was okay.

"Well, you'd better watch out, or you might get hurt." Gina took off, the volume on her ear buds loud enough for Amanda to hear the music.

She noticed the shiny silver label on the back of the young woman's running shoes.

It took Amanda another block to cool down. The image of Gina in the same outfit worn by the runner who had pushed her down and left the warning letter had stayed with her. Except right now Gina wore neon green runners.

Did she also own a black pair? Had literally running into Amanda truly been a coincidence? Or did Gina want to reinforce the message that Amanda should back off?

Amanda frowned. Maybe the police had acted on her anonymous tip about Gina's longtime hatred of Olivia, and she suspected Amanda was the source?

Well, that wasn't going to stop her.

CHAPTER 21

Amanda shook off her encounter with Gina and hustled home, more than ready for a delicious dinner. Joe had texted her he'd take on tonight's meal and promised it would be extra-special.

When she walked through the back door, Joe was holding a menu from Manny's Pizzeria in one hand and his cell phone in the other. "I'd like the 18-inch extra-special," he said into the phone.

Not sure whether to laugh or cry, Amanda discreetly rolled her eyes and headed for the stairway. "Brittany, your favorite Manny's pizza will be delivered in 30 minutes," she called up to her daughter.

"Sorry, Mom. I should have texted you," Brittany's cheerful voice echoed down. "Patrick's taking me to dinner."

Amanda held back from doing a happy dance. It was a good thing she'd talked to him this morning.

With a spring in her step, she headed back to the kitchen, where she saw a dozen red roses in a glass vase on the dining room table. For a moment, she hoped they were for her. Then she noticed the fancy Blooming Blossoms Flowers logo on the miniature white envelope leaning against the vase. No chance her loving but frugal husband would have sent the bouquet from the pricey Oak Hills florist shop.

Amanda paused, not seeing a name written on the envelope. *Hmm.* Just maybe she was wrong, and this was a special apology for the credit-card mishap.

She slipped the miniature card out of the envelope. It took a moment to decipher the shaky handwriting.

Brittany - Looking forward to tonight - Patrick.

Amanda broke into a grin. He must have been nervous when he wrote it. How sweet.

"Mom, can I borrow that fun necklace you bought last month? The red and gold one?" Brittany called down from the top of the stairway.

Amanda slipped the card back into the envelope, carefully setting it back in its original place. "Sure. And thanks for remembering to ask me first."

"You're welcome, Mom."

Amanda felt triumphant. Her daughter had asked first. A small but important win. It had always been one little step at a time with Brittany, ever since she was a baby.

She was also relieved Patrick hadn't let Brittany's thoughtlessness this morning deter him. But how did Brittany feel about Patrick?

Amanda's mother had been very suspicious of Joe. "No job, no decent clothes, and no future" was her mother's assessment the first time she brought him home. But Amanda had known he was the one for her and it would all work out. And it did.

She was picturing Brittany and Patrick walking down the aisle when her brain flashed a red stop sign. It was a little premature to make that appointment at the bridal salon just yet.

As if on cue, the doorbell rang. Once again, Patrick helped Brittany with her coat. She kissed his cheek and thanked him for the flowers. He practically glowed.

"You two have a nice evening. I'll shut the door behind you." Seeing them walk arm in arm down the front steps, Amanda smiled. The romance was back on.

She happily walked back to the kitchen and met Matt and Chloe coming in through the back door. "Hey, Mom, I saw Patrick's Porsche at the curb as we pulled in. Is he still here? I have to ask him something about David's GoFundMe campaign."

"He and Brittany just left. He's taking her out to dinner."

"Again?" Matt groaned.

"Now be nice. I think it's great Patrick wants to take your sister out to nice places."

"Just saying, not all of us make the big bucks like Patrick. But he's doing a super job with the GoFundMe accounting. We'd be hurting without him." Matt frowned. "I was a little surprised the guy volunteered. I didn't know that he was a friend of David's. Or that he's got this really weird sense of humor."

He put his arm around Chloe and smiled. "But on to a different topic. I've asked Chloe to join us for dinner."

Chloe wore a white sweater with a big pink heart across the front. She gave Amanda a little hello wave. "I hope that's okay."

"We'd love to have you."

Amanda felt a tug at her heart as Matt put his arm around Chloe and gave her shoulder a caring squeeze. The gawky, shy kid was gone.

But she couldn't help but notice that something seemed off. Chloe had shrugged off his arm. And did she also seem a little cool toward him?

Amanda pulled out placemats and plates, trying hard not to dwell on what she had just witnessed. It never failed. When one of her kids was on the upswing, the other would be headed for a crash.

Soon the four of them sat at the kitchen table, chowing down on Manny's extra-special pizza. Everything seemed right between Matt and Chloe, and Amanda relaxed. Probably nothing more than her imagination, she decided.

Matt caught his mom's attention. "I talked to David today. I told Chloe all about it when I picked her up. But I'm sure she won't mind hearing it again."

Chloe nodded yes, caught mid-bite.

"I'm all ears." Amanda felt pleased her son wanted to share his news with her.

"When I told David we set up the GoFundMe campaign, he said it felt great to know his friends were behind him. Then he said he first heard about our campaign from his great-aunt. And then again when you visited him in jail. He mentioned you also asked questions about other people who might be considered suspects."

Matt frowned. "I can't believe you didn't tell me you talked to David."

Amanda saw Joe's surprised expression and raised her hands as if it were no big deal. "I told you that I'm keeping my ears and eyes open and sending in tips to the Citizen Watch program when I find anything out. So, yes, I talked to David about it. And you're helping him financially, which is very important."

"As long as we're both helping him in different ways, I guess it's all right," Matt said. He didn't appear convinced.

Amanda realized Matt wasn't as grown-up as she had thought. Right now, especially in front of Chloe, wasn't the time to call him out.

"Amanda, I want to bring up something else," Joe said. "Ever since you started at the Dark Roast, I'm getting cheated out of my morning cup of coffee." He pouted like a six-year-old who'd been told all their Halloween candy was all gone.

Amanda gave him a raised eyebrow back. "I told you I'd get free coffee at the Dark Roast this week, remember? Besides, you can make a pot for yourself. It's easy."

"But I like the way you make it."

"Sorry, but you'll have to make your own cup of joe, Joe," she replied with a snicker.

He chuckled. "Nice comeback. So I'll have to make my own java. Or should I call it mud? Or brew?"

Chloe piped in with other coffee nicknames. Bean Juice, Jitter Juice, Wakey Juice, Morning Jolt, Liquid Energy, and Caffeine Infusion.

Matt added Cupped Lightning, Rocket Fuel, Worm Dirt, High Octane, and Brain Juice.

"I heard a new one this morning," Amanda said. "C8H10N402."

Three perplexed faces stared at her.

"I give up," Joe said. "What's that?"

"It's the name of the caffeine molecule. A customer wanted to know if we could add it to our menu board. I was clueless and he loved it. He confessed he's a chemist and likes to stump baristas. I told him he'd succeeded with me."

"That would have stumped me, too," Chloe said.

Amanda pushed back her plate. "That's enough talking shop. Who wants to help me clean up?"

Matt and Joe collected the plates and deep-sixed the pizza box before they headed out the back door to check out the funny sound Matt's car had been making on the way home.

"I want to tell you, I think it's great you're trying to help David," Chloe said, tossing out the paper napkins.

Amanda nodded. "Thanks, I appreciate the encouragement."

"If you ask my opinion, the police should talk to Gina again," Chloe said. "She's been living with her sister, who owns a condo in our building. She always has a sob story about being kicked out of her latest apartment, so she stays there a lot. It's on the third floor, 309. Right down the hall from Olivia."

Chloe emphasized "sob story" as if it were a melodrama.

Amanda didn't interrupt. Who knew what new details her son's girlfriend might add to what she already knew?

"The association is super strict about occupancy," Chloe continued. "Gina's sister has a studio, which is limited to one person. You can have one guest for a maximum of two weeks. Gina always stays much longer. She keeps under the radar by avoiding the elevator and using the stairwell, usually carrying a stuffed shopping bag instead of a suitcase. Her sister gave her a key to the back entrance, too. They share a front-door key card—which again, they're not supposed to do."

Amanda perked up. "How do you know all of this?"

Chloe slid a glass into the dishwasher's top rack. "I've seen Gina on the stairwell when the elevator is out of order. A lot. Two weeks ago, as she was lugging up boxes, I asked if she was staying with her sister again, and she barked back it was none of my business. Typical Gina."

She shrugged. "But if you add Gina's continued hate of Olivia to her open access to the building, I'm thinking she could be the murderer. And she should be the one in jail, not David."

Amanda studied Chloe. Had she heard a softening in the girl's voice, almost a tenderness, when she'd said David's name? David's friends had come to his defense. Had that loyalty rubbed off on Matt's girlfriend?

"How do you enjoy living at Valley Lane Condos?" Amanda took her time loading a plate in the dishwasher to keep Chloe talking.

"It's great. Close to my job and an easy commute to school. I live on the top floor, in 504. My parents bought the unit for my grandmother. When she passed away, they let me move in rent-free while I finish my degree." She smiled. "That's why I'm able to live there on my own and only work part-time at the Dark Roast."

"Did you hear or see anything the day of Olivia's murder?"

"No. I worked that morning and had classes until early evening."

"And if I remember right, you were interviewed by the police that night, right?

"Yes. They canvassed the condo units. The police cleared everyone, as far as I know."

"Did you tell the police about Gina having free access to the building?"

"No, I didn't. Do you think it's something I should mention to them?"

"The more information the police have on other possible suspects, the better. Check out the Citizen Watch site online if you don't want to speak to them in person."

Matt and Joe soon returned with the car fixed, and the young couple headed out.

As she wiped down the kitchen table, Amanda rehashed Chloe's revelation. It meant that anyone living in Olivia's building could use the back door and not be seen in the lobby. Including Chloe. Amanda stopped. Chloe didn't have a reason to kill Olivia.

Amanda chastised herself for forgetting to ask Chloe if she'd ever hung out at the Happy Bean—in particular the day David and Olivia had their tussle. She'd ask Chloe during tomorrow's shift.

She still needed to contact Olivia's neighbors. But once again it was too late. She'd definitely call tomorrow, just before mealtime, when the odds of them being home would be greater.

Kitchen table now spotless, she decided it'd be a good time to ask about their two credit card issues. She casually walked into the living room and asked Joe for an update as gently as she could.

He threw up his hands. "Amanda, I know you're frustrated. I'm just as frustrated. But I promise you, I'm working on it. I'll give you an update as soon as I can. You know how those credit-card companies operate."

"Okay, but are you sure you don't want me to talk to them? Maybe I—"

"No!" Joe said firmly. Then he was off to the garage and Baby.

She wanted to think he wasn't avoiding the topic. And dealing with customer service could be challenging. She'd give him the benefit of the doubt. For now.

CHAPTER 22

The next morning at exactly 9:40 a.m., Amanda told Zak she was taking a short break to test out a new marketing idea. Heading out of the Dark Roast on her mission, she focused on not dropping the tray of two steaming hot coffees she carried along the four-block walk to the Oak Hills police station. She mentally crossed her fingers that her timing would be right.

Virginia Smith stood just outside the station's front entrance. Amanda nodded at her and Virginia turned away, as if waiting for another friend.

Amanda tried not to be nervous as she walked into the police station lobby. Officer Lee wore a neutral expression as she approached the front desk.

"Yes?" he asked. Amanda ignored the wary tone in his voice.

"Good morning, Officer Lee. I'm wondering if you'd taste-test our newest brew. It's a combination of espresso with a touch of cayenne pepper. It's called 'Kick Up Your Day' because that's how it'll make you feel."

"Amanda Knightly, you and Stedman's great-aunt caused me a lot of trouble last Friday." He crossed his arms. "What's the catch with this supposedly free coffee?"

"There's no catch. The Dark Roast wants villagers to taste our exciting brews, with free delivery thrown in."

The officer raised a suspicious eyebrow ever so slightly. "What do I have to do?"

"It's easy. Sample this delicious cup of coffee. Then stop by the Dark Roast and give us your feedback. If you bring in your empty cup, you'll get a free refill."

"Sounds reasonable. But you have two cups."

"The other one is for the chief."

The officer shook his head. "I'm sorry, but Chief Grady isn't available right now. And he has a 10:00 a.m. appointment."

Amanda wanted to shout YIPPEE! "My bad luck," she said instead.

According to the *Gazette*, Chief Grady and the village department heads were right now at the mayor's monthly meeting. The mayor had told a reporter the packed agenda might make the one-hour monthly meeting run late.

Just what Amanda hoped.

"Here's your cup." She placed it on the desk. "I can leave the chief's—"

As if on cue, the front door of the station opened and little voices filled the lobby. Amanda was delighted. The chief's 10:00 a.m. appointment had arrived.

Sarah Morrison led the same swarm of children who had invaded the Dark Roast two days ago, followed by her now-mint-green-haired assistant. The children's chatter echoed off the walls, accompanied by their teacher's ever-patient voice.

"Children, remember what I told you before we left school? Inside voices only!" She raised her index finger to her lips. "Shhh!"

A collective movement of children's index fingers met their lips. "Shhh!"

Sarah chuckled. "You're all so good. Let's greet the police officer like we practiced."

Giggles, wiggles, and googly eyes gazed at Officer Lee, followed by "Good morning, Officer." Amanda watched Lee break into a grin.

"Good morning, children." The beaming officer turned to Sarah. "I'm afraid the chief is running late."

"I hope he can still meet with us. The children would be so disappointed if—"

Amanda couldn't hear what Sarah Morrison said next. The lobby reverberated with the sounds of small running feet and shouts that drowned out their teacher's voice. Sarah waved to Amanda and mouthed something, but whatever she said got lost in the pandemonium.

Officer Lee had lost his smile.

"Hold on a minute. Let me see if I can find out when he'll be back," Lee yelled over the bedlam. He grabbed the phone.

Amanda stood to the side, quietly cheering the déjà vu. Although the two teachers attempted to corral their students, today they couldn't offer hot cocoa as a bribe.

She recognized the little boy who had run behind the front counter at the Dark Roast and taken off with the computer mouse. She silently sent him vibes to repeat the same move. He didn't disappoint her.

He screamed an attack command, charged the station's front desk, grabbed the mouse, and took off. Lee yelled for him to come back. When that failed, the officer chased after him, leaving the front desk temporarily empty.

A little girl hopped into his chair and pressed every button available on the console, phones, and computer.

Amanda crossed her fingers.

Suddenly the twin security doors on either side of the front desk swung open. Seconds later Virginia Smith hobbled in through the front door of the station, leaning heavily on her cane.

"Help me! I twisted my knee," she called out. She teetered forward before collapsing in a heap on the floor.

Officer Lee stopped chasing the children and ran back across the lobby to Virginia's side, followed by the two teachers.

Amanda clutched the tray with the remaining cup of coffee and hurried through the open security door as it snapped closed behind her. Officer Lee, his back to her, seemed oblivious to her stealth move.

Alone in the back corridor, Amanda headed straight to the Chief's office. The door was open and the office empty.

Nirvana.

She hustled in and slowly lifted the cup out of the carryall container as she scanned the folders on his desk.

The label on the top folder, handwritten in thick black permanent marker, jumped out at her: HAGER CASE. Amanda did a brief mini dance, giddy at her luck, and almost dropped the coffee cup. Cautioning herself to stay on task, she carefully lowered the cup onto the one tiny open spot on the Chief's desk, careful not to spill a drop.

Amanda picked up the top folder, flipped open the cover, and skimmed the top sheet.

CASE SUMMARY had seven dated entries with a checkmark next to each.

Confirmed: Wednesday, March 30, David Stedman left the Happy Bean at 5:00 p.m. to deliver debit card to victim's home per manager's interview the next morning. In same interview, manager made statement of an attack two weeks prior by Stedman on victim, although no report filed.

Confirmed: Wednesday, March 30, 5:30-5:45 p.m. Witness heard heated shouts coming from inside victim's condo. ID'd David Stedman leaving victim's condo wearing Happy Bean blue polo minutes later.

Confirmed: Wednesday, March 30, 9:45 p.m. Witness contacted 911 and requested a wellness check of victim's unit.

Confirmed: Wednesday, March 30, 10:15 p.m. Victim's body

found in condo along with debit card belonging to victim on kitchen counter.

Confirmed: Thursday, March 31, 8:00 a.m. Victim's cause of death was stab wound to neck, per coroner's report. Time of death estimated between 5:00 p.m. and 7:00 p.m. on Wednesday, March 30.

Confirmed: Thursday, March 31, 10:25 a.m. David Stedman arrested without incident at Dark Roast.

Confirmed: Monday, April 4, 8:00 a.m. Forensics matched patent index fingerprint found on kitchen counter to David Stedman. Added to evidence collected.

Amanda's heart sank. A patent print probably meant blood. Regardless how David claimed his finger had been cut, it would be damaging evidence.

Reading on, she halted at "*Pending.*"

Locate 9-inch-blade chef's knife that killed victim, per coroner's report. Note: Knife block on victim's kitchen counter had one empty slot. Assume it held murder weapon.

She gasped. A chef's knife was the murder weapon. And a missing piece of missing evidence!

At the sound of footsteps, Amanda's adrenaline shot sky-high. She quickly closed the folder.

The footsteps grew louder. She gingerly returned the folder to the top of the pile.

The footsteps were feet away from the open door. Amanda picked up the coffee cup and assumed a pose, as if ready to put it down on the desk for the first time.

"What are you doing in here?" The chief stood in the office threshold, scowling.

Amanda flashed her best customer service smile.

"Chief Grady, I'm so glad to see you. I was afraid your 'Kick Up Your Day' coffee sample would get cold. But no worries now." Amanda stretched her smile. "It's our newest blend, and today we're marketing it to a few select people. As

Oak Hills' well-known police chief, we'd especially like your feedback."

Amanda watched his scowl deepen.

"How did you get in here?" he asked, his voice cold.

"The children in the lobby overwhelmed Officer Lee. They are so cute but so hard to handle at that age, aren't they? Enough to rattle anyone." She gave a little shrug and upped the wattage on her smile.

He didn't move. "You didn't answer my question. How did you get in here?"

"Well, somehow the security door opened. To help Officer Lee, I thought I'd deliver the coffee to your office. Like I said, I didn't want it getting cold. I was just putting it down on your desk."

At that moment, Evans's head popped around the doorway. "Chief, the Fun Times preschoolers are here and—oh." She took a step back.

Grady's scowl deepened more. "Amanda Knightly, this is the second time you've come through the security door unescorted. Don't you have any regard for procedure and rules? Or are you trying to test how to get through our security system for some unknown reason?"

Amanda vigorously shook her head. "No. Not at all. I was only trying to boost the Dark Roast's business. Honestly, I think you'll like this blend. I'll just leave it here and—"

"Not so fast." The chief raised his hand as if halting traffic on First Street. "You're trespassing in my office." His eyes were as icy as a January snowstorm.

Amanda's stomach twisted into knots. Getting caught hadn't been part of the plan.

Pretend he's an unhappy customer who needs soothing. A REALLY unhappy customer. "I'm so sorry. I hope you understand, I didn't mean to impose—"

"Stop right there." The chief's continued glare alarmed

Amanda. "In the state of Illinois, trespassing is a misdemeanor, with 30 days to six months in jail and a maximum fine of five hundred dollars. Officer Evans, please transport Amanda Knightly to a jail cell while we start the paperwork."

Neither woman spoke as Evans steered Amanda through the empty back hallways. The officer was in full professional mode. Amanda alternated between trying not to cry and holding her head up, proud that she'd taken a chance for justice.

After passing through three security doors, they entered a room with three jail cells lined up in a row. David looked up from his cot in the first cell, his face drawn and pale. "What the …"

"David, this is all a misunder—"

"No talking," Evans ordered.

Amanda turned away, knowing her cheeks burned red. She was supposed to get David *out* of jail, not become his jail mate.

Evans locked Amanda in the cell next to David's. When she shut the security door on her way out, silence echoed down the row of cells.

Amanda collapsed on the cot, thankful for the solid wall between the cells so she couldn't see David's face. No talking to him either, per Evans order.

The knot in her stomach tightened. Joe had told her not to end up in a jail cell next to David. And here she was.

A long ten minutes later, Officer Evans reappeared. "I'm escorting you out of the police station. The chief requested you not return unless invited to do so." Her sharp tone sobered Amanda's relief at getting released.

She glanced at David as she passed by his cell. He was in his own world, rocking back and forth with his arms wrapped around his body. His lawyer would know what she'd read in the folder. Which meant David knew.

She wanted to shout, "Hang on, David! Don't get discouraged!" But she didn't want to alienate Evans any more than she feared she already had.

————

"Amanda, what were you thinking?" Officer Evans tapped her foot as they stood outside the police station, out of the earshot of passersby. Virginia Smith sat on a nearby bench, swinging her legs back and forth, fully recovered from her supposedly injured knee.

"I wanted the Chief to sample our new coffee flavor, and I took a shortcut." She couldn't confess her real reason for being in the chief's office to Evans or anyone else.

Evans gave Amanda a wary gaze. "Not sure if I totally buy that excuse. You're lucky the chief didn't actually file charges. I guess he only wanted to scare you."

"He succeeded. When I'm allowed back in the station, I'll never walk through those security doors without a police escort again."

"Good. Because I'd hate to see you get in serious trouble, especially with Grady. I know Nicki would feel the same."

Amanda winced. "I need to tell her about my new marketing program."

"What will you tell her?"

"That I went overboard with a personal delivery to Grady's office, but all is well." Amanda frowned. "Do you think the chief will call Nicki and complain about what I did?"

"Not if you stay out of his way. But if there's a next time, I'm sure he will." Evans glanced over at David's great-aunt, sitting six feet away, still swinging her legs as if she didn't have a care. "Virginia over there made a remarkable recovery. She refused paramedic help after she fell. Said she was fine."

The officer smirked. "I'm sure you had nothing to do with her stumbling into the station, claiming she hurt her knee, then collapsing on the floor at the same time the security doors opened. Do I have that right, Amanda?"

Amanda hoped her face broadcast a clueless expression. "Absolutely. And thanks for your help, Officer Evans."

"You're welcome. See you at the Dark Roast, Amanda." She hesitated before adding, "And stay away from the station for a while."

"Got it."

Amanda watched the officer walk back into the station, with one question foremost on her mind.

Where had the murderer hidden the chef's knife?

Amanda's heartbeat settled down as she ushered David's great-aunt to her car.

Virginia couldn't quit crowing about the way they'd pulled off their plan. "We really got Grady's goat this time." She snickered and leaned toward Amanda. "What did you find out?"

"That we're on the right path," Amanda whispered, raising her finger to her lips. Before closing the car door, she reminded Virginia to tell no one about the secret recon they'd just pulled off. Virginia winked at her before driving away.

As she walked back to the Dark Roast, Amanda was glad she hadn't told Virginia the missing murder weapon was a chef's knife. If someone leaked that key information, it needed to be the police.

And she wasn't going to leak anything about her brief incarceration, either. Evans had escorted her through the vacant back hallways of the police station on their way out. Hopefully that meant no one had noticed. *Thank you, Evans,* she said silently.

She was glad she also hadn't mentioned to Virginia that she'd seen David in his cell. He had seemed so very down that she couldn't help worrying.

Who wouldn't be, after having been falsely arrested and jailed?

Amanda tugged her ponytail tighter and quickened her steps. She needed to work even harder now to find Olivia's killer. And when she did, she and David would toast each other with extra-large Panda Bears at the Dark Roast. Then she was sure he'd celebrate with Matt and his other friends over something a lot stronger.

Amanda felt a chill, and it wasn't from the outside temperature. Her bestie would not be happy she'd used the Dark Roast name without her okay. Could she really trust Grady not to call her best friend and complain about how she'd walked unescorted through the security doors and ended up in his office bearing coffee? Remembering his angry expression, she pulled out her phone and tapped Nicki's name.

"Hi! You've reached Nicki Lenzini, owner of the Dark Roast, Oak Hills' number one coffee shop. Sorry I missed your call. Leave a message and I'll call you back. Be sure to stop by for a great brew!"

Amanda left a voicemail asking Nicki to call her back. She crossed her fingers her bestie would get her message before Grady's, if he decided to call her. Checking the time, she quickened her pace back to the Dark Roast. Getting jailed had blown her timetable.

Zak's flushed face and the line of waiting customers sent her scurrying behind the counter and back into manager mode. Late morning and lunch hours continued to be busy.

During a brief slow spot, Zak asked how her marketing idea had worked with her friend. Luckily, he didn't ask which friend. She downplayed it, saying it would probably be best to wait for Nicki's return. And apologized for taking a longer break than she'd planned to.

She gave Zak a side glance as he waited on the last customer in a long line. Today his laid-back demeanor seemed like the Zak she knew. Something good must have happened to him. Had he passed that constitutional law test? Met someone he liked who liked him back? Or was he happy because he thought he might get away with Olivia's murder?

Amanda immediately threw up an imaginary stop sign. Until she found substantial evidence, her suspicions wouldn't prove anything.

She decided it would be a good time to ask Zak about the next coffee tip on his list. He thought for a moment, then said, "I'm going to turn the tables on you for this one. I want you to guess what country drinks the most coffee."

Amanda threw out multiple guesses: USA, Italy, Spain, Colombia, Brazil. Zak said no to each one with a smug smile.

A regular at a nearby table who had overheard their conversation started throwing out guesses: Argentina, Chile, Russia, Honduras, Venezuela. Zak said no to each.

"You each get one more guess," he said. "And no peeking at your phones!"

The customer thought for a moment and guessed Germany. Zak shook his head.

Amanda crossed her arms. "It has to be France."

"Wrong again."

Amanda and the customer both groaned. "Okay, what's the answer?" she asked.

"Finland. Almost 28 lbs. per person, in fact. Norway comes in second, followed by Iceland and then Denmark. It gets cold in Scandinavia, so no surprise, they like hot beverages."

Amanda thanked Zak for making a game of it, and the customer said the same. Watching Zak pass by Chloe when she arrived for her one o'clock shift, Amanda hoped she'd never find evidence that he'd murdered Olivia.

The Dark Roast cleared out as Chloe settled in for her shift. A quiet afternoon lull hung over the empty shop with no customers and just the two of them.

Seeing Chloe's pink headband reminded Amanda to ask her about the Happy Bean, but the front door flew open first.

Gina Rohmer strutted in wearing a blue jean miniskirt, high boots, low-cut sweater, and a signature Gucci purse slung over her shoulder. The gold-etched heart locket was missing from her neck. She halted at the front counter. Her eyes blazed fire at Chloe.

"I knew I'd find you here, you little—" She slapped her hand across her mouth, pretending to be shocked. "Oooh, I won't say that nasty word in public. Especially to Miss Pink Princess."

Chloe planted her hands on her hips. "What can I get you, Gina?" she asked with a twinge of sarcasm.

"I don't want any of your stinking coffee. I want you to come clean," Gina spat out.

"About what?"

Gina rolled her eyes. "Okay, I've heard all the talk about David Stedman proclaiming his innocence. But now the police are asking *me* questions. They made me late for work. Somebody gave them my name on that stupid tip line and I'm not guilty of anything."

Amanda silently cheered the police acting on her tip, although she felt a bit guilty Chloe was taking the heat. Luckily, it was still just the three of them in the shop.

The two young women were in a staring contest, like sworn enemies facing each other on a battlefield.

"I don't know what you're talking about," Chloe said, standing her ground.

Gina leaned in closer. "Yeah? I know who gave them my name. Someone who's eager to get their boyfriend cleared. The boyfriend no one was supposed to know about. The one she kept tabs on at the Happy Bean because Olivia was always after him. Am I right, Chloe?"

Chloe didn't move.

Amanda's mouth dropped open. So, Chloe *was* the young

woman in pink at the Happy Bean. And David had been her secret boyfriend. But what about Matt? Had Chloe shrugged off his arm last night because her feelings for David had rekindled? Or had they never gone away?

A sudden coldness shot through Amanda.

Chloe lived two floors away from Olivia. She could have easily knocked on Olivia's door and demanded that Olivia leave David alone. It could have escalated until Chloe grabbed the chef's knife and stabbed Olivia in anger. She could have quickly returned unseen to her condo by using the stairs, then lied to the police about being at school, hoping they wouldn't confirm it. Matt had said he couldn't get in touch with Chloe the night of the murder.

The coldness turned into shivers. Chloe had motive, opportunity, and possibly access to the knife that had killed Olivia Hager.

"It's *your* problem if the police are after you, Gina, not mine. So, unless you want to place an order, I suggest you leave." Chloe's even tone matched her level stare.

"No, it's your problem, Pinky. Because I'm going to tell the police they should be asking you the questions, not me. Brace yourself, Miss Priss. The cops will be coming for you soon." Gina turned toward the front door, then swung back around.

"Don't forget to tell your current lover boy you're just using him until you hope they find David innocent. Well, they might find David innocent, but I bet *you* aren't. Oh, and don't bother coming to Le Grand Café. I don't care if you're with Matt or David or anyone else. I'll make sure your evening is miserable." She lit up. "I love revenge."

Amanda was too stunned to say anything.

Chloe didn't move, except for a slowly arching brow. "Is it my turn to talk now, Gina? It's always impossible to know when you've gotten to the end of one of your famous rants."

Gina just sneered.

Chloe threw her head back and laughed. "David had no interest in you, no matter how many times you flung yourself at him. That really bothered you, didn't it? And even now you go on and on about Olivia stealing your boyfriend and prom date five years after we graduated. Plus, everyone knows you've been freeloading in your sister's condo, conveniently down the hall from Olivia's place."

Her mouth curled into a Cheshire cat grin. "So, Gina, you could have easily murdered Olivia."

Amanda blinked, but the action didn't wipe away the theatrics she was witnessing. No surprise Gina acted like a drama queen. But Chloe's response had shown a side that shocked her. It was hard to believe this same person had chatted, laughed, and chowed down on pizza last night at their kitchen table.

Gina's face turned red as she squared her shoulders. "You think you're so smart, you double-dealing sneak. Well, you haven't heard the last from me. Or from the police." She spun on her heels and stomped out of the coffee shop.

Somehow Amanda found the strength to look at Chloe. She took a deep breath. "Chloe, I want the truth. Did you kill Olivia?"

"Of course not."

"Have the police contacted you since you first talked to them?"

"No. That's Gina talking trash, as usual."

"I only ask that you be honest with Matt, David, the police, and especially yourself."

Chloe's eyes glistened. Her voice was soft. "Gina likes to say a lot of crazy things. Yes, David and I got back together several weeks ago, but we kept it to ourselves. And yeah, I kept going out with Matt at the same time. But neither of them knew I was dating the other. I'm not proud of what I did. It's just something that happened."

To Amanda's relief, a customer walked in. Seeing Chloe brighten up as she asked for the person's order, Amanda knew the young woman was just as eager as she was to get back to work. She also knew she'd never totally trust Chloe again.

Thankfully, Chloe wasn't scheduled to work the next two days, so there wasn't a chance for a repeat confrontation with Gina in the Dark Roast. After all that she'd just heard, Amanda needed a break from Chloe. She suspected Chloe felt the same way about her.

Amanda headed to the storeroom with the excuse of confirming the cup supply. Going through the motions of checking the boxes, she tried to sort out the scene she'd just witnessed.

There was no good news. Chloe's revelation of Gina's one-sided pursuit of David added a second woman who had been after him. Plus, he was secretly dating his best friend's girlfriend. All entanglements that could muddle things.

Even worse news: Gina's accusations gave Chloe a motive to kill Olivia.

Amanda slumped down on a box. Practically every week, one of the many real-life shows she watched told the sad story of a sweet young woman no one suspected had killed another woman over a man. It could be Chloe's story.

And why had Chloe seesawed between David and Matt in the past month? Where did her true feelings lie?

Amanda ached for Matt. You could shield your child from getting hurt on a playground. But you couldn't shield your grown child from getting a broken heart.

The fairy tale idea of Chloe becoming her daughter-in-law had dissolved into thin air, replaced with hard questions. Did Matt's girlfriend, who was also David's secret girlfriend, belong on her suspect list? Was there enough proof to send in a tip to the police?

Amanda held back tears. First Zak, now Chloe.

How had she ever thought becoming the Sleuth Lady wouldn't affect her? That she could stay above the fracas, and all the pieces would simply fall into place?

For the rest of the afternoon Amanda knew the forced pleasantries between herself and Chloe were obvious, even to the customers. The clock moved at a snail's pace as she waited for the 6:00 p.m. close.

Worse, with everything that happened today, she'd made zero progress in discovering where the murderer had hidden the knife.

CHAPTER 24

Amanda turned on the CLOSED sign, locked the Dark Roast's front door, and hurried the four blocks to the Oak Hills Library. Finally! She'd put this trip off way too many times. And she needed the walk to get recharged.

Thank goodness for the reference librarian. He showed her how to sort through the rows of microfiche files for archived editions of the *Gazette* that weren't digitized. She stopped herself from shouting "Bingo!" when the front page of the July 27, 1944, evening edition revealed her grandfather's story.

Today, the Honorable Judge William Harris sentenced twelve-year-old Henry Allen to five years in the Chicago Juvenile Correction Center for fatally shooting a Brinks armored truck guard on June 10, 1944.

The bullet that killed the guard matched those in the rifle carried by young Allen. He pled not guilty and told his story to the court. The judge struck down Allen's alibi that he was hunting small game for supper as a surprise for his mother and stumbled by accident onto the crime scene.

The defense did not provide any witnesses to support Allen's story. The defense also could not provide evidence that another party had planned the robbery and shot the Brinks guard.

As young Allen was led out of the courtroom in handcuffs, his mother and father wept in the gallery.

Amanda sat back, overwhelmed with sadness. Her grandfather, Henry Allen, had been falsely convicted and spent five years in the Juvenile Correction Center, a place as bad as Chicago's Cook County Jail was now. No wonder the family never wanted to talk about him when she asked questions. That also explained why her mother had seemed so pained when Amanda brought it up.

She combed the edition dated the day her grandfather was due to complete his five-year sentence. She almost gave up, until the possibility of an early release for good behavior occurred to her.

She found a small article dated six months prior stating that Henry Allen, then seventeen, had his sentence reduced because he was a model prisoner. Amanda silently cheered. At least her grandfather's sad story had a bit of a positive ending.

Yet there was no mention of Raymond Cartel in any of the *Gazette's* articles. How did he know about the story?

Deep in thought on her walk home, Amanda pulled out her phone. She couldn't wait until next Sunday to report her news.

"Amanda, why are you calling?" her mother asked after a quick hello, her voice guarded.

"I want to tell you what I just learned happened to my grandfather in 1944." She relayed all she'd uncovered at the library.

There was a long pause on the other end until her mother said, "So the story I heard all those years ago was true." She hesitated, then said, "I learned something today. But I wasn't sure I should tell you."

Amanda frowned. "Why not?"

"It's upsetting."

"I still want to know."

Another long pause followed.

"If you insist. But brace yourself."

After their talk this past Sunday, her mother had remembered a pile of dust-covered boxes in an attic corner and thought they might unveil more about their family in 1944. Digging through them, she found an envelope from Henry Allen addressed to his future descendants. The wax seal was intact. The letter had never been opened.

"I decided it was time to open it. And I'm glad I did."

Henry Allen had written the letter the week before he died, over fifty years ago. He described his hard life after being wrongly convicted of shooting a Brinks guard.

"That part I told you about, Amanda. But what I didn't know was that your grandfather had saved a young boy from drowning at the same time the Brinks guard was killed a quarter mile away. The two of them heard the shot. He told the boy to run in the opposite direction, and your grandfather went to check it out. That's when he stumbled onto the crime scene at the wrong time. Worse, your grandfather's rifle matched the killer's."

"What happened to the boy?"

"He vanished, never to be seen again."

"What was his name?" Amanda asked.

"George Franklin."

"Did he say anything about a Raymond Cartel?"

"No." Her mother paused, as if to catch her emotions along with her breath.

"Amanda, I called because I wanted you to hear your grandfather's words. He ended his letter by saying he realized saving the young boy's life was one of his proudest moments, despite the consequences. You must do what feels right for you about helping that young man you say has been falsely accused."

Amanda felt herself tear up again. This was the first time in years her mother had shown compassion for others.

After a quick goodbye her mother hung up, but not before

Amanda heard a quiver in her voice. They'd both been touched learning her grandfather had saved a life. She needed to follow his lead.

Recharged, Amanda hustled toward Valley Lane Condos and tapped Maria Sebastian's phone number along the way. It bothered her the name sounded so familiar.

A woman answered, not sounding happy that a stranger had called her. Amanda used her Deli Lady persona to calm her down and confirmed she was talking to Maria Sebastian.

Fortunately, Maria went from cross to flattered. "Yes, now I recognize your voice. But why are you calling me?"

Amanda decided it best to keep it simple. She was an acquaintance of Olivia Hager and heard Maria was her neighbor. She wondered if there was more to the story of the woman's murder than the news reported.

"I know everything that happened that night," Maria said, with a superior tone in her voice. "You've come to the right person." Amanda had reached the building's tiny entryway and was buzzed in.

When the woman opened her condo door, Amanda immediately recognized her face.

She'd hit gold.

Maria Sebastian was one of the biggest gossips in Oak Hills. She never failed to yak on and on about trivial happenings in the village when she was at the deli counter. She could also be condescending and mean spirited. Amanda tried to avoid her and gladly kept to Bob's policy to avoid small talk with customers whenever she got stuck waiting on her. Right now, it was a different story.

"I must apologize for not returning your call," Maria said inviting her in. "I just got back from my trip and found your message on my answering machine. I'm one of those dinosaurs who still have a landline," she chuckled. "But please sit down.

I'd love to tell you everything I saw that happened that night." Her chuckle had turned into a smirk.

Seated in Maria's living room, Amanda started to ask how well she knew Olivia. Maria leaped in, cutting her off.

"Well, she kept to herself just about all the time." She gave a knowing nod. "But I have to admit, underneath that tough exterior, I believe there was a decent person. In fact, just last week, she knocked on my door and asked if I had lost a glove. She'd found it in the hallway. And I had." Maria frowned. "Honestly, her death shocked and saddened me."

Olivia's neighbor also confided that she'd talked to the police the night they found the body. She had told them about suspicious activity earlier in the evening.

"What kind of suspicious activity?" Amanda asked. The case file on Chief Grady's desk had mentioned a witness, which she decided was probably Maria.

Maria leaned forward as if sharing a secret. "There was lots of shouting. I heard Olivia's voice and then a male voice that sounded like David Stedman's."

"How do you know David's voice?" Amanda focused on keeping her own voice calm.

"I know him from the Happy Bean, where he's a barista. My book club meets there weekly. I often saw Olivia there, too." Maria's expression turned pensive. "It was obvious she was infatuated with David. But he avoided her like the plague." She spat out the word.

Amanda purposely didn't react. "Could you hear what they said that night?"

"No. Only that her voice had a snippy, almost nasty tone to it. His voice sounded upset and, well ... I'd almost say desperate."

"What time was that?"

"Like I told the police, it started before six o'clock and went on for a few minutes. I know because I always watch *Family*

Feud, which starts at six o'clock. I never miss my favorite show."

Amanda nodded. "Then what happened?"

Maria flashed a '*wait until you hear what I have to say next*' look.

"Well, I heard Olivia's door whoosh open, as if it had been yanked in anger or haste. I admit I got nosy and spied out my peephole. That's when I saw David shut Olivia's door. Very quietly. He looked back and forth several times, as if checking to make sure no one saw him. Then he rushed down the hallway and opened the stairwell door. It has the most annoying squeak. Then my show started."

Maria folded her hands together. "But I started getting worried. Olivia usually plays music every night. Rap, jazz, classical, pop—it runs the gamut. I have to admit, I rather enjoy the nightly concerts. But I heard nothing that night. I knocked on Olivia's door and didn't get a response, so I called the police and insisted on a wellness check. They arrived around 10:15."

Maria pulled her sweater tighter. "If I'd known she was in danger, I would have called 911 right away. I get the shivers all over again knowing she died."

Amanda had the shivers too.

"Just so I'm clear, did you see or hear anyone else in the hallway between the times when David left and the police arrived?"

"No. But it's a quiet building, so that's not unusual. And I had the TV volume up."

When Amanda asked if Maria knew Phil Wharton in 303, the woman rolled her eyes. "Phil is never home. He's one of those businesspeople who are either constantly traveling or on vacation. For the last three weeks, he's been hiking in New Zealand. That man has the life!"

"How about Max Paxton in 307?"

"Max sold his unit a couple of months ago and moved to

somewhere in California. There's a new fellow in there who mostly keeps to himself, just like Olivia did. I've been at my daughter's home in Wisconsin a lot lately, so I still don't know his name or what he looks like."

"But Max Paxton's name is still in the directory downstairs."

Maria threw up her hands. "Honestly, the management company is terrible about updating names. Olivia's name is still listed, too. I'm going to demand they take it down." She let out a self-satisfied, "Humph."

"Do you know who else the police spoke to?"

"I don't." She pouted, crossing her arms. "They wouldn't tell me what anyone else said or heard. I didn't know until afterwards that they arrested David for Olivia's murder."

Amanda had heard enough and thanked Maria for telling her story. She made sure the woman had firmly shut her condo door before she scurried down the hallway to the stairwell door.

Slowly pushing it ajar to lessen the squeak, she peaked in. Two flights of stairs looped around above her. They led to the fifth floor, where Chloe lived.

She was ready to check things out when a nearby condo door opened and Gina's voice rang out. "Fine. Be that way. I'll clean up my mess in the kitchen, then I'm out of here. No way am I cleaning up your stuff." The door slammed shut.

Amanda took that as her cue to head out herself and quickly closed the stairwell door. With all that had happened today, she wasn't up for another confrontation with Gina, who sounded like she was already in a snarly mood.

Walking home, she couldn't push aside the scenario running through her head. On the night of the murder, David and Olivia probably had that tough conversation Olivia had insisted on earlier in the day in front of Amanda and everyone else at the deli counter. But according to Maria, it hadn't gone well.

And David had acted suspiciously when he left Olivia's

condo, as if he hadn't wanted to be seen. He could have sneaked up the stairwell to Chloe's condo on the fifth floor.

Amanda wanted to believe David had left Olivia alive and unharmed. But from what Maria had heard and seen, he sounded guilty. And … Chloe could even have aided him.

She unconsciously turned up the collar on her coat. Had David and Chloe—her son's current girlfriend—colluded in Olivia's death? Impossible to believe.

The thought numbed her.

———

When Amanda walked into the kitchen Brittany and Joe were chowing down on subs from Your Favorite Sandwich Place.

"We bought one for you." Joe smiled ear to ear. "Matt's working late and getting his own. He said something about trying to see Chloe, too."

Amanda felt a pang of hurt for her son. Gina was probably gleefully spreading the rumor that Chloe had been dating David at the same time she was dating Matt. She hoped Chloe would tell Matt herself before he found out the hard way.

She didn't let Joe and Brittany in on the upsetting news. It was Matt's place to tell them.

Joe finished first, smiling like he'd won the Mega Millions.

"You're in a great mood. Is there anything you want to share?" she asked.

"It's been another beautiful spring day. Why shouldn't I be happy?"

"Just wondering. And don't stay out in the garage all night," she added as he rose from his chair.

"Whatever you say, Amanda." He headed out the back door, the smile still plastered on his face.

For Amanda, seeing Joe smile was the best thing that had happened all day. Even if he was headed to the garage again.

As she savored the last bite of her sandwich, Brittany leaned back in her chair as if wanting to talk. Amanda's mom-antenna went on high alert.

"How are things going with you and Patrick?" she asked, deciding it'd be best to be direct. Plus, Joe wasn't there to give her none-of-your-business daggers.

"Mom, I like him, but not 100%."

"You've only been on a few dates together. It takes time to get to know a person."

"I know that, Mom. But he's a complete neat freak." Brittany pushed her plate to the side.

"How so?"

"He's always washing his hands and brushing the slightest piece of lint off his clothes. He's very finicky about his leather jackets. Doesn't want any scratches. And he has a whole collection. Even a red one. He even stashes loose things in those clear slider bags. On top of that, he's really protective of his car. I can't believe I have to check the bottom of my shoes before I get in. The worst thing is he insists on always being on time. Sometimes even early." Brittany made a face.

Knowing Brittany's carefree attitude and Patrick's fastidious ways, Amanda pictured the two of them standing on opposite rims of the Grand Canyon.

She put her empty plate on top of Brittany's. "Well, you need to be honest with yourself and with the other person."

"You're right, Mom. Although I have to admit I've loved the dinners out, the flowers, and all the attention. Every day he sends me lots of texts. It's nice to feel wanted."

"Yes, it is." Amanda thought back to how Joe had opened up her world when they met. "But I have faith in you. You'll do the right thing."

"Thanks, Mom. You know, we haven't talked like this for a long time. I'm glad we did tonight."

"Me, too." Hearing their mother-daughter talk had gotten the seal of approval from Brittany gave her a lift.

Patrick probably wouldn't get a long-term seal of approval from Brittany, she sensed. A pang of disappointment got squashed by her conscience. This was Brittany's decision, not hers. She needed to support her daughter's choice. Period.

In her head she could hear Joe's voice say, "Finally. We agree."

Brittany offered to clean up, which warmed Amanda's heart. Perhaps her daughter was finally growing up.

As Amanda snuggled into the living room couch, her phone signaled a call from Nicki.

"What's up, Amanda? I got your asap message. Sorry I didn't get a chance to return your call until now," Nicki said.

Although Evans had reassured her that the chief wouldn't tell Nicki what happened, Amanda knew she had to. She confessed she'd messed up by not calling Nicki about her marketing idea for a new brew that added just a kick of cayenne pepper to their popular espresso. On a whim, she'd debuted it at the Oak Hills police station that morning. She also mentioned her mistake of upsetting the chief when she delivered his personal cup to his empty office.

She left out the part about snooping on the chief's desk. And being briefly locked up in a jail cell. Those were post-vacation topics, if ever. She was counting on the chief never wanting anyone to know what really happened.

Nicki chastised her, rightly so, for not getting her okay. Amanda followed with an apology. The awkward silence ended when Amanda asked about Nicki's vacation. Another long silence on the other ended with, "Good."

"Still only good?"

"Let's just say the Orlando area probably isn't the place to go at the end of March if you're single. It's spring break, filled wall to wall with families and kids. Don't ask me what I was thinking."

"But you love your condo and the swimming pool."

"Also packed with families. I can't get a lounge chair unless I claim it at six in the morning. Totally killed my dream of sleeping in."

"That's a bummer."

"Today I made the mistake of venturing to one of the many theme parks. The place was a total zoo, saved only by the cute seashell sunglasses I found in one of the trillion gift shops." Amanda heard a long sigh. "But enough about me. I want to mention something I remembered about Gina that might help with your crusade for David."

"What's that?"

"Several months ago, one of my staff let it slip that Gina really liked a barista who worked at the Happy Bean in Schaumburg. But it was a one-way thing on Gina's part. That infuriated her, of course. I think the guy was David."

Amanda confirmed she'd heard the same today. And added she'd learned Chloe had been dating David.

"Wow! Chloe, Gina, and Olivia were all going after the guy at the same time. I didn't realize he was such a chick magnet," Nicki said.

"We could have had our own Bachelor of Oak Hills reality show," Amanda added. "Except someone took things way too far."

"It still makes me shudder, Amanda. And even though I keep telling you the Dark Roast is your top priority; I hope you find Olivia Hager's true murderer."

"So, you agree that David is innocent?"

"I'm still not 100% convinced. But whoever it is, my money's on you to figure it out."

"Thanks. I needed that encouragement. Today I learned

something very sad about my family's past." She gave her bestie a quick version of her grandfather's story.

"Now it makes sense why you want to help David," Nicki said. "Helping people is in your genes!"

CHAPTER 25

With Thursday's dawn on the horizon, Amanda headed down First Street to the Dark Roast. When a sheet of paper blew across her path, she swooped it up without losing a beat. Her first thought was it could be another *Stedman is guilty* letter. Seeing it was blank, she tossed it into the trash bin at the corner.

Then she screeched to a halt.

The status report in Chief Grady's case folder had said nothing about the *Stedman is guilty* letters left at Oak Hills businesses. Nor was there anything about the letter Raymond had turned over to the police at the hospital. Evans hadn't given her an update since she'd turned in her letter two days ago, either. The only update in the *Gazette* about the letters said police had asked Oak Hills businesses to turn in any security camera video.

Amanda jammed her hands into her pockets. One thing was for sure. Yesterday's revelation that both Gina and Chloe had been infatuated with David meant neither of them was likely to have created crazy letters saying he was guilty of murder.

But what if, just maybe, the letters weren't from the murderer? Maybe someone thought it would be fun to mess with people's heads. Like the prankster who'd sent in the Elvis tips to Citizen Watch.

Shaking her head, she continued down the sidewalk. Why would a prankster attack both her and Raymond on Monday night and leave her a personal message? Why would they take the time to leave letters around the village that said David was guilty? Only someone who wanted to make sure David took the rap would invest that much effort.

Amanda's pace quickened with her thoughts. The letters made everything a lot more complicated. If only she could talk to a TV sleuth like Aurora Teagarden or Jessica Fletcher or Mabel Mora. They always made solving murders look so easy.

But it might be worth a try to ask Evans.

With the Dark Roast in view, Amanda switched to manager mode. When Zak arrived right behind her, she was glad he seemed back to his usual self.

Throughout the morning, the two of them seamlessly filled customer orders. Most villagers seemed confident Oak Hills was once again safe with David secured in jail, although they were a little nervous about the attack on Raymond and the suspicious letters. Even so, friendly talk, lots of smiles, and a sense of community flowed through the shop.

That confidence wasn't shared by David's great-aunt, his friends, or her family. They all believed the real murderer was still out there. But right now, she needed to focus on the Dark Roast.

In between customers, she asked Zak for the next coffee tip on his list.

"This one has always amazed me," he said. "The caffeine that's taken out to make decaf blends is sold to soda companies in a brown powdered form."

Amanda's mouth dropped. "Wow. I never knew that."

"Yep, it's true. Remember that the next time you drink a diet soda. A part of it comes from coffee beans."

"I definitely will."

Her heart sank a few minutes later when Zak started a heated discussion with a customer, just the way he had on Sunday morning. Once again it concerned a Chicago sports team, this time the Blackhawks.

Amanda stepped in when the customer abruptly announced he was leaving without ordering. She offered an apology for the misunderstanding, along with a handful of Dark Roast complimentary coupons. The man was a regular. No way did she want him walking out for good.

When Amanda pulled Zak aside and reminded him of the Dark Roast's philosophy that the customer is always right, he shrugged it off. "Okay, maybe I was a little harsh. But he was too."

She couldn't decide which bothered her more: the way Zak had acted with the customer or how he'd tossed off her guidance. Something was still out of whack with him.

A rush of customers wanting special orders kept Amanda and Zak on their toes for the next half hour. Large nonfat latté with caramel drizzle; decaf soy latté with an extra shot and cream; iced, half-caff; and hot, no caff with cinnamon were some of the easier orders.

Amanda kept the line moving and the patrons happy. Zak shook off his funky mood and joined in. "I see you're becoming an ace barista. I need to up my game," he teased.

She'd turned away for a second but whipped back around when a familiar voice said, "I'd like a medium decaffeinated black coffee. To go, please."

Bob Early stood at the counter, with his Bob's Finer Foods employee shirt on full view underneath his jacket.

"Thanks for stopping in," Amanda said, telling herself to keep calm as her nerves zoomed to high alert. "I'll have that for you right away."

As she grabbed a cup, nonstop questions percolated in her

head. How long had he been in the shop? Was he checking up on her? Reporting back to Nicki? Or did he truly just want a cup of coffee?

Although it was the simplest of orders, Amanda was so rattled she almost reached for the super-caffeinated pot. Luckily, she caught her slip-up in time.

"Here you go. On me." She slid the steaming cup over the counter.

Bob nodded. "Thank you. I've been sitting in the back corner watching everyone come and go. Seems like the Dark Roast is doing okay."

How had she not noticed him? At least he'd given her an "okay." He'd probably witnessed how she'd jumped in and calmly defused the situation with Zak's irate customer. Bob hated unhappy customers, anywhere or anytime.

All she could do was breathe a sigh of relief when he walked out the door, coffee in hand. She hoped he'd give Nicki a positive report.

By mid-morning the shop had emptied except for a sole patron, head down on his laptop and wearing earplugs. The perfect time to ask Zak the question she kept putting off. *Where were you last Wednesday between 5:00 and 7:00 p.m.?*

Amanda quickly nixed that idea. It wouldn't be smart to give any hint that she considered him a potential suspect during the middle of his shift. Or possibly ever. After all, she was here to run a business. Nicki had been very clear about the no-hunting-for-suspects-while-on-duty policy.

Half an hour later, when no new customers had walked into the shop, Amanda confirmed the OPEN sign hadn't shorted out and asked Zak what had happened to the usual mid-morning crowd.

"Every once in a while, we get hit with quiet times, as Nicki calls them. Based on experience, I bet we won't get another customer for at least ten minutes," he said.

"I'm going to think positive. I bet someone walks in the front door in less than five minutes."

"What are we betting?"

"The loser has to make the winner a Beachy Keen," Amanda said.

"You mean that specialty coffee with brown sugar around the rim to mimic sand in honor of Nicki's vacation?"

"That's the one."

"Including the little paper cocktail umbrella perched on the side of the cup?"

"Absolutely!" Amanda grinned.

"Game on," he agreed.

The countdown started. Both kept a close watch on the clock, passing good-natured jabs back and forth.

Just past the four-minute mark, Patrick walked in.

"I win!" Amanda said, waving her hands above her head. "And don't forget the—"

"Yeah, I know. You don't have to remind me." Zak groaned as he plucked out a tiny yellow umbrella. "Hey, bro. You made me lose a bet," he said as Patrick stepped up to the counter. "And aren't you a regular at the Happy Bean?"

"I'm a regular at both shops. We must be missing each other."

"Well, no time to chat right now." Zak nodded toward Amanda and gave her a wry smile. "My boss is waiting for her winnings."

Amanda gave Zak a friendly eye roll, then turned to Patrick. "It's nice to see you again. Everything going well?"

"Everything is great, especially after we talked on Tuesday morning. Thanks again." He grinned.

"Glad I could help. Now what can I get you?" *If only Brittany would have a change of heart about this guy,* she thought.

While Amanda and Zak prepped the coffees, the two guys grumbled about the Cubs' opening weekend series being sold out and the jacked-up scalper prices. The discussion grew heated, with Zak blaming the team owner's greed and Patrick pointing to player contracts.

The two got so riled up they both turned beet red. Zak seemed especially agitated.

Amanda held up her hands. "Hey, you two. Calm down."

Zak and Patrick stopped, their shoulders dropped in unison, as if they were a duo act performing on *America's Got Talent*.

"Sorry," Patrick said. "I went a little overboard. My apologies." Amanda gave him a plus in her book.

After a pause, Zak added, "Me, too." His lingering frown made Amanda suspect he didn't truly mean it.

"I know where you can find some cheap entertainment," Amanda said, glad to redirect the conversation. "One place that's still free is Cook County's Busse Woods. It's close to Oak Hills, and it stretches for several miles in all directions. With the unusually warm forecast they're predicting for the next couple days, it's a perfect place to have fun. All those biking paths, picnic groves, fishing holes, and open fields. You could even have your own baseball game. Joe and I used to be regulars at Busse Woods. The price was right for us."

"I heard it can get crowded." Patrick raised a doubting eyebrow.

"You don't have to worry if you use the entrance off Golf Road." She slid Patrick's coffee across the counter. "And it's fun to watch the model airplane competitions. There's an airshow field just inside the park."

"That sounds like a good idea." Patrick reached for a splash stick.

Amanda felt something under her elbow. It was a sheet of white paper with stick-on letters and a too-familiar message.

Stedman is guilty.

Amanda froze. "Zak, where did this come from?"

"I meant to tell you about that. I found it outside the front door when I walked in this morning and stuck it over on the side counter. Guess it's like the others that have been popping up around Oak Hills."

"Did you see anyone loitering around the front of the shop when you arrived?"

"No." Zak shrugged.

"I was wondering when the Dark Roast would get one of these letters. My question is, why didn't we get it until now?" Amanda asked.

Zak shook his head. "It has to be crazy high school kids doing random drops. It's spring break and they're bored. I wouldn't sweat it."

"I'll go with your theory for now," Amanda said. "In the meantime, before we contaminate it any further, hand me one of those clear slider bags. We need to preserve any fingerprints."

She grabbed a napkin and picked up the letter by one corner. Then she dropped it into the bag Zak handed her and sealed it. "I'll let Nicki know. And we need to alert the police."

"You don't think it's a prank?" Patrick asked. "Or a copycat? A lot of other stores have found them, like Zak said."

"Could be. But the police have the equipment to verify it. I'll take it over to them."

"Since I discovered it, shouldn't I be the one taking it to the police?" Zak asked. "In case they have questions or something?"

Amanda studied him. She wasn't exactly welcome at the police station right now, but Zak could have concocted the letter campaign to keep the spotlight on David and away from him. He hadn't been on shift Monday night, so he could have been the person in black who not-so-gently delivered letters to her and Raymond.

She sneaked a quick glimpse at his feet. He wore black running shoes with the shiny silver label on the back, identical to the pair worn by whoever had knocked her down. Was it a coincidence?

He still hadn't connected her with the UPS deliverer accused of stealing Olivia's necklace, even though she'd asked him multiple times. Was that deliberate? Or part of his scheme? Or was he just forgetful, like Brittany?

And a few minutes ago, she'd seen him lose it again. Had he gotten carried away with Olivia last Wednesday and killed her in a rage when she rebuffed him again?

Would Nancy Drew hand over evidence to someone whose innocence she once again doubted?

The front door swung open, followed by three mothers with little ones and lots of commotion. Behind them were four men in business suits.

"Game time," Amanda said, switching back into manager mode once again.

Patrick raised his hand. "I can drop the letter off at the police station. I'm going by there anyway."

"That would be great, Patrick, thanks. The sooner, the better," Amanda said. "Can you tell the police I'll follow up with them?"

"Consider it done." He slipped the clear slider bag with the letter into his satchel and was out the front door in a few quick strides.

After the rush quieted down, Amanda thought about David and how she'd failed so far at finding the true murderer. Her shoulders drooped as if someone had deflated her spirit with a pin.

A chorus of laughter from a nearby table revived her. The Dark Roast buzzed, and she felt pride in her accomplishments as a manager. She'd gotten multiple thumbs-up from patrons and staff, along with many positive online reviews. And Nicki had been delighted that the online financial reports showed revenue had held steady all week.

Amanda stood a little taller and gave her ponytail a twirl. Pretty darned good for less than a week on the job.

Okay, so maybe there'd been a little confusion when she adjusted the staff schedule and four part-timers showed up for the same shift. But she'd quickly worked it out, making sure no one got upset. And when she'd left the cream out overnight, a fast trip to Bob's with her credit card before opening had solved the issue. There was also that large customer order she'd gotten wrong, but free refills for the rest of the day had smoothed those ruffled feathers.

She broke into a smile. Not to brag, but yeah, she had this manager thing down pat.

And in only a week, she'd alerted the police to several strong suspects in Olivia's murder.

Okay, there had been those few minutes in the jail cell that had probably freaked David out. But now her feet were totally on the ground, and she was making solid progress.

She wouldn't stop until David walked out of jail as a free man.

CHAPTER 26

Amanda waited until the lunchtime rush ended to check up on Raymond, who Nicki had alerted her was now home from the hospital. The two part-timers on duty assured her they had everything under control.

As she hurried down First Street, she hoped Raymond would be up to answering her questions. After her trip to the library and her mother's update, they danced around in her head like popcorn kernels in a microwave oven.

Seeing the Valley Lane condo building in the distance, she made an impromptu decision to check the back entrance. It'd take only a few minutes, she told herself. Then she'd know for sure if a key was needed to get in.

As Amanda neared the building's front walkway, a UPS truck pulled up and parked curbside. The driver hopped out, toting a small package. Amanda recognized him as the regular at Bob's deli counter, the one she'd almost collided with on her way to work the morning of David's arrest.

Then it hit her. He could also be the UPS driver that Zak knew. The driver Olivia had accused of stealing her necklace.

"Excuse me, are you Sam Robertson?" she asked.

"Yeah." He appeared confused for a moment, then brightened up. "Wait, I know you. You're the Deli Lady." He gave her a sheepish glance. "I need to apologize for almost running into you on the sidewalk last week."

"No problem. I figured you were having a bad day."

"I sure was." He frowned. "Hey, I haven't seen you at Bob's this week."

"That's because I'm helping at the Dark Roast."

"Ah! Then you're working with my friend Zak."

"I am and I'm hoping I can ask you a question."

He glanced at his phone. "Sure. But make it quick. I have to keep on schedule."

Amanda nodded. "Zak mentioned you regularly make deliveries to Valley Lane Condos. I was wondering if, by chance, you made a delivery to the building that day?"

Sam's face hardened. "Why do you want to know?"

"I'm asking for a friend. David Stedman's aunt hopes someone saw something suspicious beyond what the news reported." Which was true. She didn't add she was looking for other suspects. Like him.

There was a long pause. "I don't like to talk about how I was dragged into that horrible murder. But my little girl loves you because you always give her a sample of her favorite tapioca pudding, so I'll make an exception."

Sam explained he didn't know about the murder until he started his route the next morning. "My first delivery was to Valley Lane Condos. I was surprised to see the yellow crime-scene tape around the building. I could tell a couple of police officers were looking around for something. They gave me a lot of heat. Said they might want to talk to me again."

He growled. "They finally let me leave. I had to hustle like a madman to get back on schedule the rest of the day. That's why I was so grumpy when I almost bumped into you that morning. Sorry again about that."

"I understand," she said. "So, you didn't see anything suspicious the day of the murder?"

Sam took a step toward the building's front entrance. "Nope. There wasn't anyone around when I made that delivery at 3:30 p.m. She buzzed me in and accepted the package at her door. The time is stamped on the photo we have to take with each delivery. She's in the picture with the package."

That meant the timing on the photo cleared Sam. The police report on the chief's desk had said Olivia was killed between 5:00 and 7:00 p.m. But Sam wouldn't have known that. So why did the police still want to question him?

Sam reached for the handle on the front door. "Can you let Zak know I'm going to make good on that pizza and beer I promised? He helped us move into a new apartment in Chicago last week. North Side."

"What day was that?"

"Last Wednesday. The day of the murder. Right after I made the 3:30 p.m. delivery to Olivia Hager, my shift ended and I headed to the new place. My wife was relieved I got there around 4:30. Zak arrived around five. He helped us until midnight and then crashed on our sofa. We couldn't have done it without him."

Amanda did a quick calculation. Both Sam and Zak had an hour drive to Chicago's North Side in rush hour traffic. Which meant both had a solid alibi. She held off doing an impromptu jig as she mentally crossed both their names off her suspect list. This didn't help David still in jail.

Then it hit her. Maybe the police wanted to talk to Sam about that other incident.

When she asked about a necklace that Zak said had been lost, he gave her a suspicious look. "Why do you want to know about that?"

"I might be able to help find it." She already had a strong hunch who could have stolen it.

His suspicious look changed to hopeful. "If you do, that'd be great. It's a 14-carat gold, 24-inch-long necklace with a round locket. Here's the picture from the merchant's online site. I keep it handy in case I find it somewhere around the building. You'd be surprised what people don't realize they've dropped."

He pointed to the photo on his phone.

Amanda tried not to show her disappointment when Sam's picture revealed a round locket that definitely didn't match the gold-etched heart locket she'd seen Gina wearing. So, it wasn't evidence of Gina's guilt.

"If you hear anything about the necklace, let me know," Sam said. "I want to permanently delete that false accusation from my company record and get the police off my back about it." He slipped his phone back into his jacket. "Now I really gotta go. Our delivery schedules are timed. And I'm running late."

Amanda watched Sam hurry past the fake cameras, get buzzed in, and head toward the elevator. She was glad she'd heeded her instincts and hadn't submitted Zak's or Sam's name to the Citizen Watch site.

A powerful reminder that she needed to confirm all the facts before sending in an anonymous tip.

Amanda scurried around the perimeter of the building. She still needed to confirm Chloe's claim that entry through the back door required a key.

As she rounded the corner, a large sign warned: *We Prosecute Trespassers to the Fullest Extent of the Law.* She dismissed the threat with a wave.

A loud click, followed by the whoosh of an opening door, punctured Amanda's bravado. She leaped behind a line of shoulder-high arborvitae shrubs that stood like soldiers at attention as they guarded the parking lot. Crouching, she peeked through the branches.

Chloe stepped out the back door and into the sunlight, dressed in black running gear and, surprisingly, nothing pink.

The door automatically snapped shut behind her. She stretched, then jogged away from Amanda's hideout. Her black running shoes had a shiny silver label on the back. Amanda stood up, trying to comprehend what she'd just seen. Hearing a second loud click and whoosh, she quickly ducked back down.

This time Gina stepped out the back door, also wearing black running gear. She jogged toward Amanda, then abruptly turned just short of her arborvitae cover.

Once again Amanda peeked through the branches. The back of Gina's black running shoes flashed the same shiny silver label as Chloe's.

Amanda steadied herself. Both women were runners. Both wore black gear. Both had the same branded shoes as her attacker.

Either could have attacked her or Raymond Monday night. Yet it still didn't make sense. They were both crazy about David. Why would either of them leave a letter saying he was guilty?

Amanda sat back on her heels, her brain clicking.

If Gina had murdered Olivia after five years of wanting revenge, she could be pointing the finger at David in retaliation for his lack of interest in her.

If Chloe had murdered Olivia, could she hope the letters would draw sympathy for David? How?

Amanda shook her head. She needed concrete evidence for either of those thin theories.

With no one in sight, she hurried across the parking lot to the building's back door. She jiggled the lock, but the door didn't budge. Well, there was her confirmation: A key was needed to get in.

The murderer would need to live in the building, like Gina or Chloe. Or work in it, like Raymond. Or get buzzed in through the front door, like Sam or Zak when they delivered packages.

Amanda stopped. She hadn't considered someone getting

buzzed in by Olivia *after* David left her place. Another avenue to investigate.

Checking the time on her phone, she fast-tracked it down Valley Lane toward Raymond's, sorting out her suspect list along the way. Zak and Sam Robertson were now officially off. Three names remained: Gina at the top, Chloe next, followed by Raymond. She added a question mark for an unknown person who could have been buzzed in by Olivia after David left.

Turning the corner onto Birch Court, Amanda spotted Raymond walking up the front steps of his house. His steady stride spoke of a strong recovery from getting hit in the head. She called out his name and waved, but he headed inside.

She ran up the front steps and knocked on the door. "Raymond, it's Amanda Knightly."

No answer.

Another knock. "Raymond, I'm here to check up on you."

Still no answer. She started to get nervous.

"Raymond, if you don't open the door, I'm calling the paramedics."

The door swung open. Raymond stood there, clutching a Bob's Finer Foods brown plastic grocery sack.

"Hold your horses, young lady. I'm just fine. And you're just the person I want to see." He stepped onto the porch and slammed the door behind him. "We need to start walking. I gotta turn something in to the police."

Raymond hustled down the front porch steps as if he'd been dunked in the mystical Fountain of Youth. He picked up speed as he turned onto First Street.

Amanda kept up behind him. She had to know what he wanted to turn in.

She followed his shortcuts as he zigzagged through an empty lot, cut through an alley, then shot diagonally across a small park opposite the police station. She was soon out of breath.

Only a final burst of energy let her beat Raymond to the front entrance of the police station.

"Okay, we're here. So, what's in there?" She pointed to the grocery sack as she caught her breath.

"It's what I think that person who clobbered me on Monday night was after." He reached inside the sack and pulled out a large, clear slider bag.

It contained what looked like a chef's knife, several inches in length, caked in something dark red. Next to it was a slip of paper with the typed message "Stedman killed Olivia Hager with this knife."

Amanda gasped as her hand flew to her mouth. She yanked open the door. "You first," she ordered, her nerves sky high, remembering Evans had said it might be wise to stay away from the station for a while.

She pushed her apprehension aside. "I'll be right behind you."

CHAPTER 27

Amanda shadowed Raymond as they walked up to the front desk inside the Oak Hills police station. Her emotions zoomed from elation that the alleged murder weapon had shown up to dread of what it might reveal.

"May I help you?" the officer at the front desk asked. Amanda wondered what had happened to Lee. And relieved for the friendly greeting.

"My name is Raymond Cartel, and I want to turn in this here knife." He laid the clear slider bag with the knife inside on the counter as he tucked the now empty Bob's grocery sack under his arm. "I found it in my yard. The note inside says it's the one Stedman used to kill Olivia Hager."

The officer's face went blank. Amanda saw his hand drop under the edge of the counter.

Within seconds the secured side doors clicked open, followed by Evans and Lee, hands on their guns. "No one move," Evans announced.

Amanda froze, not surprised to see Lee staring at her. He said to Evans, "I don't trust her."

Evans didn't react, which also didn't surprise Amanda.

"I brought this here knife in." Raymond nodded at the counter.

"Thank you for bringing it to us, Mr. Cartel." Evans acted as calmly as if it was a casual exchange about the weather. "Can you also lay what's under your arm on the counter?"

"Okay, but there ain't nothing in there." As he put it down, he patted it to show the sack was empty. "See, I told you so."

"Yes, you did," Evans said. "Now I'd like to ask both of you to step back while we collect what you brought in."

Amanda knew Evans would act cautiously. She was also impressed that she was keeping the situation calm. It could have gone otherwise.

Lee slipped on gloves and carefully picked up both items.

"Thank you again." Evan said, unruffled. "We'd like to ask you both a few questions, if you don't mind. Officer Lee and I will escort you to separate interview rooms."

"I thought I'd drop this thing off and leave, but if I have to stay and answer some questions, then okay. But she's coming in with me or I'm not talking." Raymond jerked his thumb in Amanda's direction.

Amanda tried not to flinch. Would she get tied into the murder? Tossed into a jail cell next to David's again?

Don't borrow trouble, Amanda heard her conscience say.

"It's better if we talk to each of you separately."

"Well, you should know I found the grocery sack with that knife in it all on my own. I invited her to come to the police station with me."

Amanda nodded in agreement, but Officer Lee ushered her into a separate interview room. Chief Grady walked behind Evans as they led Raymond across the hall and shut the door.

Sitting down, she got a jolt from the familiar cold metal chair and willed herself not to shiver. Best not to attract even the slightest amount of unneeded attention, she decided.

When asked, she reiterated what Raymond had said at the front desk, adding that she had stopped by his house to make sure he was okay after being discharged from the hospital. After several more questions, Lee escorted her back to the lobby, then hurried off.

She plopped down on a bench, relieved she'd been cleared. But why was Raymond taking so long?

It seemed like forever before Raymond was escorted back into the lobby. It was clear the burst of energy he'd had on the way to the police station was long gone. He slumped down on the bench next to her.

"How'd it go?" she asked.

"I told them the total story," he said. "On Monday morning I turned over the dirt next to my garage to get my garden started. I was determined to grow vegetables this year. There's nothing like those sweet tomatoes right off the vine, you know," he said with a weary smile.

Then he explained how he'd hit a rock buried in the soil. And underneath the rock was the grocery sack.

"I felt a few drops of rain, so I shook the dirt off the sack and brought it into my house. I could tell there was something inside. But I got interrupted by a phone call. Then a neighbor stopped by to chat. I stashed it under the sink so the neighbor wouldn't see it. He's a nosy guy, likes to gossip. And I didn't want any part of that.

Raymond shook his head. "He also never takes the hint it's time to leave. I was about to make up some excuse when his wife called to tell him supper was ready. When he finally left, I made myself a nice dinner. I barely started to eat when I thought I saw someone nosing around my backyard. And then, well, you know what happened next."

Amanda nodded. "So the knife has been in your house for the last four days?"

"Yep. When I got home from the hospital, I hit the hay. Slept until this morning. This afternoon I felt good enough to start back in the garden. And then I remembered the sack and pulled it out from under the sink. That's when I knew I had to bring it to the police. And then they asked me the dumbest questions."

"What'd they ask?"

"They wanted to know if I'd touched it. I said how could I have brought it here if I didn't touch it?" Raymond grumbled. "What kind of crazy question is that?"

Amanda bit back a smile. She could always count on Raymond to get cranky. "What else?"

"They said they knew I'd touched the Bob's grocery sack, but did I touch the knife?"

"Had you?"

"Oh sure. I couldn't figure out what it was at first. When I realized it wasn't a rusty old knife, but a knife with dried blood-stains and that note, I put them both back in the slider bag. You know, these days it's easy to reseal those bags. They have nifty pulls on the top. You don't have to use twist ties anymore."

Amanda envisioned Evans's controlled interview posture as the officer tried not to react to Raymond's meandering story. Chief Grady might not have been as stoic. Their missing evidence had shown up, but it had been handled and could have been tampered with. Or maybe Raymond was hoping to pull a fast one on them.

Right now, she wasn't totally sure herself.

"Then they asked if I'd seen anyone in my backyard recently. And I told them not until that creep hit me on the head and put me in the hospital. I told them that could have been the person who was after that knife. Otherwise, why would they have hit me?"

Amanda nodded. "Makes sense to me."

"And that's when they took my fingerprints. I asked them to hurry up. I want to get home and finish tilling my garden before the weather turns."

"Did they ask any other questions?"

"Yeah. Chief Grady asked me where I worked. I mentioned Valley Lane Condos and a bunch of other places. Then he asked where I was working the day of the murder. I told him I had the pay stubs to prove I wasn't at Valley Lane Condos that day. I don't know who killed that girl, but it wasn't me."

His eyes narrowed. "And then I told the chief he should be thanking me for turning in the knife."

"What did he say to that?"

"He didn't ask me any more questions. But he did say I need to steer clear of the patch where I found the bag and the police would check it out. He also said they might want to talk to me again." Raymond let out a humph. "I told him not to worry. I have nowhere to go."

Despite his bravado, Amanda didn't want him walking back home alone. Minutes later she stood outside the station, scanning for Raymond's rideshare. "I need to get back to the Dark Roast," she said. "I'm sending you home in an Uber."

"I've heard about those things. Ain't they someone's car that they say is a taxi?"

Amanda chuckled. "Something like that. But before it gets here, does the name Henry Allen sound familiar to you?"

Raymond frowned. "Why are you asking?"

"I'm looking into my family history. He was my grandfather. Lived in Oak Hills back in the 1940s. I thought you might have known him."

"Nope, can't say I did."

Amanda thought he answered a little too hastily.

The Uber pulled up to the curb. Amanda waved goodbye and started to walk back to the Dark Roast as unanswered questions swirled in her head.

Why did she still not totally trust Raymond? Was he holding back from telling her something?

With the Dark Roast in view, she pushed her questions aside.

It was way past the end of her half-hour break. Time to focus on the coffee shop.

———

Over family dinner, Amanda was delighted to learn of Matt's plans for later that night. The GoFundMe campaign for David had reached 90% of their goal, and all of David's friends planned to celebrate at the local beer garden. It was a perfect evening to enjoy a few brews while rocking to the Four Bad Bros, a popular local band. Matt hoped to collect the last 10% at the gathering so they could retain David's lawyer.

Three hours later, the back door of the Knightly home blew open and Matt staggered in. Amanda first thought he'd had too much to drink. But when Joe sat him down at the kitchen table, Matt blurted out that their celebration had turned into total chaos.

"All was going super. Great band, great beer, and the donations were rolling in. Until the middle of the second set." Matt shook his head.

The drummer had invited his cousin, who invited a bunch of his gang friends. One patron with too much to drink and not much common sense decided he'd let the Four Bad Bros know, in very crude language, he didn't like their last song. He stood up and announced his distaste to the entire audience. The gang took immediate offense. The fight erupted like a volcano.

"Dad, I have never been in a bar fight. Everyone was in it: guys, girls, even the bartender. Fists flew left and right, chairs and tables were pushed over, beer splashed everywhere. Just like you see in the movies. It was wild."

It didn't surprise Amanda to hear her son's excitement—mixed with unease—as he told the story. He'd always liked to watch fight scenes on TV, even as a little kid. He'd just learned reality was much different from movies.

"Matt, I've been in bars where fights broke out." Joe smiled at Amanda. "Don't worry, it was a long time ago."

He turned back to Matt. "I know they can be, uh, interesting, but the smartest thing is to get out of there as fast as you can. I hope you did that."

"I tried, but the police showed up. They made all of us stay until they could piece things together. It took forever. At least I wasn't charged, or any of my friends."

"Was your sister there?" Amanda asked, trying not to sound too anxious.

"Brittany wasn't, but Chloe was. And Gina too." He paused. "I was surprised Chloe and Gina were so upset. Neither was in the fight. But they didn't want to talk to the police, almost like they had something to hide." He shook his head. "Then all of a sudden Chloe left in an Uber before I could ask her about it."

Amanda was relieved Brittany had missed the commotion; she'd talked earlier about going to the party. She tucked away Matt's comment that neither Chloe nor Gina had wanted to talk to the police. Their reluctance confirmed their positions on her suspect list.

Joe put his hand on Matt's shoulder. "Next time, make sure you leave as soon as the first fist flies."

"I will. It's a one-and-done experience for me."

Amanda's heart once again ached for Matt. She didn't want to ask if Chloe had told him she was also dating David. Maybe he was silently working through it.

She turned away so he couldn't see her face. Sitting on the sidelines, watching the drama of your children's lives unfold, was hard.

When Matt walked out of the kitchen, she gasped. He wore the same black running shoes with the shiny silver label on the back as Chloe. And Gina. And Zak. The same ones worn by the jogger who had shoved her down.

"Matt, when did you get those?" She pointed to his feet.

He shrugged. "I dunno. Everybody has them. Even Chloe has a pair. You should try them, especially with being on your feet so much at your job."

Amanda's brain felt fried. What she'd thought was a strong clue to the murderer turned out to be practically useless.

CHAPTER 28

Amanda's mood matched the cloudy sky as she hurried down the sidewalk on Friday morning, stuffing her chilly hands into the pockets of her spring coat.

Her week in Paradise would soon be ending.

Only two more days at the Dark Roast. Then she'd be back under Bob's ironclad rules. No chatting with customers to hear leads. No stretching lunch breaks to find clues. No impromptu errands to confirm hunches.

Seeing a passing Oak Hills squad car compounded her downer frame of mind. This morning's *Gazette* had reported the guard's strike at Cook County Jail had been settled. Small holding jails, like Oak Hills, would be transporting their detainees there starting tomorrow. That gave her only one more day to find Olivia's killer before David would be locked up in one of the roughest jails in the country.

Amanda let out a long sigh. Even with finding the probable murder weapon and now the *Stedman is guilty* letter left at the Dark Roast in police hands, it didn't guarantee they'd uncover Olivia's true killer. David could still be tried for her murder. One piece of good news: Matt had told her they'd hired that lawyer for David.

Amanda's mood nosedived further when Zak rushed into the shop ten minutes before opening.

"The police sure took their time letting us leave after the bar fight last night," he said. "Guess Matt told you about it. I got home really late and overslept." He glanced around the shop. "But it looks like you already took care of everything." He gave an "oops" gesture without offering an apology.

Amanda held back from calling out his cavalier response.

Yesterday she'd been thrilled to scratch Zak's name off her suspect list after talking to Sam Robertson. But today he was back to Bad Zak. She didn't ask for her coffee tip of the day, and he didn't volunteer one. Whatever was bothering him hadn't gone away.

By mid-morning the flow of patrons slowed as the regulars settled in. A bright sun had pushed the clouds away, and the temperature had risen way above typical spring readings. Normally the ground would still have lingering patches of snow.

Amanda was cleaning the front counter, grateful for the brief lull, when Virginia Smith walked in.

"We need to talk." The older woman's voice was strained. "Privately."

Amanda quickly poured Virginia's decaf with room for cream and handed it over the counter. Not the time to honor David's promise to give his aunt special service.

"I'm all ears," Amanda said as they sat down at a table in the back corner.

Virginia took a slow sip of her coffee before setting it down. "There's something I forgot to mention about the five thousand dollars Olivia lent David."

Amanda got a sinking feeling. "What's that?"

"The day before the murder I told David I'd give him the five thousand dollars so he could get Olivia off his back."

"What was his reaction?"

"He thanked me but said he planned to pay that money back to Olivia in his own way. I'd told you that part already."

Amanda nodded. "Yes, I remember. But what did he mean by 'in his own way'?"

"I figured that was his business. I didn't tell you or anyone else, including the police, about offering him the money. Just because, well, I like to keep my personal finances personal."

Amanda leaned forward. "You need to tell the police what you just told me. That could rule out money as a motive. Plus, it would back up David if he made that same claim."

"You're right. I wasn't thinking straight when they interviewed me. I'll contact the police right away." Virginia began to rise from the table.

Amanda held up her hand. "Hold on. I need to know if there's anything else you haven't told me."

Virginia sat back down and fidgeted in her chair. "Well, David swore me to secrecy."

Amanda's sinking feeling grew. Would this be another whammy?

Virginia played with her coffee cup before continuing. "The night before David was arrested, he confided that he and Chloe had gotten back together a few weeks earlier. I knew they'd been crazy about each other in high school. Chloe was the one who insisted they not tell anyone. David didn't understand why, but he honored her request."

Amanda shook her head, relieved that was old news. To her, anyway. "You don't have to keep it confidential anymore. Gina broadcast David and Chloe's secret relationship right here in the Dark Roast two days ago."

"So now everyone knows." Virginia's regal posture returned, as if she were ready to make a proclamation. "But I know who really murdered Olivia."

"Really? Who?" Amanda asked, leery of what the woman would say.

"Gina Rohmer hated Olivia Hager." Virginia's eyes narrowed. "Enough to kill her."

"What's your proof?" Amanda asked. Virginia was currently 0-2 in telling the truth, and this claim could make it 0-3.

"Well, I know for sure David couldn't stand either Olivia or Gina, even though they were both after him."

"Okay. What else do you know?"

"Gina lived down the hall from Olivia, so she had opportunity. Olivia was her rival for David, so that was her motive."

Amanda gave the woman a wry look. "That reasoning could also be used against Chloe. She lives in the same building and had the same opportunity. Once she and David were back together, Olivia was also Chloe's competition. Which means she had motive, too."

Virginia's eyes got teary, and the regal stare vanished. "Chloe would never kill someone. She's just not that kind of person."

Amanda wasn't ready to admit to Virginia she'd thought the same at one time.

Right now, she ached for her son. She'd seen no signs that Matt knew anything about Chloe and David. Amanda didn't feel it was her place to tell him.

"Is there anything else you haven't said that I should know?" Amanda asked, still feeling uneasy.

Virginia hesitated for a moment. "Yes, there is. But it has nothing to do with the murder."

"Tell me anyway."

"That same night David told me he and Chloe were back together, he also said he had a bigger surprise."

Amanda froze, like she'd stepped into a walk-in freezer.

Virginia leaned forward. "They were going to elope once he'd finished his week filling in at the Dark Roast. They planned to tell their friends when they got back."

Now Amanda's heart lurched, as if pierced with the knife that had killed Olivia Hager.

"Oh dear, you've turned pale. Are you okay?" Virginia reached her hand out to Amanda's.

"I'm fine," Amanda said, catching her breath. "I didn't realize they were … that serious."

"Trust me, I was surprised too. And now, if we can't prove David's innocent, they'll never be able to marry. I'm only telling you this because of all you've done to help him. But please keep their plan a secret."

Amanda nodded her agreement.

Zak signaled a HELP look and she ended her conversation with Virginia.

She watched the woman head toward the police station, wanting to believe Virginia would really come clean with the police on all she knew.

Chloe was another story. She seemed clueless how the huge secret she was keeping could hurt others. Especially Matt. If by some quirk of fate Chloe became her daughter-in-law, it would be very hard to trust her.

Amanda was still reeling from Virginia's revelations when Joe walked into the coffee shop.

He gave her a big smile. "Thought I'd stop in for a quick cup."

Seeing her husband perked her up. "It's about time," she teased, wagging her finger and giving him a mock scowl. "You haven't come in once this week."

"You're right," he said. "But there's also something I need to tell you. Can we talk outside for a minute?"

This was the day for confessions, Amanda thought. First Virginia and now Joe. Was there something in the water?

She saw he had the jitters. *Uh-oh.* Was there still a problem with that over-limit credit card?

She glanced over at Zak, who shooed the two of them out the door. "I've got this," he said to Amanda.

"Okay, so what's this big thing you want to tell me?" Amanda braced herself for more bad news as she and Joe stood together on the sunny sidewalk.

He took a deep breath. "I have a new job."

Amanda stepped back, shocked. "Wow. That's a big surprise. You didn't tell me you were job hunting." She held up her hands. "But don't keep me in suspense. Where? And when did this all happen?"

He explained that he'd accepted a position as lead accountant at a prestigious firm in downtown Chicago, with a big bump in salary. Plus, it was a hybrid company: three days in the office and two days remote, with minimal on-site client visits. Best of all, he was excited about the job.

"Remember when I was grinning like a fool on Wednesday night, and you asked me why?"

"Yes."

"Well, that day I got a call back. I was at the top of their list of candidates. I didn't tell you because I didn't want to jinx it before I got the formal offer."

"It's official then. Congratulations." Amanda wrapped her arms around him. "Did you give your two-week notice?"

Joe's smile evaporated. "Uh, that's my other news."

She cocked her head. "You don't seem happy about the other news."

A red streak began to creep up his neck. "I was going to tell you that part tonight, but well, you need to hear everything now. Something happened that I let get out of hand."

Amanda's arms dropped to her side. "Is … is there someone else, Joe?" Her heart began to race. For twenty-four years she'd never, ever thought she'd have to ask that question.

"Oh, no. Nothing like that." Joe quickly swatted away the idea. "That's something you never need to worry about."

Amanda slowly let out a sigh of relief, but her heart still raced. "What's this other news?"

The words spilled out of Joe's mouth faster than air rushing out of a punctured tire.

He'd been laid off from his job three months ago. His stories about visiting client sites weren't true. He'd camped out in libraries and community centers searching for leads and dressed for potential interviews. If nothing came through on a particular day, he'd send out resumés and head home early. That's why she'd found him so often with his head under Baby's hood when she got home from work.

"I guess my pride stopped me from telling you." The red streak had moved up to Joe's cheeks.

"Go on." Amanda said quietly, not moving.

"Those cheapskates that laid me off only gave me one month of severance. They wouldn't budge."

Amanda frowned. "Without your salary for the last two months, how did you pay our bills?"

"I figured I'd get another job right away, so I didn't file for unemployment. As a temporary stopgap, I drew down on our family savings account. That kept us on top of the mortgage payments and the home equity loan we took out last year. But a new job didn't come through as soon as I'd thought, and we still had our monthly expenses. So, I kept drawing down more from our savings until it was practically empty. I also learned that filing late for unemployment is its own quagmire."

The red streak headed north toward Joe's hairline. "With so much extra time on my hands, I kept working on Baby and maxed out the Super Fuel and the household credit card. I couldn't make the minimum monthly payments on both of them. That's when you found out there was a problem." Joe shook his head. "I can't believe I'm an accountant and made all the classic wrong moves."

A long stretch of silence passed between them. Finally,

Amanda asked, "Were you ever going to bring me in on what was happening?"

"Yes, once I was employed again. I thought I was a shoo-in for one job, but heard it went to a friend of the hiring manager. Nothing came through after that. I was getting really nervous. I know how you feel about money, and there I was digging our financial hole deeper."

"And lying to me." Amanda took a deep breath. "When did you find out you had the new job?"

"The offer officially came through ten minutes ago. I had to rush over and tell you my good news and confess to the bad stuff."

"That's the first positive thing you've done in this whole mess." Amanda stared at her husband in disbelief.

"I'm sorry to say it's going to take a few months before we get our savings back where it should be and our credit back on track," Joe said.

Amanda took another deep breath. "Joe, I'm happy about your new job. But do you know how mad I am right now?"

He glanced down at the pavement before looking up again. "I can only imagine how you feel."

"Multiply that a thousand times."

"I'm so, so sorry, Amanda."

She knew he was telling the truth. But still.

"What about Baby?" she asked. "Is she in good shape now, at least?"

Joe nodded. "For now, Baby is drivable. But I promise, I won't be tinkering with her much going forward. To be honest, I can't wait to get back to work. I guess that means I'm not ready for retirement."

"With the financial hole we're in, we'll both be working until we're ninety." Amanda crossed her arms.

Joe winced. "I'll make it up to you," he said. "And I'll never keep something this important from you again. I promise."

"I'll take you at your word. Now is there anything else you want to tell me before I get back to work?"

"Well, this may sound like bad timing, but with this surprise warm weather, I'd love to take you for that test ride tonight. Baby's waiting in the driveway. What do you think?"

Amanda raised an eyebrow. "Can we afford the gas?"

"Well, Baby's almost on empty, but we can make it a really short ride."

Amanda weighed his offer. Joe had confessed. He had a new job that he was excited about. They would be okay. Life needed to go on.

"The Dark Roast closes at 6:00 p.m. Have her waiting in the driveway," she said.

He pulled her into a hug and tried to add a kiss.

Amanda pushed him away. "Not so fast. I'm not over being mad at you."

"Are we still on for that ride?" he asked.

Amanda nodded. "I want to see the end result of your little spending spree."

"Touché," Joe answered, offering a tentative smile.

She watched Joe head out of view as she tugged on her ponytail. How had she missed all the signs that he'd lost his job?

And what signs had she missed that pointed to Olivia Hager's true murderer?

CHAPTER 29

By that afternoon the sun was shining, the sky was cloudless, and the temperature had reached a record-breaking 77 degrees. Everyone in Oak Hills seemed to be outside before a cold front was due to hit late evening.

"I can't believe it's this warm." Amanda fanned her face with her hand. Nicki hadn't changed over to AC yet. No surprise, the Dark Roast had emptied out an hour ago.

When she offered her part-timer the option of leaving early, he zipped out the door before she could say goodbye. That left Amanda alone in the coffee shop. She swore she could hear the digital clock ticking.

Spotting a top-down convertible cruise by the shop's front window gave her a kick. The driver sported a tartan plaid cap, like Cary Grant in those classic movies. The woman in the passenger seat could have been Marilyn Monroe's double, with a 1950s aqua-blue scarf tied under her chin. Amanda envisioned a scarf buried in her closet that would be perfect for Baby's test ride with Joe. It'd make the drive around the neighborhood a little more fun.

Antsy to take advantage of the unexpected weather, she started checking off shutdown tasks a half-hour early, primed to lock the coffee shop door at exactly the posted 6:00 p.m. closing time.

But she couldn't stop thinking about David, who would soon be sent to Cook County Jail. And Patrick hadn't stopped in today to update her on what the police had said when he turned in the *Stedman is guilty* letter yesterday. Had Brittany already ghosted him, and he couldn't face her mom?

When a young mother and her little girl walked in, Amanda was happy to have customers. She delivered an iced coffee and an apple juice to their table in record time.

"I'm so relieved we left the Dark Roast just before that, uh … commotion last Thursday," the mother said. "Honestly, I thought the new barista was the perfect employee. Nice guy. Great with kids. I never would have guessed he'd be a murder suspect."

That lit a spark in Amanda. "By chance, did you notice anything unusual happen in the shop that morning?" she asked.

"Well, I was a bit surprised when I heard Nicki tell the new barista she needed to run an errand and he'd be on his own. The shop was busy but, like I said, he seemed to be doing a great job. I remember checking my watch and it was 9:45. That meant I still had time to chat with my friends before I needed to leave for my 10:30 appointment."

Amanda's Sleuth Lady antenna went up. Nicki had insisted that David was fine before she'd left to run her errand. But when Amanda had arrived about fifteen minutes later, she'd noted that he wasn't acting like the David she knew.

"Did anything unusual happen after Nicki left?"

The mother nodded. "It turned out to be a big day for my Madison." The mother gave her daughter a good-girl smile. "I was at the side counter, picking up extra napkins, when a young guy walked in and placed an order. He had a terse conversation with the new barista and then left in a hurry. The barista, who'd been all smiles, headed toward the back hallway, leaving the front counter empty. He seemed to be really upset."

"Did you hear what they said?" Amanda asked.

"No, I didn't."

"Can you describe the young guy?"

"Tall and thin. I didn't get a good look at his face, but he wore a sharp black leather jacket. I remember it because that's the style of jacket I want to give my husband for his birthday."

Amanda inwardly groaned. Another muddy clue. Many young, tall, thin guys wore black leather jackets: Matt, Zak, Patrick, probably even David had one. She remembered David's boss at the Happy Bean also had a black leather jacket hanging off a chair in his office.

The mother held up her hand. "But I remember that day for another reason. The young man paid with a credit card. He dropped it, and Madison ran to pick it up. I shooed her back to the table. She loves helping others, but she's gotten into this horrible habit of picking up things people drop on the floor and handing them back. I keep telling her to let the person know they've dropped something and not touch it." The woman shuddered. "All those germs."

"But Mommy, I never pick up things strangers drop anymore," the little girl said proudly. "Germs are yucky."

"Yes, Madison. And you're doing a perfect job." She signaled to her daughter it was time to leave. They waved goodbye as they walked out the front door.

Amanda was happy the little girl had stopped her bad habit, and happier the credit card might give her a clue to the identity of the young man who had so upset David.

On her way to Nicki's office to dig through the credit card receipts, Amanda halted when Raymond Cartel lumbered into the shop at the pace of a sloth.

He pulled out a faded red bandanna, wiped his brow, then jammed it back into the pocket of his farmer jeans. "I have something to say to you, and I need to sit down when I do."

Another request for a private talk. Amanda hoped this one would go better.

After she guided him to the closest table, Raymond folded his hands and stared straight at her. "I want to make amends, no matter how much time has passed."

"I'm listening," she said. Was this about 1944 or Olivia's murder? Or both?

"You asked me yesterday if I knew your grandfather, Henry Allen. I said I didn't. But I did."

Amanda felt like she'd been sucker punched. "Why did you lie?"

"I like to think of it more as not telling the whole truth. The past is hard for me to talk about. Still, it's something you need to hear."

"I'm still listening."

"Henry Allen saved a five-year-old boy from drowning in Salt Creek back in 1944." Raymond paused. "That boy was me. And Henry suffered for it."

Amanda pulled her chair closer to his.

"I'll try to give you the short version," he began. "A local gang pressured my dad into making me their decoy for a Brinks truck robbery on the outskirts of Oak Hills. But the plan fell apart when I didn't show up, and a Brinks guard got shot and killed by one of the gang members. They all scattered like scaredy-cats, while the truck with the money in it screeched off to Oak Hills."

He took a deep breath. "It was hotter than the dickens that day. Tired of waiting for the Brinks truck, like any little boy would do, I snuck off to take a quick dip in Salt Creek. I was probably a quarter mile from where I was supposed to be waiting. I was lucky Henry walked by the creek just as I tumbled on the slippery rocks. I hit my head, and he saved me from drowning. Then we both heard a rifle shot in the distance. Henry said he'd go check it out and I should run the other way. And that's what I did."

Raymond rubbed his chin. "Henry walked into the crime scene just as the police arrived. The gang came out of the woods and pointed the finger at Henry. In those days, they only matched the type of rifle with the bullet. They couldn't match a specific bullet to a specific rifle. Anyway, he was arrested for the murder and sentenced to five years in the juvenile home."

Raymond wiped his brow again with his bandana. "His arrest was all my fault because I ran off."

Amanda sat quiet for a moment, processing what Raymond has just told her. "You didn't tell anyone what really happened?" she finally asked.

Raymond shook his head. "I was going to, but right away my dad heard the gang was furious they hadn't gotten their money because I wasn't where I was supposed to be. He worried up a storm they would take revenge on our family. As soon as it got dark we skedaddled to Washington State, stopped being the Franklins, and became the Cartels. My first name changed from George to Raymond. Easy to do in those days. My folks didn't live long after that. I was on my own for many years. Never married. I didn't want anyone to know about my story or my original name."

He sighed. "I've always felt guilty about Henry getting the short end of the stick."

A stillness hung over the shop as Amanda reached out and touched Raymond's arm. "I never met my grandfather. And although this was painful to hear, thank you for telling me. But why did you wait all these years to tell your story?"

"I didn't want what happened to your grandfather to happen to David Stedman. I'm thinking someone else killed that young woman. I'd seen him around the Valley Lane condos. Nice guy and always friendly. I knew he visited a young lady living on the fifth floor quite a lot lately. I even saw him walking into her condo the day before the murder."

Amanda offered a weak smile. Gina wasn't the only person who had known about Chloe and David.

"Yesterday, when I finally opened that grocery bag and found the knife with the note, I knew in my heart whoever killed the young woman was trying to pin it on Stedman instead. I wasn't sure what to do. I didn't want to give the police anything they'd try to use against me, either. When I was lying in that hospital, they kept asking me questions." He made a long face. "Police still make me nervous."

"But yesterday you turned in the knife."

"It was the right thing to do. And then before we parted company outside the police station, you mentioned your grandfather's name. I realized I needed to be honest with you.

Raymond wagged his finger at Amanda. "Never think harshly of your grandfather having to serve time in the juvenile home. He saved my life and got cheated out of his own. I don't want David Stedman to get cheated out of his life."

"With all that happened years ago, why did you return to Oak Hills?" Amanda asked.

"I thought coming back here might make me happy again. And it has, a little. But the hurt is still there."

"Thank you for telling me the true story. I'm going to tell my mother. Henry Allen was her father. She needs to know what really happened."

"Well, I'm glad I did one thing right today. And now I'm going to do a second right thing. I'm going to head over to the police station and ask them how to fix their records on Henry Allen. I don't know the name of the gang member who killed the guard. But I do know it wasn't your grandfather." He pulled his shoulders back and sat up straight. "I feel better coming clean. Now I guess I have to face the music."

An old saying popped into Amanda's head as Raymond left, a lot steadier and faster than when he'd walked in.

Better late than never.

It was the same for finally taking his name off her suspect list.

CHAPTER 30

Amanda was heading back to Nicki's office to dig into those credit-card receipts when a phone call from her bestie stopped her.

"Amanda, I'll make this quick. I just remembered something before I—"

"*Boarding Flight 251, Group 9.*"

Amanda frowned. "Where are you?"

"I'm at the Orlando airport, getting ready to board my flight."

"I thought you were flying home tomorrow."

"All I want to say right now is that alligators are more mobile than people think."

"Alligators? Are you okay?"

"I'm fine, but I'll tell you later."

"I can't wait to hear *that* story," Amanda said.

"You will. In the meantime, there's something I forgot to tell you about. You need to check the merchant credit-card receipts for the past week."

Nicki explained that unsigned merchant credit card receipts meant she wouldn't get reimbursed for the sale amount. Her processor was very fussy about that. She couldn't wait to upgrade to the new tap-and-go machines that didn't require signatures.

"You'll need to go all the way back to the day the police arrested David. You should have nine days' worth, counting today. All you have to do is pull out the unsigned ones. They're usually for small amounts, but they add up. I spent more than I thought I would this week, and I don't want to lose out on any money I'm rightfully owed. I'll contact the customers. You don't have to worry about that part."

"No problem. I'll find the receipts." Amanda couldn't believe her luck. Nicki wanted her to check the same credit-card receipts she hoped would uncover the name of the customer David had talked to just before his attitude had changed so radically the morning of his arrest.

"*Final boarding call.*"

"Wait. One more thing." Nicki's words sped up. "Last night, I remembered something one of my staff told me. A couple of weeks ago a nice guy tried to pay for a girl's order, and she lit into him. He stormed out. The person who mentioned it didn't understand why she was so nasty and felt sorry for the guy. The girl was Olivia Hager. The guy, I believe, was that friend of Matt's. The one who was my first customer after I reopened last Thursday."

"*The doors close in one minute.*"

"Gotta go. Bye."

Before Amanda could ask anything more, Nicki hung up.

She stared at her phone. Nicki's tip had just connected Patrick and Olivia. That was a surprise. He sounded just like Zak, who had a liking for Olivia that wasn't returned. Definitely something to check into. But right now, she was on a mission.

Hustling to Nicki's office, she grabbed the merchant credit-card receipts bin and shot back to the front counter in the still empty shop.

She quickly sorted them into piles by date, checking for customer signatures. The unsigned receipts totaled $155.25. Absolutely worth the effort.

Except there was a problem. Last Thursday's receipts, the day of David's arrest, were missing.

Amanda looked up as the front door opened and Officer Evans peered inside. "Any chance I could get one last cup of coffee to go? I'm on the late shift."

Amanda waved the officer in. "You're in luck."

She pushed the merchant receipts out of sight and grabbed an empty cup. "I heard about the big fight last night at the beer garden."

"Mm-hmm." Evans said nothing more as she reached for the cream pitcher.

"Anything you can tell me about the knife Raymond Cartel brought in yesterday afternoon?"

Evans picked up a stirrer and a lid. "You know I can't tell you anything unless it's been deemed public record." She gave Amanda a wry glance.

Amanda nodded. No surprise Evans was tight-lipped. But she wasn't giving up.

"What about the letter left at my feet by that jogger who pushed me down Monday night?" Amanda pushed the steaming cup across the counter.

"Again, no. But might I add again, you need to be mindful of your surroundings, especially after dark."

"Did you check out the letter we found yesterday morning outside the shop?" Amanda asked. "It has the same message as the other anonymous ones left around Oak Hills businesses."

Evans shook her head as she stirred in cream. "I wasn't aware of an additional anonymous letter being turned in. Especially from the Dark Roast. No one said anything about it at the daily briefing."

Amanda frowned. "That's odd. Patrick said he'd drop it off."

Evans snapped on the lid. "Thanks for the heads-up, Amanda. I'll check on it." Her phone rang. "Sorry. Have to get this." She turned her back to Amanda. "Evans here."

Amanda tried not to listen, but she faintly heard the words *"bring in for questioning"* come through the phone.

"Okay, I'm less than five minutes away on foot. I'll meet you there." Evans grabbed the cup of coffee from the counter and rushed out, throwing Amanda a brief goodbye wave.

Amanda watched through the front window as Evans disappeared down the sidewalk in the same direction as Valley Lane Condos. Was that where she was headed? Who were the police bringing in for questioning—and why?

Amanda hoped fresh evidence had surfaced. She wasn't ready to give up on David.

When she picked up the shop's procedure manual to put it away, a stack of rubber-banded receipts with last Thursday's date fell to the counter.

Her heart leaped.

The missing merchant receipts had shown up!

How they'd gotten stuck in the procedure manual wasn't her concern right now. She needed to find the receipt time stamped after 9:45 and before 10:06 a.m.

She shoved the procedure manual back into its assigned place. When she turned, she saw a police car barrel down the street.

Were they going to the same place as Evans?

In one swift move, Amanda grabbed her coat, dropped her cell phone into a side pocket, and stowed the merchant receipts from last Thursday into the other pocket. She would check the names and time stamps once she figured out what Evans and the police were up to.

She flipped off the lights, switched the OPEN sign to CLOSED, and locked the front door.

As she scurried down the sidewalk, Officer Evans dashed

past the *Welcome to Oak Hills Business District* sign and turned down Valley Lane. She was soon out of sight.

Amanda doubled her speed. Hearing Brittany's text tone, she pulled her phone out of her coat pocket and slowed down.

Going to Busse Woods with Patrick to watch model airplanes.

So, Brittany hadn't ghosted Patrick. Then what had he done with the *Stedman is guilty* letter? She added it to her list of open questions and shoved the phone back into her coat pocket. Back on a fast pace, she turned down Valley Lane.

Ahead, Amanda spotted a squad car in front of the main entrance to the condo building. Evans stood on the sidewalk.

"Please, please don't let it be Chloe they want to question," she said aloud to herself. Evidence had pointed to Chloe, yet even two-timing Matt hadn't completely wiped out the soft spot she'd built up for the young woman.

As if answering her plea, Chloe exited the front door. Then she calmly walked to her car in the side parking lot and drove off as if nothing were amiss.

None of the officers who glanced in Chloe's direction reacted.

Amanda felt a twinge of relief. As a regular customer at the Dark Roast, Evans would have recognized Chloe. She wasn't the reason the police were here. Was it for Gina? Or someone else?

Catching up to Evans on the sidewalk, Amanda tapped the officer on the shoulder. Evans swung around.

"I can't talk to you now, Amanda. We're here on official police business," Evans said in a firm, no-nonsense voice.

Amanda didn't move. "I have new information. It concerns David and a customer who stopped in at the Dark Roast just before I arrived the morning of the arrest," she said. "They told me something I think you might want to know."

Evans frowned. "I'd advise you to move away."

"You don't understand—"

"I don't want to say this again, Amanda. Move away and let us do our jobs, please." She turned back around and focused on the tablet in her hand.

Disappointed, Amanda stepped back as Officer Lee scurried out the front door of the condo building toward Evans.

"Our person of interest isn't here," Amanda overheard him say.

"Did you have the right unit?" Evans asked.

"Yes," he said. "There was no answer at 309."

Curiosity washed over Amanda. Why did the police want to talk to Gina Rohmer or her sister?

Whichever. If this had to do with Gina, Amanda knew something Evans needed to know. Right away. Tentatively walking up to the officer once more, Amanda cleared her throat loud enough to get her attention.

Evans glared. "Amanda, didn't I tell you to leave?"

Amanda nodded. "I'm sorry, Officer, but it's important. I'll keep it short. The person currently staying in 309 uses the stairwell a lot."

Evans gave her a puzzled look, then hustled toward Lee.

Amanda heard her say, "Make sure you do a thorough check of the stairwell."

Yes, Gina, you're right, Amanda told herself. *Revenge can be sweet.*

On the short walk home, she pulled the stack of last Thursday's merchant receipts out of her coat pocket. She still needed to confirm who'd caused David's demeanor to change so drastically that morning.

It was a smaller stack than the other days. No surprise. The Dark Roast had been closed for almost an hour after David's arrest, and Nicki had complained that customers had been scarce for the rest of the day.

Amanda quickly skimmed through the receipts. Only one was timestamped between when Nicki left David in charge of the

Dark Roast at 9:45 and Amanda had her Panda Bear in hand at 10:06. The name roared out at Amanda. She halted abruptly.

Her hands shook as she pulled out her phone. An online search revealed the person's address as Valley Lane Condominiums, Unit 307. The unit next door to Olivia Hager's. The unit that had recently been sold to a new owner, whose name hadn't been added to the building's directory.

Amanda gulped.

This person had upset David at the Dark Roast just before his arrest last Thursday morning.

This person had been publicly embarrassed by Olivia.

This person had probably volunteered to help on the GoFundMe campaign, so it looked like they were David's friend.

This person could own a pair of the popular black running shoes with the shiny silver label on the back.

This person never turned in the *Stedman is guilty* letter left outside the Dark Roast to the police and had probably written all the letters.

And right now, this person was driving her daughter to Busse Woods.

Amanda so hoped she was wrong.

CHAPTER 31

Amanda dashed the rest of the way home as if in hyperdrive, propelled by shock, dread, and fear.

She gulped air like a marathon runner crossing the finish line. It was bad timing that the neighbor she least wanted to see popped up out of nowhere.

"Hey, Amanda. Didn't know you were into jogging. Ha, ha." Frank snickered.

Bent over, trying to catch her breath, she waved him away as she frantically scanned the driveway.

Where was the van?

"Well, I can tell someone's in a bad mood." Frank crossed his arms. "If you're looking for Joe, he took the van to get a leak fixed in the front tire. You just missed him."

Amanda spied Baby parked in the driveway, facing the street. The exterior paint job on the 1964 Ford Mustang gleamed, and the windows sparkled. The car was ready for Joe's promised test drive after she got home from work.

She ran into the house and grabbed the Mustang's keychain off the rack. For a moment she hesitated. Would Joe be furious if she took his beloved pony car without asking?

Amanda shrugged off the question with a yank of her ponytail. Their daughter was in danger. Time to take action first and ask for forgiveness later. Plus, Joe had said he wanted her to take a test drive. He just wouldn't be the driver.

Frank's jaw dropped when she opened the Mustang's driver-side door. He ran to the front of the car and flung his body, spread-eagled, across the hood.

"No, you don't! This is Joe's car," he cried.

Amanda blurted out the first response that popped into her head as she slipped into the driver's seat. "If you don't get out of my way, Frank, I'll run you over." The engine roared with the first turn of the key. Frank leaped off the hood, landing on a side patch of grass.

She slammed the door shut, threw the gearshift into drive, and stomped on the gas pedal.

The car surged forward.

Amanda's body shot backwards, despite the buckled seatbelt. She tightened her grip on the steering wheel. Glancing in the rearview mirror, she saw Frank standing at the edge of their driveway, jaw hanging open.

Eyes on the road ahead, one hand on the steering wheel, she pulled out her phone. She had to let the police know where the probable killer of Olivia Hager was headed.

As she sped down First Street, it dawned on her that the 60-year-old car didn't have a Bluetooth connection. She couldn't wrestle with her cell phone while driving Joe's revved-up super-charged sports car.

She tossed it on the passenger seat and gripped the steering wheel with both hands.

She'd call at the stoplight.

The first light stayed green. Amanda sailed through.

The second, third, and fourth lights also stayed green, as if she'd won the green-light lottery. That never happened.

Her luck hit a snag at the gridlocked intersection in front of the Oak Hills Senior Center. The Spring Fling, advertised as a late afternoon event on the poster the Logans had taped up at the Dark Roast, must have just ended.

Amanda's stomach sank.

The scene in front of her looked like a road rally gone horribly wrong. Multiple cars littered the intersection and more streamed out of the parking lot, adding to the chaos.

A small gap widened in the middle of the deadlock. She stepped on the gas at the same time a shiny, newer-model white Cadillac rambled directly into Baby's path. Trying to swerve out of the way, Amanda couldn't stop the Mustang from clipping the Caddy's front bumper.

Of course it would be the Logans' car. They glared at Amanda through their front windshield. She gave a little "so sorry" wave and maneuvered Baby through the rest of the tight opening. She'd confess to fleeing the scene of an accident once she knew Brittany was safe.

Back in the clear, she put pedal to the metal. The Mustang sprung forward.

"Nice job, Baby," she said, patting the dashboard.

Her green-light lottery streak ended at the next light.

Amanda hit the brakes, squealed to a stop, and lunged for her cell phone lying on the passenger seat. She'd already decided calling 911 could lead to a lot of explaining and delay. Telling Evans directly what she just uncovered and her concern for Brittany's safety would mean the officer could react immediately.

"You have reached the Oak Hills Police Station. Please listen to this message—"

Amanda punched 0 to get to a live person.

"Oak Hills Police Station. May I help you?" the monotone voice asked.

"It's urgent I talk to Officer Evans. Tell her it's Amanda Knightly calling."

"Please hold."

Silence.

Hurry it up, Evans.

As the traffic lessened, the line of cars behind her honked a not-so-gentle reminder she could turn right on red. A glance in the rearview mirror showed a driver shaking his fist as a familiar voice finally came through the phone.

"Amanda, it's Officer Evans. What's the emergency?"

"I know who killed Olivia Hager."

There was a short pause before Evans said, "David Stedman was arrested and charged and is being arraigned for the homicide."

"I know that. I'm only asking you hear me out."

"Is this a hunch? Or something solid?"

"I believe it's solid. On top of that, my daughter could be harmed." Amanda couldn't hold back from breaking into sobs. Saying her fear out loud had made it more real.

"First you need to calm down, Amanda. Then tell me what's going on."

Amanda quickly gave a *Reader's Digest* version of why and where she was going.

"This isn't something you should handle on your own," Evans said sharply. "I'll call in a squad. Wait where you are and we'll connect with you."

Amanda briefly considered staying put. Then she tossed the phone back onto the seat beside her and took off. It made more sense to keep going and apologize to Evans later for not waiting for the police. She could lose precious minutes, with Brittany in grave danger.

That was when Amanda glanced at the fuel gauge and tried not to panic even more. The arrow pointed way too close to EMPTY. Joe had said Baby was low on gas, but she couldn't stop now.

The last mile seemed like an eternity. Amanda finally caught sight of the familiar rectangular sign for Busse Woods. Budding trees and open fields of green grass greeted Amanda as she took a fast left turn into the entrance and sped toward the parking lot near the model plane airshow field.

The small lot was crammed full of drivers in pursuit of a parking spot.

She checked the gas gauge once again and groaned. The arrow had moved way past EMPTY. Baby was running on fumes.

Things didn't look good.

She clutched the steering wheel and pressed on. There had to be a space tucked away somewhere.

A distant, intermittent buzz pulled Amanda's focus upward. A model airplane soared in the sky, close enough for her to make out its red, white, and blue colors. A second yellow-and- black-striped plane joined, and the two maneuvered as if on a dance floor. Soon squadrons of small planes of all colors surrounded them, plummeting and then swooping skyward, filling the wild blue yonder.

A crowd had gathered on the edge of the airfield, cheering as if watching a dogfight between enemy aircraft in an old-time movie. There had to be several hundred onlookers.

Patrick and Brittany could be anywhere in this crowd. At least her daughter might be safe surrounded by other people, she reasoned.

Getting more uptight by the second, she continued to inch Baby forward without luck. Finally, she spied a tiny opening halfway on the asphalt and halfway on the grass, wedged between two parked monster trucks. It definitely wasn't a legal spot, but finding her daughter beat obeying the rules. Heck, she'd already left the scene after a car accident.

Amanda pointed Joe's pride and joy toward the opening. But the harder she pressed the gas pedal, the slower Baby moved.

The screech of scraping metal from the Mustang's underside made her wince. The car let out a last gasp and stopped dead.

Baby had run over something. And run out of gas.

"It doesn't matter," Amanda told herself out loud. "I'm here."

Then she spied the black car that had been parked in front of her family's house several times this past week.

Patrick's Porsche.

Please don't let me be too late.

———

Amanda sprinted up the deserted hill that bordered the overflowing parking lot and the airshow field. Stopping at a picnic shelter to catch her breath, she scanned the bodies milling at a distance below her, watching the show on the field.

Recognizing a neon-orange baseball cap on the tail end of the crowd gave her hope. It was identical to the one Brittany often wore. The young woman, with her back to Amanda, had her daughter's height and hair color. Then she noticed the guy, built like a linebacker for the Chicago Bears, his arm draped around the girl. That definitely wasn't Patrick. And looking closer, she saw it wasn't Brittany, either.

Amanda did a 180-degree turn and spotted another couple, just inside another shelter about a hundred feet farther up the hill. They weren't watching the model planes; they were staring at each other. And they were alone.

This time, she knew for sure it was Brittany's silhouette. Patrick faced her daughter, wearing a red leather jacket. Amanda could clearly see his deep frown. He glanced back and forth between the ground and Brittany as if confused and looking for better answers.

Brittany backed ever so slightly away from him.

Amanda dived behind a tree and peeked around the trunk. She watched Brittany plant her hands on her hips, signaling the conversation had ended. Patrick reached for Brittany's hand several times, but she vigorously shook her head and waved him away. His look of confusion quickly turned icy.

Amanda shot a worried glance back at the parking lot. No police cars were in sight. She hadn't heard sirens, either.

She reached into her pocket to alert Evans where she was and silently groaned. She'd left her phone on Baby's passenger seat.

Patrick's glare grew darker, setting off alarm bells in Amanda's brain. She couldn't wait for the police. She had to protect her daughter before things got worse. But she needed to be smart about it.

Amanda made a beeline into the woods. Under the cover of the trees, she quietly crept forward until she was close enough to hear the couple's conversation.

"Patrick, you don't seem to get what I just said. I've had a wonderful time with you this past week, but I'm not sure about our future." Brittany turned away, as if not looking at him would soften her message.

"If you felt that way, why did you agree to come here with me?" Patrick snapped, so sharply it was all Amanda could do not to gasp out loud and blow her cover.

"I thought it would be a nice way to end our dating relationship, but not our friendship."

"Friendship?" Patrick threw up his hands. "Is that all you think this is? The expensive dinners, going to clubs?" He wagged his finger at her. "And don't forget the flowers I sent you. Why do you think I did all that?" he sneered. "Because we were *friends*?"

Brittany didn't answer.

Patrick's right hand reached up to Brittany's chin and turned it toward his so they stood face to face again. His lips had drawn together into a tight line, but Amanda could see only her daughter's back.

"Boy, was I stupid," Patrick went on. "I should have recognized the signs when you stood me up for coffee Tuesday morning. It was the start of a change in attitude I am very familiar with."

"I'm sorry," Brittany said. She gave a little shrug.

Patrick jammed his hands into his jeans pockets. "Okay, I get it now. We can be friends, but nothing more. How about it's not you, it's me? Or it's just not the right time? Trust me, I've heard them all."

"I didn't mean to hurt you." Brittany stared down at the ground. Amanda was glad Brittany had been honest. But it wasn't what Patrick wanted to hear. Which made her nervous.

She scoured the parking lot again. Still no police.

Suddenly Patrick grabbed Brittany's left arm, spun her body around, and pinned her to his left side, giving Amanda a full view of her terrified daughter.

"Let go of me. What do you think you're doing?" Brittany cried out as she struggled to yank her arm out of his grip.

Amanda leaped out of her hiding place and charged full force toward the couple, her heart pounding like it would burst out of her chest.

CHAPTER 32

Patrick's jaw dropped in surprise as Amanda charged toward them. Brittany shrieked.

In one swift move, Patrick jerked a pocketknife out of his jacket and brought it up to Brittany's neck. "Don't come any closer, Mrs. Knightly," he warned, his voice steely.

"Mom! Help me!" Brittany screamed, struggling to lean away from the knife's blade.

Amanda halted. Her stomach rolled. Her heart was in her throat. She told herself to keep things calm as she held up her hands. "Take it easy, Patrick. I'll do whatever you say. You don't need to hurt Brittany."

Patrick smirked. "Why shouldn't I? She's just like all the other girls. I take them to expensive restaurants and clubs. I send flowers and try to be the perfect boyfriend. But in the end, I get tossed aside."

Seeing his bitter expression up close, Amanda cringed. This was a side of Patrick she'd never witnessed. Or thought possible. It set off more alarm bells.

"Your daughter is no different from the rest. She thought nothing of using me," Patrick added with an edge of sarcasm.

Amanda feared if she shouted for help, he might use the knife on Brittany. If she could keep him talking, it might temper his anger until the police arrived. Very soon, she hoped.

She lowered her hands slowly and took a deep breath. Then she said gently, "I'm sorry that things haven't worked out the way you wanted."

Patrick's tone turned matter of fact. "Well, they didn't work out the way I wanted with Olivia either. But I didn't plan to kill her. It just happened."

Amanda froze at Patrick's nonchalant confession. He'd admitted what she dreaded. With no sign of remorse.

She watched the color drain from Brittany's face and willed herself to stay strong.

Patrick continued to press the knife against Brittany's now ghost-white skin. "Just like all the others, Olivia accepted my dates. She made me believe that she liked me. Maybe even loved me."

He tightened his arm around Brittany. She didn't move, but her eyes pleaded with Amanda.

"Then what happened?" Amanda concentrated on keeping him talking—and her terror from showing.

"When Olivia suddenly became busy whenever I called or texted, I knew what would come next. She seemed to enjoy embarrassing me. Like that time at the Dark Roast. And then that day at the Happy Bean when she brutally put me down and then hung around the front counter, trying to get David's attention. He was the big jock in high school, the rugged outdoors guy, the one all the girls fell all over. Not me. Not the math geek who couldn't throw a decent pitch. Not the shrimp everyone made fun of. Olivia made it clear it was David or nobody."

Brittany tried to wiggle out of Patrick's grasp. He pulled her closer.

"That must have been hard to hear." Amanda nodded as if she were on his side.

"It was. And that's what Olivia called me when I stopped by her apartment that night after David left. A nobody. Can you believe that? After all the money and time that I spent on her."

Patrick let out a jarring laugh and tightened his grip on the knife at Brittany's neck.

Brittany let out a sob. Her body shook as she sucked in air.

Amanda wanted to run to her daughter and wrap her arms around her. But she dared not move or take her eyes off Patrick.

He wasn't finished. "If that knife hadn't been on Olivia's kitchen counter, maybe nothing would have happened. But she taunted me. Told me I was crazy if I thought she'd be interested in an accounting nerd like me." He added a snarky emphasis on *nerd*, and his face hardened. "She only wanted David. That tipped it for me."

"Then what happened?" Amanda said carefully, as Brittany's sobs got louder.

"I picked up the knife and took a swipe at her, just to scare her. But somehow the swipe turned into a deep slash." He shook his head. "I couldn't believe what I had done."

"Did you try to save her?" Amanda steeled herself to stay composed on the outside while shaking on the inside.

"It was too late. I could tell she was dead. I grabbed the knife and slipped out with no one seeing me. Somehow, I missed getting blood on my clothes." He said it as emotionlessly as if describing something he did daily.

Amanda froze. Patrick had confessed to killing Olivia. And Brittany had heard his full confession as a second witness. If the trauma didn't erase it from her memory. Amanda wondered if not remembering would be better.

"You need to tell your story to the police, Patrick," she said. "But don't hurt Brittany. That won't help you."

"I don't want to hurt her. So don't make me," he sneered.

"I won't." Amanda slowly edged closer as Brittany sobbed softly.

"Well, we've got that settled." Patrick's sarcastic smile transformed into a frown. "But David? I wanted him to rot in jail."

Amanda steeled herself and pressed on. "I thought David was your friend. You even helped set up his GoFundMe campaign. You were the go-to person for tax questions."

Patrick shrugged. "You're right. I don't hate David. I hate what David represents. Everything I'm not."

A stream of silent tears rolled down Brittany's cheeks.

Patrick hadn't finished. "After I snuck out of Olivia's condo, I returned to my place. I had to get rid of the knife. I took a quick jog and buried it in the backyard of a deserted house where I thought it wouldn't be found. I even included a stupid typed note saying David was guilty."

"And then the police showed up at Valley Lane Condos," Amanda said.

Patrick nodded. "I was getting nervous having Olivia's dead body right next door to me. But one of the neighbors had already called for a wellness check, the police said when they knocked on my door. It was easy to point suspicion toward David, since I saw him shove Olivia at the Happy Bean not too long ago. Even the manager knew about it. David wasn't always so perfect," he added with an ugly twist to his mouth.

He shook his head. "Of course, no one suspected me. I guess being known as a geeky accountant who had a hard time getting dates even though I had a cool car finally worked to my advantage."

Brittany was silent.

Even though she was boiling inside, Amanda kept her cool. *Keep him talking. The police should be here any minute.*

"The next morning you stopped in at the Dark Roast and said something that upset David."

"I was trying to be funny. Made a crude remark about Olivia's murder. You know, be a tough guy. But David got all crazed."

"And you knew David had been arrested when you came back a second time to the Dark Roast, but you acted surprised about it. Do I have that right?"

"Yes. I had watched the whole thing from across the street. When the police arrested David, I figured I'd be in the clear."

"And you created all those *Stedman is guilty* letters."

He let out a cynical laugh. "Yep. I even personalized one for you, Mrs. Knightly. By the way, I didn't mean to knock you down, only frighten you. Sorry about that."

Amanda gave him a withering stare. "You're lucky it was my knee instead of my head that hit the sidewalk." She frowned. "That same night you also attacked Raymond Cartel, correct?"

"Right again. But it was his own fault."

"How's that?"

Patrick shrugged. "When I found out it wasn't a deserted house, and that some old man lived there, I went back to dig up the knife. But it was gone."

"Did you think you'd get it back by hitting him in the head?"

"I just wanted to get the knife back. I had already decided burying it was a dumb idea. My new plan was to toss it into Lake Michigan to make sure it could never be found."

"Fortunately, Raymond will recover," Amanda said. "But back to the letters. You never turned in the one we got at the Dark Roast to the police. Am I correct?"

"Right again, Mrs. Knightly. I took it home and shredded it. I realized the letters might be traced back to me, even though I wore gloves when I made them. Plus, those messy stick-on letters should be left to dumb little kids." He laughed as if he'd told a clever joke.

His laughter stopped as quickly as it started. "I thought I had it all figured out," he said flatly. "But with you snooping around, Mrs. Knightly, not believing David killed Olivia, I got worried it was only a matter of time before my luck ran out. Word had already surfaced that a suspicious knife had been found. I decided I needed to disappear quickly to where I wouldn't be found."

"Where would that be?"

"I hadn't figured that out." Patrick shook his head. "Ha! What a joke. I had my car packed, ready to leave, but I wanted to give Brittany the chance to run away with me. Accountants can be romantic and do spur-of-the-moment things. But I guess that won't happen now, will it?"

Brittany flashed a weak but flirtatious smile. "Why would you say that? Of course I want to go away with you."

Amanda silently applauded Brittany. Her daughter had pulled herself together to take Patrick off guard.

Patrick appeared confused. Then he smirked.

"Nice try, Brittany. If only you had said that earlier. But now I know it's all an act." Patrick yanked her closer to him. "You only want to be my friend. Well, I don't want to be just friends."

He tightened his grip on her. "I need to get out of here, and you and your mother are going to help me."

"Not so fast." Amanda held up her hand. "There's two of us and one of you." She didn't say the police were on their way. He might do something horrific out of desperation.

Patrick chuckled and shook his head. "But you see, Mrs. Knightly, I've got a knife. And your daughter. So, I'm calling the shots. And we're all going to walk down the hill, nice and slowly, to my car."

Patrick took two steps toward Amanda, with Brittany cocooned in his left arm. His right hand held the small knife, discreetly pointed at Brittany's neck. "Please join us, Mrs. Knightly. Here, on my right side. We'll walk together to the parking lot at a steady pace so as not to draw attention. Don't forget, I can easily hurt your daughter if you decide to do something stupid." His clenched lips broke into a grim smile. His voice had a hard edge.

Amanda had no choice. She couldn't let her daughter go

anywhere with that madman. She gritted her teeth and fell into step next to Patrick.

He continued to hold the pocketknife against Brittany's neck as they started down the hill. Brittany walked stiffly with a look of panic on her face.

Amanda took a quick account of the scene in front of them. The buzz of airplanes overhead had not let up. Spectators, bikers, and vehicles dotted the landscape. The parking lot was jammed. Was this why the police hadn't showed?

With the crowd focused on the final dramatic minutes of competition in the sky, no one glanced in their direction as they headed toward Patrick's car, now less than fifty yards away.

Amanda's heart beat like an out-of-control drum.

She didn't know how she'd stop Patrick, but one thing she did know.

Her daughter would only be forced into Patrick's car over Amanda's dead body.

CHAPTER 33

Amanda hid her fear behind a blank mask as she trudged next to a determined, angry Patrick and a weeping, shaking Brittany.

If she screamed, Patrick might do something drastic. Then she and Brittany would be in an even worse predicament. If she kept quiet, it might buy more time for the police to arrive. She scanned the perimeter of the field. No security in sight.

The squadron of model airplanes continued to whirl and dive skyward. Amanda tried to mouth "HELP" as they neared the outskirts of the crowd. She gave up. All eyes were on the sky and the beginning of the grand finale.

The buzz from a single model airplane caught Amanda's attention. The whirr grew louder and louder. Directly ahead of them, an errant plane vroomed sharply down, then zoomed up, then down again.

It was on a collision path towards the three of them.

"Watch out!" Amanda yelled.

She leaned right, Brittany leaned left.

Patrick dropped his grip on Brittany, along with the pocketknife.

Amanda grabbed Brittany's hand, and the two of them ran. Neither of them looked back as they frantically maneuvered between spectators watching the show in the sky.

They had to get somewhere safe. And what better place than Baby, which sat like a fortress in the parking lot, currently immobile but impenetrable to Patrick's knife.

As she pulled her daughter toward the parking lot, Brittany's hand was ripped away. Amanda turned, startled to see Patrick. He had swung Brittany toward him, once more wrapping her tightly against him.

Amanda gasped as Patrick once again aimed the knife at her daughter's throat. She had to stop him.

"I warned you," he said through gritted teeth as Brittany struggled to get out of his grasp.

"And I'm warning you," Amanda said. She landed a sharp kick to his shin, as hard and as swift as she could.

Patrick let out a yelp. The knife slipped out of his hand and fell to the grass. He gave Brittany a sharp shove.

She cried out, then fell forward. Her body hit the ground hard.

Patrick stared in disbelief for a brief moment, then spun around and disappeared, limping, into the crowd.

Amanda dropped on her knees next to her daughter, who was lying way too still.

For a moment she panicked. Why wasn't she moving?

Then Brittany's eyes opened ever so slightly. She sat up slowly, breathing hard. "Where's Patrick?" she asked in a panic.

Amanda put her arm around her daughter. "Don't worry about Patrick. He staggered away and left the knife behind. Right now, you need to stay where you are."

Brittany nodded and added a weak smile. "Mom, I can't believe you kicked him so hard. You saved me."

"You also need to thank your dad. He's the one who gave me the idea."

A sudden wail in the distance made Amanda turn her head. Were those police sirens? Finally.

She gently unwrapped her arm from Brittany and stood up. Taking a 360 scan of the area, she was relieved to see Evans and three officers emerge through the crowd. Spectators gawked as the police hurried her way.

"Amanda, there … you … are," Evans said before catching her breath. "We had to ditch our squad cars because of the jammed lot."

Evans immediately took charge, looking like a maestro poised at the podium at the start of a symphony performance.

"Tell me what happened," she directed Amanda.

Amanda blurted out, "Patrick Williams threatened to stab my daughter with a pocketknife. I fought back with a quick kick to his shin and he ran away. But before all that happened, he confessed to killing Olivia Hager. Right now he could be anywhere."

Her hand reached out to Brittany. "I'm very worried my daughter's badly hurt."

Brittany, still sitting on the grass, shook her head. "Patrick gave me a rough shove and I fell to the ground. I think I got the wind knocked out of me. But I'm feeling better now."

Evans looked down at Brittany. "The EMTs are following us. They'll take care of you." She looked back at Amanda. "Is Williams still armed?"

"He dropped the knife. It's over there." She pointed to where it had fallen on the grass. "I don't know if he's carrying anything else."

"Tag it and bag it," Evans directed the nearest officer, who hurried toward the knife. She then asked Amanda, "Where was he headed?"

"He melted into the crowd." Amanda nodded toward the black Porsche. "That's his car. It's blocked in by a pickup truck. He's probably somewhere on foot."

"What's he wearing?"

Brittany looked up. "Jeans, black running shoes, black T-shirt, and a red leather jacket."

Evans directed a second officer to Patrick's car. "Wait there in case he tries to flee in it."

She pointed to the third officer. "Find whoever is running this show and tell them they need to stop the grand finale but not frighten the crowd. They should ask everyone to leave Busse Woods. Quickly and orderly. We don't want a stampede. I'm calling in more support."

Call made, Evans turned back to Amanda. "Tell me what led up to this attack. Start at the beginning when you arrived."

"I found Patrick and my daughter Brittany in a heated discussion up there." Amanda pointed toward the isolated shelter on the hill where she had first seen them.

She had just finished giving Evans a quick recap when an announcement echoed across the field that the airshow had ended. Everyone was asked to exit safely. Amanda heard grumbling as the crowd moved en masse toward the parking lot and the Busse Woods exit.

Suddenly out of the corner of her eye, Amanda caught a streak of red, highlighted by a sudden shaft of sunlight. A very familiar figure in a red jacket was running east toward a grove of trees.

Patrick. It was as if the sun had signaled his location to Amanda. And he'd lost his limp.

"There he is!" Amanda pointed. "In the red jacket. He's headed toward Golf Road."

Evans instantly directed the officer who had just returned with the tagged and bagged knife to head the pursuit. The officer posted at Patrick's car was directed to join him. The third officer followed them.

"I'll stay here in case Williams swings back," Evans said.

"I just hope they catch him," Amanda stooped next to her daughter. "How are you feeling now?"

"I can stand up, Mom. I'm back to breathing okay."

Amanda grabbed Brittany's hand and pulled her up. She wrapped her arms around her, wishing she could never let her go.

"Mom, I had no idea Patrick was this messed up," Brittany said weakly.

"Me neither. We'll talk about it later." Amanda knew there would be a lot of talking later, on all sides.

"I've just been notified they're closing in on Williams," Evans reported. "He's cornered, and I need to join them."

"Brittany and I will be safe in my car," Amanda said. "I'll keep watch for the EMTs."

Evans nodded, then hustled toward the path where officers were closing in on Patrick.

Amanda held her daughter's hand as they hurried toward the safety of Baby. Every fiber in her body remained on high alert.

With Baby in sight, Amanda's panic lessened. The crowd had dispersed and the parking lot was almost deserted. They'd be safe in Joe's car.

Then Amanda froze. Out of the corner of her eye, a streak of red ran by the isolated shelter on the hill where she'd found Brittany and Patrick.

Patrick! How had he slipped away from the police?

She pointed toward the red jacket moving in the *opposite* direction from where Evans and the other officers were headed. "Brittany, look over there. What do you see?"

Brittany gasped. Her hand flew to her mouth. "That's Patrick."

Amanda tried to keep calm as her heart raced. "He must have

sneaked through the police line somehow. We've got to alert them. I need your cell phone."

"I left it in Patrick's car," Brittany wailed.

Amanda tossed Baby's car keys at her daughter. "Your dad's car is steps away. My cell phone is on the passenger seat. Call 911. Tell them it's a matter of life or death. They must alert Evans that Patrick is now headed in the opposite direction from where we first saw him running."

"What about you, Mom?"

"I'll keep Patrick in sight in case he switches back again. Now get to Baby and make that call."

Amanda's adrenaline shot sky high as she kept watch between Patrick's in-flight red jacket and Brittney's dash to Baby. When her daughter safely slipped through the Mustang's door and slammed it shut, Amanda turned her full attention to the fleeing Patrick.

She ran faster than she ever had in her life. She didn't know what she'd do if she caught up to him, but she'd figure it out.

Patrick looked back over his shoulder in surprise. He motioned her to stay back.

She kept running toward him.

He ducked behind a tree, and she briefly lost sight of him. Until he made the mistake of sidestepping into a small clearing and, once again, the red jacket alerted Amanda of his position.

He was almost to Golf Road and she wasn't far behind.

Traffic on the congested road flew by at 45 miles an hour.

Patrick halted at the edge of the road. His head turned left, then right, then left again, judging how to cross the four lanes of cars and trucks.

He took advantage of a slight break in traffic in the first lane and safely charged across.

Stopped on the white line dividing the first and second lanes, he once again checked both ways.

Amanda saw a small, empty stretch open up in the second lane, created by a long-haul truck switching gears.

Patrick took two steps forward.

She cringed as his left foot slipped out from under him and he fell headfirst toward the pavement.

The squeal of braking truck tires echoed down Golf Road as Evans and the other officers ran up next to Amanda.

CHAPTER 34

"Enjoy your Panda Bear. It's on the house." Nicki slid Amanda's favorite latté, with an extra drizzle of chocolate, across the counter.

Amanda touched the cup. Extra hot, but not too hot. Just right. She grinned at her bestie. "Thanks. Can you join me?"

Nicki glanced at the line behind Amanda. "I will, once things slow down."

Four weeks to the day since David Stedman had been arrested and shouted for her help, Amanda settled into her favorite table in the Dark Roast Coffee Shop. She pulled today's *Gazette* out of her backpack and zeroed in on the short front-page article titled "**Update on Hager Murder Trial.**"

Yesterday, the grand jury determined that the Illinois State Attorney's office presented sufficient evidence to set a trial date for the murder of Olivia Hager. The accused, Patrick Williams, remains hospitalized with two broken legs, a cracked jaw, a broken nose, and a dislocated shoulder, from injuries sustained while trying to flee from law enforcement on the perimeter of Busse Woods. A medical consultant stated that Williams could physically stand trial.

Additional charges of kidnapping and attempted murder are being processed separately. A nuisance charge for the anonymous letters left outside of Oak Hills businesses is being assessed.

Amanda rubbed her arms, feeling a chill. Patrick had almost gotten away with Olivia's murder. And almost Brittany's too.

"I thought I'd find you here, Mrs. K."

David stood in front of her, wearing a smile that stretched from ear to ear. "I had to thank you one more time before I head to Colorado."

"You've thanked me a million times already. But what's this about Colorado?" Amanda motioned to the chair next to her. "Have a seat. Tell me more."

"I need a fresh start," he said, plopping down. "It'll be hard to leave Oak Hills, and my great-aunt isn't too happy about it. But the Rockies are calling me."

"What's your plan once you get there?"

"I reconnected with a college friend who opened a small coffee shop just outside of Denver. We're forming a partnership to start up additional shops. My car is packed and ready to go. I leave tomorrow."

Amanda's smile matched David's. "I'm happy for you. But you'll be missed." She paused, then asked, "Do you need my help?"

He shook his head. "Thanks, Mrs. K. Not this time. The GoFundMe account took care of my legal bills. And I'm going to be living very frugally for a while."

"What happened to the coffee shop equipment you bought with Olivia's five-thousand-dollar investment?"

"Turns out Olivia had a will that left everything she had to an abused children's non-profit. I sold the equipment and donated the money from the sale to their capital campaign in Olivia's name. I figure that's what Olivia would have wanted me to do."

Amanda nodded. "I agree." *That's the David I know.*

"I'm telling Matt and the rest of my friends tonight about moving to Colorado. Don't spoil my surprise, okay?"

Amanda held up her hand. "I promise not to spill the beans, as they say in the coffee business."

David chuckled, then turned solemn. "I still can't believe Patrick's credit card was a key clue. No way did I think he could have murdered Olivia. Even after he made that nasty remark about her death when I waited on him just before the police showed up and arrested me."

"No one did," Amanda said.

"I'm forever grateful you didn't give up on me." Amanda heard a catch in David's throat. He pushed back his chair. "If you're ever in Colorado, I'll treat you to all the coffee you can drink as you take in the views of the mountains."

"Beautiful scenery and coffee on the house? I like the sound of that," she said with a smile.

David hesitated. "I don't need your help, but Great-Aunt Virginia might."

"You don't have to worry. I have a standing invitation for lunch at her house every Tuesday. She wants to treat me to her delicious homemade soups. Trust me, I'll be keeping my eye on her." They both chuckled.

After one last thank you, David hustled out of the Dark Roast. She watched him disappear out of sight, thrilled he was moving on to a new life. But she was also sad to see him go.

Nicki slipped in where David had sat. "Rats. I missed saying hi to David. How's he doing?"

"Great." Amanda bit her tongue. She'd promised to keep his Colorado move a secret until he told his friends.

"And how are all the Knightlys?"

Before Amanda could answer, Nicki got called up to the front counter and scampered off.

Taking a sip of her Panda Bear, Amanda was glad for a quiet

moment to ponder, once again, the impact of Olivia Hager's murder on her own family.

Thankfully, Brittany had started working through her trauma from the attempted kidnapping and threatened stabbing. It greatly helped that her friends had rallied around her.

"I let Patrick's constant attention, expensive dinners, and beautiful flowers brush aside a nagging doubt that something was off with him, until it was almost too late." Brittany had confessed to her mom soon after the terrifying experience.

Amanda loved that the two of them could support each other when called to testify at Patrick's trial. But she worried about Matt, who still chastised himself for ignoring the warning signs about Patrick that had put his mom and sister in grave danger.

"I kind of figured he wasn't telling the truth about being a friend of David's. But we needed a numbers person and he volunteered. So, I let it slide. I won't do that again," he'd told Amanda.

He'd been upfront about ending things with Chloe after learning she'd been two-timing him with David. He also confessed to suspecting from the beginning that Chloe's feelings weren't nearly as strong as his, and he'd hoped she'd change her mind.

To David's credit, he had made a clean break from Chloe when he learned she'd been dishonest with both him and Matt.

Amanda had noticed a couple of weeks after Patrick's arrest that Chloe's photo was no longer lined up with the other Dark Roast staff headshots. Nicki had confirmed the young woman had left the coffee shop and moved to downtown Chicago. It made sense she'd wanted a fresh start. Amanda only hoped Chloe had learned to be totally honest with anyone she dated in the future.

Taking another sip of her drink, Amanda vowed to stay out of her adult children's love lives going forward. But maybe she was kidding herself. Fantasizing about their future weddings would be a hard habit to break.

As for Joe, he was still glowing after his first month on the new job. She'd also been somewhat reassured to learn that their savings hadn't been as depleted as she'd feared. But she'd insisted their monthly expenditures be kept to a minimum until everything was back on track.

She'd warned him that regaining her trust after the double bombshell of his layoff and financial shenanigans wouldn't happen overnight. Setting up a weekly review of their finances was a good start, she'd told him.

Baby was another story. Yep, Amanda had developed a soft spot for the vintage red sports car. After all, the 1964 Mustang had been a lifesaver, getting her to Busse Woods in the nick of time while running on fumes. Since that fateful day, the classic car sat in their garage while Joe figured out the cost of repairing the damaged undercarriage and front bumper.

Amanda chuckled, remembering how she'd talked to Baby during that wild drive after making fun of Joe for doing the same. She gave the Mustang a friendly wave whenever she walked by the garage. When she'd suggested they call the car *"Our* Baby," Joe had agreed, although—no surprise— reluctantly.

Amanda sat back feeling a stab of disappointment seeing happy customers bustle in and out of the small coffee shop. She'd thrived in her week as manager at the Dark Roast, but now she was back at Bob's deli counter in a job she'd outgrown. Continuing as the manager at the Dark Roast wasn't an option, unfortunately, with Nicki resuming her dual role as owner/manager.

It was time to hunt for a new job. But between family, home, and her work schedule, she hadn't had time to start.

Amanda shook off her private pity party when Nicki returned to her table. Her bestie peered over the top of her daffodil-yellow glasses as she sat down again. "Did I tell you Las Vegas is my next vacation spot?"

Amanda gave her a hopeful glance. "If you need a manager while you're away, sign me up."

"Will do. We already know how to get Bob Early to agree." They both laughed. "Which reminds me. I heard there was some confusion with his grandson who subbed for you at the deli counter," Nicki said, her voice lowered. "He didn't slice the ham the right thickness on an order for the Logans. They barged into Bob's office to complain. Bob was livid. His grandson didn't go near him the rest of the day."

"I hadn't heard that one."

"Bob made me promise I'd keep it a secret. But I had to tell you."

"My lips are sealed." Amanda dragged her index finger across her mouth as her bestie chuckled. That could explain why Bob had called her into his office and given her a big raise on her first morning back. It'd been a much-needed boost to her and Joe's depleted savings, but the extra money hadn't erased her restlessness about the job.

Nicki's phone rang. "Gotta answer this. Catch you later." She hustled toward her office.

Amanda caught sight of Zak working the front counter, once again the fun barista. He'd changed overnight after dropping out of law school and enrolling in the fine arts program at Columbia College right after Patrick's arrest. Nicki had confirmed that Zak's fiery confrontations with customers had become a thing of the past.

"I can't tell you how much better I feel going down a path that's best for me," Zak had told Amanda. "Although my dad's afraid he'll have a starving-artist son instead of the hotshot lawyer he'd hoped for." He was also collecting a whole new bunch of fun coffee facts for her.

Taking another sip of her Panda Bear, Amanda watched

Nicki in action behind the front counter. She was lending a hand while regaling a customer with the saga of how she'd saved her Florida vacation condo complex from a meandering alligator. It was four feet long when she'd first told the story. Since then, the menacing reptile had somehow grown to eight feet.

Amanda saw Nicki tap a few drops of green food coloring into a coffee cup and knew she'd talked the customer into trying the Alligator Slayer, their newest specialty cappuccino. Chopped-up sugar cubes lined the cup's rim as the alligator's teeth. Amanda wasn't surprised it was a big hit. Nicki was a genius at marketing.

Spotting Evans as the officer walked into the Dark Roast, Amanda waved her over. Nicki returned to the table.

"Monica, you haven't stopped into the shop since I got back from Florida." Nicki stood hands on hips, waving her finger at the officer.

"It's not because I didn't want to. Prepping for the Hager trial has kept me stuck at the station with vending machine coffee," Evans said. "Today I rebelled. I told my sergeant I needed the real deal. Although I can only take a quick break."

"Let me get your regular, and I'll fill you in on my vacation." Nicki held up her hand. "I promise to keep it short."

Evans gave her a good-natured "Uh-huh."

Nicki turned to Amanda. "Don't leave just yet. I have something I need to tell you."

Amanda swore her bestie looked like the cat that ate the canary as she headed to the front counter.

Evans hesitated by Amanda's table. "You should know that Chief Grady was all smiles when the *Gazette* ran the editorial congratulating the Oak Hills Police for capturing the confessed killer in the Olivia Hager murder case. We've been talking about how to thank you for your part."

Amanda shook her head. "That's not necessary. I'm happy it

all worked out." Her reward had been saving David from a life-time in jail—and her own daughter's life.

Evans gestured to the front counter. "Nicki's signaling my coffee is ready. Hope to see you again soon, Amanda."

"Same here." Amanda made a last-second decision not to add "Monica." She'd keep it to Evans until given the invitation.

She settled back into her chair and turned to the Neighbor-hood News section of the *Gazette*. A small article reported that Gina Rohmer had been convicted of shoplifting from local retail-ers. She'd hidden the stolen bounty in the stairwell of Valley Lane Condos before selling it online. The article made it clear there was no connection to Olivia Hager's murder in that same building.

Reading about Gina's conviction made her think of Sam Robertson, the UPS driver whom Olivia Hager had accused of stealing her necklace. The police had found it behind a dresser in Olivia's bedroom and determined it had slipped there by acci-dent. Amanda could still see Sam's beaming grin when he told her the black mark on his work record had been erased.

As if by magic, Raymond appeared in front of Amanda. "How're you doing, young lady?" the handyman asked, giving her a friendly smile.

"I'm just fine, thanks. Good to see you, Raymond."

"I fixed a broken table leg earlier today and came back for my small, black to-go coffee." Raymond hesitated then said, "Thanks again for helping me straighten out that mess that happened way back when. But enough about that." He added with a wave, "I plan to keep you supplied with fresh garden tomatoes this summer. And if there's anything that needs fixing at your house, let me know. We're practically neighbors, and in Oak Hills, neighbors help neighbors." Without waiting for an answer, he shuffled to the front counter.

Seeing Raymond reminded Amanda of her mother. She pulled out her phone and checked her calendar. Yep, she'd added their Sunday visits with a permanent repeat—and a couple of more hours. Ever since Amanda had learned the truth about her grandfather, she and her mom talked freely over their Sunday meal at the local diner. Amanda no longer saw their weekly visits as a duty, but as time happily spent for both of them.

Returning once again to the *Gazette*, Amanda turned to the Arts and Entertainment section, ready to check out the upcoming streaming releases.

"I'm back," Nicki said, pulling out a chair. Her expression looked as if she'd won a jackpot, even before her trip to Vegas.

"You definitely have me curious. I'm guessing that you have good news." Amanda raised a questioning eyebrow.

"That phone call was from your boss," Nicki said. "He's wondering if the two of us might be interested in a business proposition."

Amanda cocked her head toward her friend. "Bob Early wants to talk to you and *me* about a business deal?"

Nicki nodded. "Turns out he was impressed seeing you handle a touchy situation between an irate customer and a belligerent barista that morning he stopped in for a coffee break. I shared with him the great customer feedback I received about you and told him how the shop was humming when I returned. He also mentioned your stellar Deli Lady reputation."

Amanda chuckled. "I'm glad I got Bob's seal of approval. I have to admit, filling in as your manager re-energized me."

Nicki leaned closer. "Here's the best part. He has an idea for a new venture bringing together my Dark Roast business chops with your Deli Lady know-how into something that's never been done before in Oak Hills."

"Sounds intriguing. Let's hear the details." Amanda nervously twirled her ponytail and told herself not to get too excited in case the news turned out to be a bust.

"I can't tell you yet. Be in Bob's office tomorrow morning at 8:00 a.m."

"Not even a hint?" Amanda gave her bestie a hopeful look.

"Mum's the word," Nicki held up her hand. "I promised."

Well, okay," Amanda said. "But I thought we told each other everything."

Nicki smiled. "Maybe not everything. Am I right?"

"Well, yes." Amanda sighed. She couldn't wait to hear more. A job combining her Deli Lady skills and Dark Roast experience seemed like a great fit. But Bob could be cagey. What exactly *did* her boss have in mind?

She polished off the last of the Panda Bear, her mind already spinning possibilities.

Would she also get another chance to be the Sleuth Lady?

THE END

ACKNOWLEDGMENTS

Serving Up the Truth would not have been published without the tremendous support I received from so many along my writing journey.

Thanks to the fledgling critique group, Write Here Write Now, who first encouraged me to turn my short story into a novel.

Thanks to fellow authors Mars D. Gill and Ilene T. Goldman, who continue to share their vast knowledge and honest feedback since those early days.

Thanks to Lisa Mathews, my smart, very patient editor, who tackled my early manuscript, asking key questions that honed it into a solid story, and upped my writing skills.

Thanks to Judith Gallagher, my expert proofreader and adviser, who found all those pesky, hidden mistakes, upped my writing skills another level, and put the final polish on my novel.

Thanks to Karen Phillips, my creative cover artist, who turned my vision into a winner.

Thanks to Sue Trowbridge, my masterful formatter, who crafted the pages of my book to be inviting to readers.

Thanks to the Arlington Heights Citizen Police Academy, who opened my eyes to what police really do.

Thanks to Sisters in Crime, Chicagoland and Guppies Chapters, Mystery Writers of America, and the Authors Guild, who educated me on writing craft, career and community.

Thanks to all my many friends and family for their unfailing encouragement from beginning to end. My novel wouldn't have become a reality without you.

Most of all, I want to thank my husband, Mark. First, for his spot-on feedback. He also kept the home front humming while I remained hunched over my writing desk. And I'm positive his fabulous baked goodies fueled my creativity. But most importantly, I know his love and unfailing backing truly made my journey possible.

ABOUT THE AUTHOR

Debra Klein is a lifelong Chicagoan, who loves everything about the city and the people within it. No surprise, the Chicagoland area is the setting of ***Serving Up the Truth***. Her short story "Ghost of a Chance" in ***Tales From The Golden State of Mind*** anthology also has a Chicago setting.

Debra is a member of Sisters in Crime and serves on the board of her local chapter. She's also a member of the Guppies chapter, Mystery Writers of America and the Authors Guild.

When she's not hunched over her writing desk, you can find her on a golf course driving for that elusive first hole in one.

A long-time reader across all genres, for Debra, walking into a book store is like stepping into a chocolate shop – she wants one of each!

Stay connected with Debra through her website at
DebraKleinBooks.com